APOCALYPSE

Caught in the Eye of the Storm

Peter & Paul Lalonde

Design Peter Wing

Published by This Week In Bible Prophecy, P.O. Box 1440,
Niagara Falls, New York. 14302 / P.O. Box 665, Niagara Falls, Ontario L2E6V5

Canadian Catalogue in Publishing Data
Lalonde, Peter

ISBN 0-9680758-2-7

I. Lalonde, Paul, 1961-II. Title

PS3562.A417A76 1998   c813'.54   C98-900130-X

Printed in Canada

To Patti, Ann and Maggie.
The three great ladies in our lives.

FOREWORD

Make no mistake. This novel is indeed a work of fiction. But just barely. The fact that these events haven't happened yet makes it fiction. But unlike other novels and stories you may read, something very unique can be said about Apocalypse. It is a book about the future based on Bible truths that will soon occur globally.

You see, the Bible paints a very clear picture of what life is going to be like in the days leading up to the glorious Second Coming of Christ. And that's what Apocalypse is all about. So fasten your seatbelt and get ready for the ride of a lifetime.

The story follows the lives of two central characters, Bronson Pearl and Helen Hannah, the leading prime time anchors for the World News Network. Neither of them are Christians and so when Bible Prophecy starts falling into place at an unbelievable pace, they are blind to what is really happening.

And then, when the greatest single event in the history of the planet takes place, they are at a complete loss to understand or explain to the world, what has happened.

Suddenly, millions of people simply vanish off the face of the earth, in a moment, in the twinkling of an eye. Cars crash, planes go down and there is absolute terror and chaos internationally. It seems, that everyone has lost at least one loved one or acquaintance!

Page after page, this compelling story keeps one on the edge of his seat. In fact, you'll feel like you're right there with Bronson and Helen as they struggle to understand what is, for those who remain, the greatest mystery in the history of the world.

In the hours and days after this incredible event, the world is lulled into a false state of security. A belief that all is well. And a belief that it was indeed God Himself who removed these countless souls from the face of the earth. So far so good, right? Wrong!

What the world is hearing is a lie. They are led to believe, by the most powerful and persuasive deceiver the world has ever known, that these millions of people have been removed because they were standing in the way of world peace.

In reality, this great deceiver is the one the Bible calls the antichrist and he convinces humanity globally that these "troublemakers" are finally out of the way. Those that remain can now experience a new age of peace and prosperity.

While Helen and Bronson are initially thankful to have been spared from "God's" cleansing, Helen has lost someone - Her God-fearing and Bible-believing Grandmother. A mysterious message that Grandma left behind is the only glimpse of truth in this new and deceptive world. But will Helen even believe it? Will she be able to resist the temptation and delusion of the new world order, and see the truth?

As you follow this incredible adventure, you won't be able to turn the pages fast enough. In fact, Peter and Paul Lalonde have made this story so exciting and so compelling that I believe many will actually read it from front to back at a single sitting. These two authors are tremendously gifted and this book proves it beyond any shadow of a doubt. It's Bible Prophecy like few have ever been able to put in words. And remember, it's a true story - it just hasn't happened yet.

And the best news of all is that this book is an absolutely great way to share the message of Bible Prophecy, and of the Lord's soon return, with unsaved friends and loved ones. So if you know someone who needs to discover the truth of this incredible story, make sure you get and give them a copy of Apocalypse.

Dr. Jack Van Impe
President,
Jack Van Impe Ministries

ONE

The Beginning

The Jezreel Valley, Israel

In the days that followed, Abdallah's lips would say what happened to his son was God's will. He would recite the words of ritual praise he had known since his own childhood, saving the tears for when he was alone with his wife.

As the days turned to weeks, the prayers continued, but as the overwhelming enormity of the other events taking place in his homeland came to pass, Abdallah's heart would come to truly believe what previously his lips had only spoken.

Father and son had left that morning invoking God's name as was the custom of so many Arabs. "You and Ahmed will not be late returning home tonight?" his wife, Perichehr, had asked.

"No. The boy has too much work to do and the journey is tiring," said Abdallah. "We will return before sunset, 'Insha'allah.'"

APOCALYPSE

The words meant "God willing," and though they were spoken frequently, they were always said with conviction. For the Bedouins like Abdallah, and for many other Arabs, God was always in control. They did not plan for the future. That was fate to be neither known nor altered. They could only concern themselves with the moment, and that morning had been a glorious day for a journey.

The trek to Megiddo, the historic site of many past civilizations, was, as always, a joyous celebration of the diversity of God's people, at least as Abdallah viewed them. He showed Ahmed Lebanese, Ja'bari, Kurds, Samaritans, Vietnamese, Masri, Syrians, Ethiopian Copts, American Mormons, Maronites, evangelical Christian fundamentalists, and many others they met as they passed a nearby Jewish Kibbutz. Everyone was drawn to the site of more than 6,000 years of history layered in a manner archaeologists had only recently uncovered.

"Do you see that mound of rocks, Ahmed?" asked Abdallah, pointing to the remains of one of several buildings. "That temple is 5,000 years old."

"Was that where Grandfather prayed to Allah when he was a boy?" asked the child.

"That temple is older than your grandfather," laughed Abdallah, "Older than his grandfather. Older than the time of the prophet Muhammad." He tried to tell the boy of the history, of the land. To him the site was the history of the Creator's hand in the lives of all men whether they knew him as Allah or Yahweh, the Lord Almighty, or any other name. The ruins showed temples and cities, each built upon the other, each bearing a time of peace and war, of love and hate, of hope and frustration, of fear and rejoicing.

The terrain of Megiddo made it a natural passageway for soldiers bent on conquest, so from time to time there were stories of the great warriors of the past. Abdallah told his son of Ahmed of Thutmose III who came to Megiddo to conquer a civilization so massive that it was written his booty included 1,929 head of cattle, 400 horses, warhorses, and colts, more than 900 carriages including two made from gold used by the Governors of Megiddo, 20,500 sheep, battle armor, military uniforms, archers' bows... The list was as endless as the history of the area.

"Each new city was built on the old," Abdallah explained. "One day you will read of men such as Thutmose and King David, Ahab and King Solomon, King Josiah and Pharaoh Necho. You will see the hand of Allah bringing peace to stubborn people who keep returning to war. You will see how each layer of these ruins, each city built upon a city past, represents new hope for the people."

The boy did not understand, of course. Abdallah knew he was too young. The boy only wanted to toss pebbles over the edge of the archaeological site to see how far he could throw them. Still, he had to begin teaching his son a different way from that of his own father, a man of passionate anger who saw his beloved Palestine as an occupied territory. The old man continued to curse the day he first heard a Jew use the term Eretz Israel, referring to the land as one promised to them by God. He cursed the Christians who saw his beloved territory as the Holy Land of Jesus but failed to acknowledge Muhammad.

Abdallah thought differently. The ruins of Megiddo, the diversity of the visitors, all were a reminder of the vast creation. Rather than being troubled by the differences in worship, he rejoiced that so many people were coming to the one true God. He had read the Bible, not just the Koran. He had seen that Mary, the mother of Jesus, is mentioned more times in the Koran than in the New Testament. He realized that there was a deeper message for those who would try to see and understand.

While others were drawn to Jerusalem, to the Temple Mount where three faiths fought over their differences instead of seeing God trying to bring them together in a common area, he came to Megiddo. The excavation made him feel as though he was in touch with the lives and conflicts of the past in a way that was preparing him for something preordained.

"You are a foolish man," his wife had lovingly told him. She knew it was wrong to speak against the teachings of the elders. But she also knew that he was a man of deep devotion, so what did it matter if he took Ahmed from the sheep and the cattle for a few hours in his young life? They would return before sunset, Insha'allah, happy for the time together.

The woman from the tourist bus saw him first. He was not in uniform, but the tour guide had explained how all Israelis are trained for the army at 18. They can be called to active duty at any time, and they frequently stand patrol in civilian dress. That was why so many men and women carried weapons, the rifles having replaced the swords of old, the Messiah not yet having returned to beat them into ploughshares.

The woman wanted a picture of the soldier and asked her husband if he thought it would be rude to ask him to pose. She had already taken a picture of the Bedouin father and son, something the tour guide admonished her should not have been done. Such casual snapping of images without permission violated the Arab culture. She did not want to offend anyone else.

"Everybody takes pictures of the soldiers," her husband told her. "They did it in Jerusalem and Tel Aviv. They did it in Nazareth. Why should this place be any different?"

The woman shrugged, then picked up her camera and turned towards the man who was now cradling his weapon in his arms. Without understanding the significance of his actions, she waved to him, trying to get him to look her way. When he started to turn, she was too busy snapping the shutter to realize at first that he was not posing but starting to aim and fire.

For an instant all was as it had been. The tour guide was holding a microphone, about to tell her charges to finish taking their pictures or buying souvenirs because the bus would depart in five minutes. Abdallah was laughing at Ahmed who had thrown a stone at a bird and was now running, covering his head, as the bird he had targeted and what looked like several friends were flying all about him, angrily squawking their displeasure. The woman with the camera squeezed off frame after frame. An Israeli couple leaned against a tree, drinking a cola before starting the walk back to their Kibbutz.

Then there was pandemonium. A bullet shattered the knee of the woman with the camera, sending her screaming to the ground in agony. A window of the tour bus exploded, shards of glass striking the driver with such force that his face appeared to have been slashed by razors. And as several Israeli men rushed to the gunman, grabbing the weapon, striking him repeatedly, forcing him to the ground and using a belt to bind his wrists, Abdallah froze with horror. Ahmed, his beloved first son, was sprawled on the ground, the earth turning red from blood pouring from a gaping head wound.

"Ahmed!" he shouted, running to the fallen child. "Ahmed!"

Abdallah knew there was no hope even before he touched the lifeless figure, even before someone from the tour bus identified herself as a retired nurse and pronounced the child beyond help.

He did not know if the shooter was an Arab or a Jew. He did not know if he was a terrorist or a man insane with the anger that had periodically been so much a part of Megiddo's past. He did not care. All he could do was cradle his son's head and cry out to the living God who had witnessed so many other deaths before this one. All he could do was ask why? His faith did not see death as an ending, a belief reinforced by the other holy books he had secretly read despite his own father's objections. Ahmed would be in a joyous place. He was going to a father who had lost his own son to senseless violence. Abdallah instinctively understood this, yet still he cried out, as much for the loss as because he had been left behind.

In minutes there were people swarming about the site, some with guns, some with medical kits. The people of the Kibbutz and others who lived in the area were always ready to deal with trauma, pain, violence, and death. Joy and sorrow were two sides of a coin of destiny endlessly flipped throughout each day. They were used to being buffeted by winds of change over which they had no control. They could only praise the Lord, believing in His ultimate wisdom and presence, burying the dead, tending to the wounded, rejoicing with each new life, each commitment to marriage and family.

Abdallah heard voices in several languages, recognizing all and understanding none. Someone wrapped his arms about his shoulders, a tourist, a stranger who did not understand that was wrong. Still Abdallah felt strangely comforted, as though his loss had touched another who needed to act with kindness even if the traditions were in conflict. Why did these foolish people need to experience such tragedy to face the love of the Creator that was in them all?

And suddenly Abdallah understood something else. He understood why so many Christians ignored the name of Meggido and chose to use the other word by which it was identified. They called the spot Armageddon.

Perhaps that was why his own son, an innocent in love with all creation, could be killed in such a holy place. Until moments before the shooting, Abdallah had rejoiced in the continuing love of the God above who, over the centuries, allowed Megiddo to be rebuilt, each new community founded on the ruins of the previous. Now he understood that the Christians were right. Megiddo was more properly called Armageddon, the place where there would one day be the last battle between good and evil. He could only wonder in his sorrow as so many arms reached out, so many tongues spoke words of comfort, if the good would respond as it had that day — too late to prevent the horror of the ever present evil.

*

Los Angeles, California

If Ginnie had asked him, Lennie could not have told her why he invited her to the prom. Not that they didn't both love dancing. They did, and with all the skill and enthusiasm of the tone deaf who stand in

APOCALYPSE

bathroom showers bellowing popular songs while the cat cringes, the dog howls, and the neighbors worry about spouse abuse.

Between them, Lennie and Ginnie had completed a collection of old Fred Astaire and Gene Kelly movies. They sat enthralled as the men danced with Ginger Rogers, Debbie Reynolds, Cyd Charisse, and so many other greats from the past. Then, when away from parents, they would start a video and transform themselves into the romantic leads of *Top Hat, Singin' In The Rain, On The Town*, and so many others.

Not that their practice had accomplished much. In all the time they had been best friends, Ginnie had sustained a broken big toe, several major bruises, and a sprained ankle. Lennie had wrenched his back, received 17 stitches when he tripped over a floor lamp and accidentally put his hand through a glass aquarium while trying to catch himself. They knew they dared not go on the dance floor the night of the prom, not unless they wanted to risk wreaking havoc on all their classmates. Perhaps they would do a slow dance or two. But while their love was big band music and jazz ballads, their classmates were hopping and bopping to groups whose names, alone, had so many foul words, the class poster committee dared not write them on the in-school ads. Their music was, if anything, worse.

Still, it was the prom, the last big dance of high school before they both graduated and went on to college. And while Lennie knew that none of the other guys would ever consider a "geek" like Ginnie with her sweaty palms, acne, and a figure that would probably be stuck in girlhood for another year or two, he visibly relaxed when she said she was available. Likewise, while Ginnie knew that the other girls made fun of Lennie's serious side, his having tried to form an after school Bible study club, his talk of how teens should best prepare themselves for the end times, she, too, was relieved when he asked her to the dance.

And so they sat in the midst of a cacophony of sounds and a rainbow of color as the other kids leaped, squatted, shook, waved, and otherwise cavorted to sounds whose driving beat reminded Ginnie of the story of Joshua bringing down the walls of Jericho. At first they tried to talk, their greatest joy in life, though neither of their parents could figure out how they could spend so many hours together on the telephone and in person and still have more words to share.

Then they tried to enjoy the music, but it was too loud, the speakers amplified far more than the carefully decorated gym could absorb. Most of the chaperones wore ear plugs. Those who didn't kept finding excuses to go to the rest room to escape the sound, if only for a few minutes.

And so they sat, Lennie's hand suddenly finding itself on Ginnie's for the first time since they became best friends. Ginnie noticed even before Lennie, despite the fact that he had moved first. For him it was natural. For her, it was a surprise that suddenly felt warm, reassuring, as though perhaps they were destined to be more of one body than two.

Neither knew when they got up to leave. Lennie said something about punch. Ginnie said something about the buffet. They walked towards the table still holding hands. Then, without either remembering saying a word or even changing direction, they found themselves outside in the open air.

9

APOCALYPSE

The high school was located near the base of a hill, and they found themselves slowly walking up a path that led to an area from which they could see a portion of the Los Angeles skyline. Or they could if the smog had lifted from earlier in the day. The full moon was still obscured, and the sunset had been filled with shades of reds and yellows that was so spectacular, some people burst into applause. It was a natural reaction for a city so attuned to the world of show business, but the sad fact was that the richer the colors, the thicker the particulate matter. Rather than being the best of God's creation, it represented the increasing destruction of the atmosphere scientists were beginning to worry about.

But it was not a night to worry about pollution, the stewardship of creation, or anything other than Lennie and Ginnie. Each realized that they were in a new phase of their relationship. Each was alive with feelings neither could express yet which each hoped the other would instinctively understand.

The couple reached the top of the hill, standing silently, looking towards what was visible of the distant urban landscape. Perhaps they stood like that for seconds. Perhaps they stood for hours. Neither was aware of the passage of time. Neither was aware when one of them turned towards the other, the silence between them suddenly becoming a bridge for emotions they instinctively understood transcended adolescent hormones.

A moment later their lips met. It was the first kiss for each, gentle, unhurried. Their hearts knew to do what their minds did not understand. Lennie felt a hand caress his neck. Ginnie felt herself enveloped in arms that had never before seemed so strong, so comforting, so right. They were both light headed, pausing momentarily, then kissing again as Lennie's glasses slipped from his face and the high school became but a blur of light and sound.

The earth moved at that moment. A gentle rumbling that seemed to radiate from their toes to their heads. Ginnie smiled, then laughed with joy, breaking from Lennie, then starting to kiss him once more. She knew that love could move mountains. She knew that...

They fell as though they had been standing on a rug that was suddenly yanked from under their feet. Her jaw struck his shoulder. His tuxedo pants tore as his knee twisted against a rock. There was a sound like a bowling alley where every lane was experiencing simultaneous strikes. Then it seemed as though a freight train was passing through.

The couple rolled with the ever growing shocks. "Lennie!" she shouted, grabbing his sleeve.

"Ginnie. I've got you," he said, reaching her arm, bringing her near, then clinging to her as they rolled once more.

The experience lasted less than a minute, though it seemed far longer. When it was over, Lennie found that the frame of his glasses was bent and one lens popped out. He adjusted them as best he could, then looked down the hill.

"Ginnie," he whispered. "Oh, my Lord, Ginnie."

The high school that had moments before been ablaze with lights and sound was now in full darkness. In the dim glow of the haze obscured moon, they could see that what had once been steel, concrete, and glass so strong that it had nurtured generations of students through adolescence was now rubble. The destruction was swift and total. It was as though it had been made of children's building blocks, then smashed with a sledge hammer.

Then an eerie light seemed to flicker, growing stronger, and bursting forth like a beacon from Hell in the night sky. The remains of the school were ablaze, as were other buildings in the area. Cars had crashed and the ground was unnaturally shifted.

"I think it was the big one," Ginnie whispered. "I think..."

The next quake was shorter but equally intense. This time they began rolling down the hill together, fighting for handholds as they also clutched each other.

They were closer to the school, and Lennie realized they would have to call for help somehow, to try and start a rescue effort. There were houses in the neighborhood, and they could hear the mournful wail of endless car alarms triggered by the vibrations. Some of the vehicles had been flipped upside down. One particularly hard hit area had a shock wave that sent a mini-van crashing onto a carport roof. The telephone lines were probably dead, but someone was bound to have a cellular phone that still worked.

And then they heard the most chilling sound of all — silence. Not from the nearby streets so alive with noise. Not from the fires which crackled and popped as they consumed everything flammable in their wake. The silence was from the school building which, in a study that would be undertaken in the aftermath of the disaster, was found to have been improperly built. It was supposed to be earthquake resistant enough to assure a safe exit. It was supposed to still be usable a hundred years after it was built.

Instead, the contractor had cheated on the materials, the quality, and method of construction, paying large bribes to city inspectors. A smaller quake would have resulted in extensive loss of life and ruinous damage. The quake that had just occurred created carnage as thorough as if a bomb had made a direct hit on the building.

Although they would tear at the rubble until their hands were bleeding and their clothing in tatters, although surviving neighbors would join them with picks, shovels, and pry bars, no one would be found alive. No one would be found to have survived the first devastating shock wave. The teens and adults were crushed beyond recognition, their bodies looking as though they were victims of a high altitude aircraft disaster.

Only Ginnie and Lennie were left alive from among their classmates. And in the days that followed, their story would be repeated hundreds of times over as Los Angeles struggled to feed, shelter, and provide water for hundreds of thousands of people left homeless. Ministerial teams, psychologists, and out of town reporters blanketed the ruins of the city, comforting the survivors or seeking their stories. Billions of dollars in losses had occurred. The death toll would prove greater than the total number of lives lost in every war Americans had fought since the Revolution.

*

Chicago, Illinois

Susan Hildebrandt knew they were money the moment they entered the leasing office of Cardwell Towers. He was tall, lean, muscular, his carefully styled black hair laced here and there with gray. The suit he wore was an Armani, and between the quality of the fabric and the way it fit his body, she suspected it was personally tailored by the designer. His shoes were so soft and supple a leather, they looked as though they had been made from unborn calf skin. His shirt had gold and diamond cufflinks, and his watch was a limited edition Rolex she had seen advertised for more money than her new Cadillac. The only unusual item was a combination overnight bag/briefcase she was carrying. It was neither expensive nor particularly remarkable, the type of item you could buy for $100 in any luggage shop.

The woman's clothing was an eclectic mix from the most respected couturiers in the world. The blouse was from Paris, the skirt was from Rome. The long scarf, large enough to be draped over the shoulders as an artistic accessory, was hand made by a designer/crafts woman in London whose work sold for no less than 500 pounds. And the shoes bore the craftsmanship of Lugano, a small shop on the upper East Side of Manhattan where one wall was filled with shelves containing casts of the feet of some of the richest and most successful women in the world. From major movie stars to CEOs of major corporations to heads of state, duplicates of their feet were carefully tagged and preserved. Then, as desired, Luigi Lugano would use some of the most exotic leathers in the world to custom fit his clientele.

Not that Susan could afford such items herself. Well paid as she was, her purchases still were made at Saks and then only during sales. However, it was her job to keep aware of the places frequented by the tiny percentage of people who could afford Chicago's Gold Coast shops pandering to those who believed in conspicuous consumption. She needed to be able to spot the differences between the merely rich and those who could afford to live in the flagship apartment community owned by the notorious Spencer Cardwell.

"We realize you're almost ready to close," said the woman, her speech pattern reflecting the New England boarding school enunciation of a number of the building's tenants. "But we have to leave for Europe tomorrow and we did want to see your suites before we left. We're spending so much time in Chicago, it seems foolish to have to constantly be paying for a hotel suite."

"There's no problem. We schedule Sunday hours to meet your needs. If this is the time you need to see a suite, I will be happy to show you what is available," said Susan. She had been working since early in the morning, having come in before the official leasing office time in order to catch up with paperwork. Her feet were tired, her back ached, and she had been planning to meet Frank at the new French restaurant everyone in the building was talking about. Since the least expensive suite was just over a million dollars, and since the bulk of her income came from commissions, Frank would just have to understand. She had a live one.

"We only need a one bedroom if it is large enough to do some entertaining," said the man. He spoke with one of those nondescript accents that hinted at a childhood spent moving among several different European countries.

"I have just the place. Thirty-fourth floor with a spectacular view of the water. It's just one bedroom, but the formal dining room and living room are almost 2,500 square feet by themselves." She did not mention price. If they had to ask, they couldn't afford it, as the saying goes. And these people obviously did not have to ask.

"That sounds perfect. We'd like to take a look at it if that's not too much trouble."

For an instant Susan thought of calling the restaurant and leaving word for Frank. Then she thought better of it. If this was a live one, the last thing she wanted was for them to feel rushed.

The couple spent an hour in the apartment and another 45 minutes touring the building. There were three restaurants, a private health club with personal trainers available to work with tenants in their suites, a full service dry cleaners, and even a private library with both books and audio/visual materials. A full time concierge staff handled any needs the tenants might have outside the building. And the security system assured that no unauthorized persons could enter the building unchallenged.

"Mr. Cardwell wanted the building to be a self-contained community, an oasis in the city for those who appreciated the best." And often had more money than brains, she thought to herself. Several of the tenants were heirs to vast fortunes they were doing their best to whittle away to nothing. A few were connected with various governments in exile, spending money that had been looted from one treasury or another over the years. There were some CEOs of major corporations, usually under investigation though not yet indicted. And there was a handful of self-made, completely honest business people who simply enjoyed a hedonistic lifestyle to which almost no one is accustomed. She had no idea to which category the couple in front of her belonged, nor did she care. They were thinking of spending more than two-million dollars plus an annual maintenance fee that would in itself be enough to support a family of four in relative luxury.

"I'd like to take another look at the suite," said the man. "If it's not too late, that is."

7:15 p.m. on a Sunday. The restaurants closed early, and Frank was liable to be gone long before that. The condominium always maintained a skeleton crew on Sunday, most of the tenants either away or spending the evening at home. There was no one who could take over for her whom she could trust to close the deal. Even with her stomach rumbling and her body screaming for a nap, she smiled and said, "I think looking at the suite again is an excellent idea."

Susan was showing the woman a section of the suite that could be adapted for a home office. It was specially wired for multiple telephone lines, cable access, and a variety of electronic devices. "Many of the tenants need elaborate computer and teleconferencing systems to effectively handle their global businesses. I think you'll find that whatever your needs, the building is equipped for..."

Somehow Susan knew she was in danger even before she realized that the object touching her back was a gun. Her awareness was a primal instinct, no different than what primitive man must have felt when confronting a saber tooth tiger or giant mastodon. There had been no change in the couple's manner, no difference in the tone of their voices. One moment they were looking at the building, the next moment there was a gun in her back.

"If this is a robbery, I think you have it backwards," said Susan, her voice breaking with fear. "I'm lucky to afford El fare. I should be robbing you."

"This is not a robbery," said the woman, stepping away from Susan. She was unarmed, but from the way she shifted her body, instinctively balancing herself so she could move swiftly in any direction, Susan suspected she was a martial arts expert. "We just need access to the building for a couple of hours, and you've been kind enough to show us what we needed to know."

"I don't understand..."

"You don't need to understand," said the woman. When she saw that Susan was not going to try and resist, she walked over to the bag and put on a thin pair of leather gloves identical to the ones Susan realized the man was wearing. It was then that Susan realized she could not recall either of them touching anything during the tour. They let Susan open doors for them, touching whatever had to be handled. She did not know what the change meant, did not want to know.

"We're going to need you to stay in this suite," said the man. "We can not be interrupted until we are finished."

Susan did not reply.

"If you cooperate, you will be left unharmed," said the woman. "If you cause us trouble, we will kill you. Your life is of no importance to us."

"Whatever you want," said Susan, nervously. She tried to force a smile, but her mouth was too dry and she felt as though she might wet herself. She had been attacked once when working for a real estate developer in New York City, late at night during the days before the 42nd Street and Times Square region had been made respectable. She had screamed when he touched her arm, throwing her to the ground. But she had grabbed his ankle and brought him down with her, still screaming. Several passers-by had come to her rescue, and the police were able to make an arrest.

She was still frightened of being out alone at night, even after moving halfway across the country, but she had told herself she had the courage to handle anything after she warded off that attack. Now she was not so sure. She was out of control with no way to fight back as she had before. And nothing about the couple with the gun made sense to her.

They left Susan helpless on the floor of the living room. There was no telephone in the suite, and the panic alarm buttons wired into the various rooms had been deactivated on the building's computer control when the place was vacated by the previous tenant. But the door locks would only prevent someone from coming inside. They would not keep someone from leaving.

Not that she could have gone anywhere. The bag about which she had been curious contained several lengths of rope along with some canisters, tools, and electronic devices. They tied her securely, the ropes so tight that she could not move without the cords biting into her wrists and ankles, her shoulders aching from the strain. The woman had looped her expensive scarf twice around Susan's face, tying it between her teeth, then wrapping it again over her mouth to firmly gag her.

Susan had to fight her panic in order to breathe. Unless she could keep calm, inhaling and exhaling carefully through her nose, she would suffocate or choke herself fighting the cloth in her mouth. She dared not try to scream out for help. All she could do was endure what they had done to her until someone came to free her. She could not think about the alternative.

APOCALYPSE

The couple left Susan and moved swiftly through the building to the maintenance area. No one questioned them. Their appearance and the fact that they had keys to every door they entered prevented suspicion by the handful of tenants and building staff they encountered.

The rigging of the canister to the blower of the duct system took slightly more than an hour, exactly what the experience of the other terrorists in London, Rome, Paris, Bonn, and Tokyo had been. The buildings were energy efficient, well sealed, constantly circulating and cleaning the air. It was an extremely costly technology, but the design was amazingly simple. Once the bacteria was released into the air, not a suite would go uninfected. It would take three days for the tenants to become seriously ill, at least another day for adequate tests to be run on those who might be the first to talk to a doctor. By the time the variety of plague could be identified, some of the richest and most influential men and women in the world would be dead.

That was why ransoms had already been paid in other countries. And because the incident could not be prevented, that was why those who did pay refused to alert the news media. Their silence had been counted upon, and it assured that the current mission would take place without a problem.

When the man had finished the wiring, the woman used her cell phone to place a call to the Middle East. She spoke briefly in Arabic, then turned off the phone and helped stash the equipment. On the way out the front lobby entrance, they told the security guard at the desk that the leasing agent was having some problems in the suite they had seen. They said that Susan had asked them to alert him to send someone up with a key and a blanket. The request puzzled the man, but not the $100 he was handed as a tip. He immediately got on the telephone to arrange for someone from maintenance to stop up as requested.

Twenty-four hours later, in response to a series of messages sent simultaneously on the Internet, by fax, and by courier, Spencer Cardwell and the city of Chicago authorized the wire transfer of fifty-million dollars to a bank in the Middle East known to have ties with Hamas. When the transfer was confirmed, the exact nature of the plague virus released into the system, as well as the appropriate antibiotic protocol to cure those infected, was provided to the authorities.

*

Korea, The 38th Parallel

The movements were noticed first by satellite. Subtle shifts roughly along the 38th parallel, the most heavily fortified border in the world.

For months there had been rumors that war was possible. The North Korean government had failed once again to find a way to handle the extensive famine devastating the country. There was discontent among the military leaders, political unrest, and a militancy against anyone connected with the government that had not been witnessed before.

At the same time, North Korea had been quietly making alliances with terrorist groups from Germany, Japan, and the Middle East. Some were connected with specific governments in the countries, such as Libya, from which they operated. Others were operating to destabilize nations in the hope that a series of violent acts would bring down governments whose philosophies they had long opposed. They believed that with terrorist actions, they could dramatically change the political face of Europe, Asia, and the Middle East. They felt they could isolate the United States, turn it into a second rate power, then attack it both from within and without.

A war in Korea would force the United States to send troops to reinforce South Korea at the same time its forces were stretched to their limits in the Middle East. It would bring Chinese troops to North Korea at a time when the United States thought old hostilities with the Communist Chinese regime were being defused because of increased economic ties. Military, financial, and economic interests would also bring Japan into conflict with several trading partners if drawn into an Asian battle. In addition, other countries including members of the European Union whose energy needs were creating previously unexpected allies in Jordan, Kuwait, Iran, Egypt, and elsewhere, would suddenly find themselves at political odds over quite different commitments they had made in Southeast Asia.

Hit squads and "moles" trained in urban sabotage had been identified in the United States and elsewhere. These were men and women who had immigrated in their late teens and early twenties, taken jobs, married, raised children, and seemingly assimilated into their new nations. Yet unknown to all but a handful of trusted contacts, they were positioned to unleash biological weapons, destroy government buildings, and severely damage critical highways and communication centers. The movement towards armed confrontation between North and South Korea would be accompanied by violent acts meant to destabilize entire cities in several areas of the Western World.

Despite occasional intelligence warnings about what was happening, United States officials at first thought that North Korea was likely to exchange peace for food and other humanitarian assistance. The United Nations assigned a task force to assess the full needs of the people, then began approaching member countries with requests for grain, medical supplies, and other essentials. Private relief agencies that had been quietly active all along were encouraged to step-up their efforts. However, the UN members decided that none of their countries' supplies would be released by their governments until the North Korean leaders ended the bellicose attitude that had existed for more than two generations. It was blackmail, but the UN member nations saw it as a means to an end.

Now the changes anticipated by the American public as a result of statements coming from the UN Ambassador supported from the Oval Office were happening in a very different way than originally expected. Rather than peace, the leaders of North Korea seemed determined to unite the people through war. The North was long suspected of having tactical nuclear weapons. Biological weapons had been in readiness for several years. Both the North and South Koreans had their elite troops facing one another, yet the truth was that the North had a far superior army in the event of a surprise attack. Thousands would die on the first day of an unexpected assault, and the shock of such a battle might be enough for the North to gain victory.

The land between the opposing forces was filled with land mines and other explosive devices, one or another of which was occasionally detonated by soldiers probing the perimeter for weaknesses. There had also been constant saber rattling, such as when the North held joint military exercises with the Chinese advisers whose troops were widely deployed. But saber rattling was quite different from what the satellite was recording. This was a tactical change, though its meaning was not yet clear.

Intelligence officers had heard rumors of shifting alliances. Both Iraq and Iran had sent emissaries to Korea. Officially there were discussions related to oil and other resources that might improve the North's ability to feed its people. Unofficially there was reference to the Arab concept that "the enemy of my enemy is my friend."

What could be discerned was that if North Korea was going to begin an assault, it would come from three distinctly different strike zones. Yet the nature of the defensive troops in place was such that they could not shift men and materials without making themselves vulnerable to something different. They had to wait for a first strike or go pro-active, initiating the violence everyone had so long feared.

Equally unsettling was the fact that several Middle Eastern leaders were rumored to have been considering a multi-front action. This would involve their making an assault against Israel while having previously unknown allies within the Korean government, and perhaps elsewhere, make simultaneous attacks against other parts of the world. American and United Nations troops would be spread so thin, only token counter-attacks could be launched with conventional weapons.

*

Near Hell's Kitchen, Manhattan, New York

Edna Williams's apartment was in the section of Manhattan that the tourist buses always avoided when showing off the theater district of Broadway, the newly refurbished and family safe 42nd Street and Times Square area, the Upper East Side museums, and the waterfront from which you could travel to the Statue of Liberty or Roosevelt Island. It was near what had once been called Hell's Kitchen, near the Lower East Side garment district, and a stopping point for junkies shooting up their latest buy, gang members proving their toughness by hassling the weak, the lame, and the elderly, and graffiti "artists" decorating the walls with as many four letter words as they could spell. The buildings were all what was known as "pre-war," a term that caused the long time residents to laugh derisively. They knew the war was still going on outside their buildings' front doors. It was the war for human souls, and from the looks of many of the passers-by, it was a war in which too many young people had surrendered.

In the fifteen years Edna Williams had lived in a small one bedroom walk-up on the third floor of a corner building, she had witnessed three murders, been among the first to discover an overdosed junkie dead in the alley near where the trash was kept, and talked with countless prostitutes, pimps, and strong arm thieves. Anyone with more money than they needed for the essentials of survival moved to other parts of the city or across the river to New Jersey. The lucky ones lived alone in one, two, and three room apartments, much like Edna's. The rest were occupied by college students who disdained the dormitory life, office co-workers sharing space while trying to rise above minimum wage, entry level jobs, and an assortment of illegal aliens, street people, and similar misfits.

Helen Hannah, Edna's granddaughter, had hated the idea of her grandmother taking the apartment at a time when the area was still classed as just "disreputable." She calmed her fears by recognizing that her grandmother was a vibrant, active woman who had single-handedly raised not only her own four children, but also three grandchildren. Helen's aunts and uncle had long ago made lives for themselves in various parts of the world, marriage and family taking them to Seattle, Montreal, and London, respectively. Only her mother had stayed in the area, marrying a rising young attorney, moving into an airy, three-bedroom rent controlled apartment in the East 80s, and living what was increasingly proving to be the good life. At least until they left their children in the care of Edna, got on a plane, and flew to London to visit her Aunt Charlotte.

No one ever did learn what happened to her parents' plane. A bomb in the cargo hold, mechanical failure from counterfeit parts sold as original replacement equipment, friendly fire from a military exercise, and a stolen missile fired by a terrorist were all theories that were offered. None could be proven. None could be denied. All that was certain was that 237 people had left on a flight for England and all that returned was horror, grief, and a lifelong ache for loved ones taken too soon and without adequate preparation.

Edna Williams stayed in her daughter and son-in-law's apartment, using the settlement the families were given in order to raise and educate her grandchildren. They attended parochial schools, Eastern colleges, and all found excellent jobs, Helen's being the highest profile as a news reporter, then anchor for WNN Television. What none of them realized until Edna moved into her current residence was that she had no meaningful resources of her own. The settlement had been substantial, and there had been insurance from her son-in-law's law firm, but that was designated for the children. She made certain they had the tools needed to become anything they wished in life, the only luxury she allowed herself was a television/VCR combination so she could watch the videotapes her pastor recommended to the congregation.

In recent years Helen had helped her financially, a way of saying thanks. She did not know if her siblings did the same, and did not ask them. They all had very different lives, very different incomes and responsibilities. She knew her grandmother would treat them all the same, no matter what any one of them might do. What she did not know was that her grandmother rarely used the money for herself.

For example, Shiata was a prostitute Edna had nightly watched work the street corner near her building. She had befriended the young woman, barely out of her teens, buying her coffee when she was done with "work," talking with her, sharing child raising secrets when she discovered the girl had a little boy she was supporting. Occasionally she convinced Shiata to join her for church, never telling anyone what the woman did for a living, never doing more than sharing God's love.

Over time Edna had convinced the girl to leave the risky profession, finding her a small attic apartment in the home of one of her fellow parishioners. Edna had helped her get by while earning her high school equivalency, helped her make the payments to become a cosmetologist. From there Shiata had earned enough money to begin paying for courses at City College where she planned to eventually earn a degree as a social worker.

Not that Edna ever talked about the girl or told anyone what she was doing. Sometimes Helen would see Shiata's little boy when her grandmother was baby sitting on those days the woman had to rush directly from the beauty shop to one of her classes. Sometimes she would talk briefly with Shiata when the two women happened to be in the building at the same time. So far as Helen knew, though, Shiata was either one of her grandmother's better neighbors or a young friend from church. That was all she needed to know. The past was over, Edna Williams always said. Jesus never condemned what you were. He just expected you to move on.

There were others as well. Pastor Holmes sometimes laughed about the "Bank of Edna Williams" when counselling with the now elderly woman about one or another of the street people she was trying to change. "You can't financially support the world, Sister Edna. You can't change all of humanity," he would say when he worried that she might not have enough to eat herself.

"The Lord has provided for my needs," she told him. "I have my Social Security, a small savings my beloved husband left me, and good friends who will never let me starve.

"But you're wrong about changing the world, Pastor Holmes. Do you think I can help just two people turn from a destructive path and embrace a life that is right with our Lord and savior?"

"Of course I do," laughed the minister. "If I didn't, I never would have gone to Bible college. I would have followed my first love in life and become a cowboy like Roy Rogers."

Edna smiled and said, "I'm serious, Pastor Holmes. And if I, or you, or anyone can change just two lives in their own lifetime, do you think that change will be enough to cause them to each influence two more people for good?"

"I would say that's a reasonable assumption," he replied, not quite certain where she was leading him.

"Then that's like one of those pyramid schemes they used to have when I was young. A man named Ponzi was arrested for one of them, I recall. The idea was to sell to two people who would each sell to two more and then each of them to two more, and so on. I think you didn't have to go very far before everyone on earth had bought into the scheme. Only this time it's a pyramid scheme for the Lord. We each change just two lives and soon we will have caused the entire world, billions and billions of people, to give their lives to Jesus."

"You're talking about the thousand year reign of Jesus following Armageddon, aren't you?"

"It doesn't matter what it's called. I'm not sure it matters what precedes it for that is in God's hands. But I truly believe that if each one of us tells the story to two others, tells it with the Holy Spirit guiding us so we touch their hearts, His kingdom will truly rule."

And so Edna stayed in the apartment, walking the streets at all hours, befriending the friendless. She was scoffed by some, ridiculed, taunted, even physically threatened. She was also embraced and loved, even by those who thought she was a crazy old lady whose ideas were from a world of which they would never be a part.

That was why she did not move, not even when Helen became successful enough to buy her grandmother a condominium in the most desirable sections of Manhattan. "This is where the Lord has put me. This is where I have friends. When He is ready to take me home, I will go joyously. Until then, please try to see my neighbors as I do."

APOCALYPSE

Helen continued to visit when she could, calling her grandmother two or three times a week. She worried about the old woman's safety, yet she also knew that somehow such concerns were unnecessary.

That Tuesday night, Helen Hannah called her grandmother fifteen minutes after the WNN Evening News went off the air. "What a wonderful newscast you had tonight, Helen," said her grandmother.

"Wonderful? Grandmother, we ran stories about housing riots in the Golan Heights, violence between families of Holocaust survivors and the Ku Klux Klan in Skokie, Illinois, a flood in Nevada causing severe food shortages and a desperate need for clean drinking water, an uprising by the generals in China, the torture trial of General..."

"Yes. Yes. I saw it all. Tragedy in Europe. Tragedy in the Middle East. Tragedy in the United States. Tragedy everywhere. A regular time of trial for many people. I hope you and your crew remembered to bless the Lord for what you were able to report."

"Grandmother, I know how your faith sustained you when Mom and Dad died and you were stuck with us kids, and I know how you live your life, but have you been buying some of the 'happy pills' your neighbors sell on the street? The news is hell these days. In my television journalism classes, the professors used to joke about how 'if it bleeds, it leads.' You look for something visually horrible — a shooting, a riot, a plane crash site — and you hook the viewer with it. Then you place happy news at the end so the viewer wants to watch you the next night.

"Do you know what our 'happy news' choices were tonight? A war in one of those unpronounceable Eastern European provinces where only 30 people died compared with 100 yesterday, and a plane

30

crash in Paris where a cat and two dogs were found alive in the
smoldering wreckage. Everything else was war, threats of war, famine,
earthquakes, plague, bad hair days for half the movie stars in Hollywood..."

"You're teasing me, dear, but I'm serious. You know what I've
been telling you about our Bible study of the end times. Yes, the world
is in a horrible mess, but that is all the more to let us see the hand of God
in our lives. The worse your news broadcasts, the closer we are to
Jesus. Some time soon, perhaps any day now, you mark my words that
there will be the rapture. After that, whoever is left behind at your
network can report on the greatest story the world will have known
since the birth of our Savior."

"I wish I had your faith, Grandmother. Every century there are
people predicting the end times. The new millennium just brings more
of them out. Do you know how many calls the network gets from people talking about the end of the world? The second coming of Jesus?
The soon to occur landing of UFOs or the imminent takeover of the
White House by little green men from Mars? Maybe not all of them are
crazy, but I don't think even you could discern which ones among them
have a vision of the future that doesn't stem from madness."

"It's not what people say. It's what's in the Bible. From Daniel
to Revelation, we're shown God's plan. I am deeply saddened for those
who are suffering, but the more our times reflect what is written, the
closer we come to the rapture."

"We've been through this before, Grandmother. I suppose I
believe in God. I suppose I believe in Jesus as our Savior. But I know
without question that my parents were good people. I needed them

desperately when they were killed. I needed their love. I needed their wisdom."

"And all you got was this old lady."

"No, that's not it, Grandma. You couldn't have loved me more. Now that I'm older, I even understand that if you hadn't been a wonderful mother to Mom, she wouldn't have known how to be so wonderful to me. Her loss wouldn't have been so devastating.

"But I also know that I would have had your love whether Mom and Dad lived or died. I wanted you all, Grandma. I wanted them *and* you. Sometimes, even now, I cry myself to sleep, questioning that God can exist and allow such a loss. Then I feel guilty for questioning His existence, my feelings turning to anger for His allowing the premature deaths of two of the three most important people in my life. And then.... And then I just hurt so much I don't know what to believe."

"I know. I really do understand. And despite your questioning, God understands as well. Your Mom was my daughter, and I loved your father like another son. There is no greater pain a parent can bear than the loss of a child. I expected your mother to bury me, not the other way around. I wanted her to grieve for me as I grieved for my mother, and she grieved for her mother before her. That should be the natural way.

"And yes, I, too, was angry with God. I would have taken her place if I could have done so. Instead, I have to wait out my years before being reunited with them. Until then you and I just have to accept His plans for us, to remember that ultimately he is in control."

"Does that really bring you comfort, Grandma? Is that why you find hope in a news cast like tonight's?"

"It truly does, Helen. And one day it will for you, too. Why else would we want to carry on if not to help fulfill His plan? You just watch. What is happening today in our lives, in the stories your network is covering, is unique in human existence. It is only a matter of time."

TWO

Bronson Pearl suspected he was going to have a problem when the flight attendant asked him to remain on the airplane while the other passengers disembarked. It wasn't a Customs issue. He had been through Customs when he flew from England to O'Hare for some work with WNN's regional headquarters. He had sent most of his baggage on to LaGuardia ahead of him, knowing the network would send a runner for it. Helen Hannah would be waiting for him in the parking area, so he kept only a couple of carry-ons to avoid having to wait at the baggage claim area. Now the flight attendant was keeping him longer than the old man in the wheelchair and the too-wise-for-her-years ten-year-old girl who was flying alone to meet her father. As she explained to everyone who would listen and several who pretended to be deaf, she fancied herself practicing shuttle diplomacy in the parent wars. "Dad owns a chain of steak and prime rib restaurants in Brooklyn, and Mom runs a vegetarian health food store in Cicero, so you see why they're divorced. I try to honor my parents by sneaking out to Wendy's for a triple beef patty when I'm living with Mom, and I eat tofu and bean sprouts with my baked potato when I have prime rib with Dad. It seems like the least I can do, what with all their guilt about the divorce and their determination to not speak badly about each other in front of me. But, honestly, absolutely everyone I know has two or three sets of parents because no one, just no one thinks marriage is forever any more.

"Not that I agree with them. I've told Johnny Connors — he's my boy friend when I'm with Mom in Cicero — that I want to elope to Niagara Falls, not telling anyone we're married. Then we'll get our own place and pretend we're just living together to make everyone happy."

But the kid was gone, the cleaning service was starting to work on the rear of the plane, and the flight attendant was standing, smiling, blocking his way and discussing one inanity or another. And Bronson felt he had to listen, had to be polite.

Suddenly the pilot opened the cockpit door and said, "Okay, Shirley. They're in place." Then he turned towards Bronson, held up a copy of Time magazine, and said, "Great picture of you on the cover, Mr. Pearl. Nice having you on board."

And then he knew. Helen had done it. Helen had really done it.

Bracing himself, Bronson Pearl left the plane and started up the ramp. He could hear them before he could see them, could imagine the looks of the other passengers and their friends in the waiting area.

There were a half dozen of them, each with a different toy instrument. Chet, the intern for the News department, had a tiny trumpet he had difficulty holding in his large hands. He had been a college football player, a massive kid with a brain to match, a compassionate heart, and a desire to see broadcast news bring change to a troubled world. Linda, the receptionist, was using a harmonica. Gareth, a newly hired sports reporter, had a toy piano. Imogene, one of Helen's researchers, had a miniature saxophone. Ian, from advertising, had a kazoo. And Afi, the new hire in public relations, was working with tissue paper and a comb.

The music was crude, off key, but recognizable. It was the theme from the "Bronson Pearl Report" on WNN, the music that led in to his weekly commentary.

He looked for Helen, not certain if he wanted to kiss her or strangle her. For years he had joked that he wasn't a success. He had been featured on the cover of *TV Guide* and on the inside pages of *People* magazine. *Broadcast* magazine had done an article on how he was able to gain the trust of so many different world leaders. And his salary had steadily increased to the point where, if he was frugal, he could retire in his forties and spend his days fishing up in the Pacific Northwest as he claimed he always wanted to do.

Not that Bronson Pearl had ever fished in his life. He had done stories about fishermen, both commercial fleet workers and average people who relaxed with a line in the water on a warm summer's morning. He thought it was an idyllic life and vowed to spend his retirement years doing nothing else.

Yet Bronson knew in his heart he would never have his fantasy life, probably never retire. He loved his work regardless of the fame and success it had brought him, and would have been just as happy covering local stories in Dead-At-Night, Iowa, as he was being a cable network star. "But I would like theme music," he said.

"What do you mean?" Helen had asked him. They had been eating at a restaurant in lower Manhattan and decided to walk back to her apartment on the upper east side.

"Theme music. Like they use on television. Haven't you ever noticed the shows where, every time the good guy goes into action, you hear music? I've never understood how the bad guys are deaf to what's taking place. I mean, it's in the dead of night, not a sound on the street except the occasional alley cat foraging for food in a back alley trash can, the good guy sneaking up on a warehouse where the bad guys have hidden their stolen merchandise, the kidnapped heiress, and the computer programmed to control the world, and suddenly his music overwhelms everything. It echoes off the walls, explodes on the street, and fills the night sky. The sound is everywhere, bold, brassy, exciting. And the bad guys never hear it. The good guy crashes through the window and karate chops everyone until they give up in terror.

"I'm on television. I have to interview bad guys. Why can't I have theme music that plays everywhere I go? Now that would be real success."

"Bronson, you're kidding," Helen had said, laughing.

"No. I'm serious. I'd give up half my salary for theme music. It would be the greatest perk a journalist could have."

"It would cost a fortune."

"No it wouldn't. The groupies would do it for nothing. They'd be honored."

"The groupies...?

"The reporter groupies. You know the ones. They're like the people who follow rock stars only more intellectual."

"And you've met these...these groupies...?" asked Helen. She had stopped, looking at him, her face both bemused and incredulous.

"Of course not. They're too reserved to approach me, more's the pity. But they're there in every airport lobby, admiring you, me, and all the other reporters from afar. If they weren't so conservative, they'd ask us for our autographs, give us a kiss on the cheek, ask for a few seconds of audio tape for a souvenir."

"Bronson, you're crazy," she had laughed.

"Maybe, but you can't tell me you haven't fantasized about something like that."

"Okay, Bronson. The day you have your picture on the cover of Time magazine, I'll get you theme music."

"I've been in *Time*. I didn't get any theme music."

"I didn't say *in* the magazine. The cover. You get the cover story and I'll make certain you have theme music."

That had been months ago, one of those times when too many long days and short nights, too many stories of man's inhumanity to man, had left them both exhausted. They had escaped to a day at a county fair, overdosing on cotton candy, hot dogs, and other midway treats, riding rides and delighting in the joy of a life away from the newsroom. It was in a moment of silliness that Bronson had made his comments. It was only after the flight attendant let him leave the plane that he realized Helen had remembered.

The make-shift band moved behind Bronson as he walked from the entrance area. They matched his step, saying nothing, ignoring the stares of other passengers, acting as though what they were doing was perfectly normal.

"Helen..." said Bronson, starting to blush. "Helen, where are you?"

And then he saw the poster. It was the *Time* magazine cover for the current week, blown up so that the cover photo was life size. "Bronson Pearl: The World's Most Trusted Newsman" was printed underneath. At first he thought it was a joke, something Helen had the production department create on their computers. Then he saw the news stand and the same issue on the rack.

"Helen...?"

Helen Hannah stepped from behind a pillar holding a piece of paper, a pencil, and a grin that told him she was delighting in his embarrassment. "Look... Over there..." she shouted, attracting the attention of passengers about to board the return flight to Chicago. "The man with the theme music. It's... It's... It's Dan Rather. I'd know him anywhere. Dan Rather of CBS News. I've got to have your autograph Mr. Rather."

"Helen. I'm going to kill you," whispered Bronson, still walking as she rushed to his side. "I'm going to marry you and then I'm going to kill you. I just hope someone is videotaping this so the jury will rule it justifiable homicide."

Helen ignored him. Grinning broadly, her voice excitedly high, she said, loudly, "Sign my paper, Mr. Rather. I'm your biggest fan."

Bronson kept walking, his face flushed. Helen kept pace, waving the paper at him, holding out the pencil, his co-workers from WNN matching the two step for step, playing the theme music over and over.

As they passed one of the bars, a rather large man who had apparently misjudged his capacity for alcohol during a flight delay, moved unsteadily from his stool and stepped out to confront Bronson. "I've been watching you, Rather," he said, angrily. "That's the trouble with you celebrity types. You're rude. I seen you on television, pretending to be so nice. Then you come here and all this lady wants is your autograph and you treat her like she stepped in something your dog dropped on the sidewalk. It's disgusting, all the money CBS pays you. Give the lady your autograph or I'll tell all the guys at the shop to watch some other station."

Helen handed him the paper, trying to keep from laughing as the stranger watched him write "Dan Rather."

"Can't you say something personal to the lady? A big fan like this?" said the man. His breath was sour, his eyes bloodshot. Bronson hoped he was waiting for a friend. If he was an airline passenger, the flight attendants were going to have a difficult time.

"How about 'to my greatest fan, a beautiful and gracious lady?' That make you happy?"

The man nodded, watched Bronson for a moment, then looked up, his face suddenly quite pale. He glanced around, spotted the men's room, and hurried off. Helen burst into laughter. The rest of the WNN crew managed to continue playing, though more shakily than before.

"I owe you," said Bronson.

"I'm looking forward to it, Bronson," she said softly. "Time magazine..." She looked at him for a moment, then cupped her hand around his neck, brought his head close to hers, and kissed him tenderly. "I'm so proud of you, even if you're not Dan Rather."

APOCALYPSE

Bronson smiled, lost for a moment in her eyes. Then he looked back at the people watching the spectacle she had created for him, and said, "Helen, could we just get out of here? I've never felt so foolish in my life."

Helen stopped, her face suddenly showing the intensely sad, expression of an eager puppy who has just discovered that the expensive new slippers his owner unwrapped the night before really weren't his newest chew toy. "But Bronson," she whined before bursting into laughter. "You *said* you wanted theme music."

*

They called themselves the Women Who Witness. They were Arab and Israeli, Christian, Jew, and Muslim. Most were in their thirties and forties. A few were barely out of their teens, widowed in one instance before the marriage could be consummated. Others were much older, having lost not only husbands and sons but an occasional grandson. In their homes some followed traditions dating back thousands of years. Others were so liberal that their diets were based on the offerings of McDonald's rather than the teachings of Leviticus. They all wore the traditional head and body covering of modest Arab women when demonstrating, the cloth serving as both an act of respect for their orthodox Islamic members who had to dress in such a manner, and to reduce the chance they would be recognized.

Sometimes they stood silently in the midst of a riot or war zone, a reminder, they explained, that there are no winners in such conflict. Violence means a loss of life, a grieving mother, wife, or daughter. God is present in the creation of each new life. To destroy that life because of where someone is born, the language they speak, or where they go to give thanks and praise to the Creator is an abomination. Neither side can claim to "win" if victory means ending a life before it was in the Father's plan to call him home.

The women said they were militant in love. Sometimes they lifted their voices in prayer and song, each speaking in her native tongue of Hebrew, Arabic, English, Russian, or one of the Eastern European languages. "God hears all," they explained. "God understands all."

Sometimes one or more spoke out angrily against the atrocities in their midst, sharing her personal story of an earlier time when a family member was maimed, tortured, or killed. They stood not as a buffer between opposing forces but as prophets whose own lives foretold more pain, suffering, and sadness if those they confronted continued the actions of the past.

Yet even in those moments when they chose to protest by their silence, their sad presence articulated the senseless horror of endless war.

At first the news media treated them as a different type of photo opportunity. They would be recorded as a framing device amidst ruins, masked youths hurling stones, and police firing rubber bullets into the midst of hostile mobs. They were not generals or kings, presidents or religious leaders. Some had attended college and graduate school. Others could barely read or write, trained in domestic chores and subservience to the husbands to whom they were betrothed before their teenaged years.

None of the women sought personal glory. None of the women used their given names. They traveled to and from their homes using routes that were constantly changing, elaborately planned, and involving a network of sympathizers, safe houses, and disguises. To do otherwise was to risk the arrest and torture of families who, in many instances, did not know that a spouse or daughter was one of the Women Who Witness.

The names they gave to the press and the authorities were those of historic women who, in their opinion, witnessed the role of God in the lives of man in a manner that changed the world. One member identified herself as Miriam. Another said she was Sarah. A third called herself Elizabeth. There was a Hannah, a Mary, a Salome', a Eunice, and several more. Each name was a reminder of a Bible story, an event that told of God's covenants with His people, of his faithfulness unto death and beyond. Each name had endured difficult times, often including extreme violence against herself or her loved ones. Sarah had endured barrenness at a time when a woman's value came in large measure from her ability to reproduce. Then she had known the pleasure of motherhood in her old age, her children destined to be great leaders working for God. Mary was the humble Jewish teenager who was favored above all others to bring the son of God into the world. Eunice, the Jewish wife of a Greek, was praised by Paul for her faith and her nurturing of her son, Timothy, a leader in the early Christian church.

At first the witnesses came together by chance. Each had lost a son, a husband, a brother, or a father to the senseless violence that was increasing throughout the Middle East. They met in the marketplace, the hospital, the synagogue, mosque, or church, sharing their stories with women of their faith, nationality, and income bracket. Then, as if guided by the hand of God, one or another of the grieving friends would encounter a woman who was officially her "enemy," seeing in the grief stricken face a mirror of her own soul. Gradually they had accomplished the "impossible," uniting in love, bonded by shared experience, transcending the cosmetic differences that once had kept them apart.

In grief they became the sisters of Eve whose one son, Abel, was murdered because of the greed, jealousy, and foolish anger of his brother, Cain, who she also lost through his forced exile. In grief they also became the sisters of Mary, the mother of Jesus, killed on the cross in fulfillment of prophecy.

It was not that they failed to see God's hand in such events. They knew all was done for His plan and that, ultimately, it would be good. But they were mothers first, and mothers grieve the loss of even a wayward child such as Cain. Thus their tears formed a communion of women that seemed to predate written history and would continue until the Second Coming.

Those early members of Women Who Witness also expressed a sisterhood with Mary Magdalene, Mary, mother of James, and Salome', the women who had discovered the empty tomb of Jesus and thus been the first to learn of His resurrection. They were the bearers of sorrow, but they could also be the harbingers of the Good News. And so they went out together, challenging the evil that seemed to be increasingly dominating all aspects of the Middle East.

Women Who Witness first appeared as a group in Jerusalem, at the site of the endlessly disputed Temple Mount, one of the holiest locations for all of Judaism, Christianity, and Islam. Riots had broken out over the issue of yet another rebuilding of what began as Solomon's Temple, was destroyed, then eventually rebuilt as Herod's Temple until it, too, was destroyed in 70 A.D. Arabs also considered the site sacred. They called it the Dome of the Rock, believing it was from there that the prophet Mohammed received the Koran.

Many Christians and Jews believed that God had once been physically present on the site and that He would return there to rule the earth. Yet in His absence, the men made an abomination of the area by constantly trying to kill each other in His name. Or so the women believed as they stood in silent prayer while rubber bullets, rocks, sticks, and tear gas exploded all around.

It was Franco Macalusso who first sensed the potential international impact of Women Who Witness. It was impossible to look at them without compassion. It was impossible to talk with them without being moved by their sincere desire for peace. Yet though they spoke as though having at least some knowledge of one or another Holy books, one or another faiths, they were not committed to any teaching. By trying to be inclusive, they no longer felt themselves to be Christian, Jew, or Muslim. A pagan was as welcome as a Catholic, so determined were they to not continue divisiveness of any kind, even in spiritual matters.

Macalusso began meeting with the women, gaining their loyalty as he discussed his own concerns for world peace. They were flattered by his attention, impressed that someone so well known and respected in the United Nations should take the time to be with them. They knew little of his history, little of his life. What mattered was that he had access to the news media, that he cared about their cause, that when they gave him their support, they were endorsing a man who understood the need for peace at any price.

Despite their tendency to try to be in the middle of escalating conflicts, none of the women were ever hurt. Some of the women said that if God was with them, who could be against them? Observers who were more cynical sneered and said that God protects fools and little children.

Over time the presence of the Women Who Witness became a bigger story than the riots, terrorist attacks, and examples of inhumanity that drew them to neighborhoods and religious sites throughout the Middle East. Their message was not political. They said they would follow anyone who brought peace to the region, regardless of religious affiliation, political party, or nationality. "Some of us would probably get in bed with the devil if our children would stop dying from this senseless violence," one of the women commented. It was a statement chilling to their detractors who instantly thought about the blind following so many dictators had enjoyed. Others found the statement uplifting, thinking of the Wise Men and Shepherds who sought out the baby Jesus.

WNN's Bronson Pearl covered the story of the women because it was the story every network had to run. At once tragic and hopeful, the women seemed like a beacon of light in one of the darker corners of the world.

Pearl noticed that the peasants and middle class, unconnected with the rich and powerful, were beginning to listen to the personal testimony of the Women Who Witness. The average man and woman on the street told Bronson that they felt they were hearing their own lives reflected in the stories of the Women Who Witness. They listened when revenge still seemed like a viable option. They listened when the men and boys in their families were still strong, virile, still capable of loving and being loved or entering combat to kill and be killed. The women especially said they were beginning to question the values of the government leaders, the military, even those spiritual leaders who seemed to justify a hate destructive to God's creation.

Soon many women who had not yet experienced the losses of the Women Who Witness aggressively began challenging their religious leaders, regardless of faith, questioning why the Creator was honored by the death of His sons. As car bombs and suicide bombs, sniper fire and commando raids turned more and more of the Holy Land red with blood, it was the women who began going to local demonstrations to stand between the violent factions. Often acting against the ways of their culture, they faced their angry husbands, sons, fathers, and/or brothers, demanding that they return home at once. They risked scorn, arrest, and floggings in some locations, but they did not care. The Middle East was rapidly spinning out of control. The leaders were shifting soldiers, stockpiling weapons of mass destruction, and calling upon nations pledged to their support to enhance the growing international military presence. Someone had to say "no," and the Women Who Witness were slowly inspiring the one force who best understood death since it was women who had been chosen by God to carry each new life to term. Or such was their image.

Not that Bronson was as impressed as many of his colleagues. "Something's wrong with all this," he had told Helen when they were eating out together one night. "Remember when we were in Ireland a few years ago, covering the women's march for peace? They were mixed Catholic and Protestant, but they were brought together by their religious faith, not just their frustration with the bombings and shooting.

They had lost friends and loved ones. Many were widowed or the mothers of dead children. Yet there was something different about them. Something..."

"Spiritual, Bronson?"

"Yes. Like your grandmother. It's not that these women aren't sincere. It's just that they seem like some of the one issue politicians in the States. I get the feeling that they would tolerate a Hitler if he stopped the fighting."

"You're getting cynical, my love. Though I must admit that my grandmother agrees with you. She doesn't even like that UN consultant you interviewed."

"Macalusso? At least his connection is understandable. He comes from the business world, and only weapons manufacturers think that wars are good for business. He's also being courted by the European Union to take some high-profile post with them, and what's an alliance like that if not about business?"

"So why are you covering them on your next Bronson Pearl Special?"

"I'm pragmatic, too. There are going to be specials on CBS, the BBC, CBC, CNN, and all the rest. I was told I could do a report first and hopefully better, or I could go back to reading the farm report at 2 a.m. in some backwater affiliate in the middle of nowhere."

"You, my love? The man who has won more industry awards than any other broadcaster at the network? You would jump through the corporate hoop just to have a regular paycheck?"

"That and so I get to be with you. Until you decide to retire and take up crocheting, you're spending so much time at the network, I have to work there or we'd never have time together."

"That's right. Lay the moral choice on me."

"What moral choice? They're sincere. Macalusso's sincere. It's a real story. I just find what's going on almost cult like and it makes me uncomfortable. But if they can ease the tensions in the Middle East by standing around as a permanent photo opportunity, who am I to say I won't cover the story?"

*

The idea that Helen Hannah was one of WNN's most popular news anchors was not so surprising as that she had settled into one job long enough to be a success at anything. Not that she wasn't intelligent. She originally anticipated majoring in the sciences and minoring in the arts. Her early career plans were to make her living in bio-mechanical research, a field that marries computer technology, engineering, and medicine. But her inquiring mind led her to take so many additional classes in anthropology, history, and art that she was in her fifth year of what should have been a four year education before an adviser suggested switching to journalism. "You have the most curious mind I've ever encountered," he told her. "Everything in life excites you. Why don't you forget saving the world and just start reporting it? Journalism is the one profession I know where you can get paid for being nosy."

Helen had been embarrassed to tell her grandmother about her plan to change careers. She knew her grandmother wanted her to be in a profession where she could help others, do good works. She had made a point of introducing Helen to women who were making careers in the ministry in one capacity or another. Some were educators. Others were choir directors, missionaries, and ministers. The idea of being in a field that combined medicine and science to help others overcome disabilities seemed to fit a number of her interests and certainly pleased the elderly woman who raised her.

But journalism had a different image. She had often heard Pastor Holmes speak out against the media. He criticized the lack of moral fiber among reporters. They would embarrass a government official, but they would rarely attack an important local business whose practices were unethical or otherwise dangerous to the public. The self-interest of advertisers and the bias of the owners seemed to motivate both print and electronic journalism, and she knew that her grandmother shared such feelings.

To her surprise, Edna Williams had enthusiastically supported her grand-daughter's interest. "Of course I'm angered by much of what I read in the papers and see on television. But that doesn't mean there is anything wrong with the media. Don't you realize that the scrolls used to make the Bible were the media of their day? And Jesus' disciple Luke was like you. His first interest was science. He was a physician, not a fisherman or laborer like the others. And he became a writer with two of his books being used in the New Testament.

"You're the one in control of your career, of where you work and how you handle yourself. There are clergy who are held in great esteem yet who act against the will of God. That doesn't mean that the ministry is a sinful profession.

"The good Lord gave us free will in every endeavor, Helen. If you are right with Him, it does not matter how you earn your living."

Helen was not like her grandmother. In her parochial school she sometimes told a favorite teacher that she loved God but she was not sure she liked Him. If the story was true, He had let His own Son die, and He had certainly let her parents die. She did not see where the media and God had much in common, but she did care that her grandmother was pleased with her choice of profession. She just did not tell her the number of times she compromised what one of her professors sneeringly called "journalistic integrity" during a Sweeps Week.

For example, while working for one station, she agreed to carry a hidden camera and wear a broadcast wire for a Sweeps Week exposé of adult oriented businesses near the airport. She took a job as a hostess in a men's club where there was a dress code for the males and an undress code for the female dancers. She and the bouncer were the only ones who were modestly attired among the staff, and she filmed some of the "entertainment" for broadcast on the evening news. The two anchors, the sports reporter, and the weather girl all looked appropriately shocked by the five day report on what was happening. They praised Helen's work on camera, talking about the danger she must have been in, the courage she had shown. Then, when the broadcast was over, several of the staff went to the very same club to see the same "disgusting" action for themselves.

It was all hypocrisy in the name of news, yet tapes of such programs helped her get better jobs when she moved into larger markets.

Helen made one other discovery as she advanced. She was becoming a skilled reporter in addition to being increasingly competent on air. At the last station where she worked before joining WNN back in New York, she was given a chance to produce some documentaries that had been nominated for regional Emmys. She did not win, though.

There was an unwritten rule in the industry that Emmys were always given to news people with at least five years in the local market. She stayed just two years, though she had been nominated for more awards than any other television reporter in the region when she left. In addition she had been given a number of freelance assignments from regional news magazines not considered to be conflicts of interest by her station, and she had won awards for that writing.

What was more important to Helen than the honors was the growing sense of control with television news. The basic broadcasts were written by herself and others, then read on a Teleprompter. The special reports, documentaries, and other features were completely her own. She would decide who to interview, what footage to shoot and show, and the way the public would perceive the subject she was covering.

Truth, Helen realized, was subjective. The reporter shaped the truth by who he or she interviewed, the questions asked, and sometimes the questions not asked. The videographer shaped the truth by what was photographed and how it was shown to the viewer. But the ultimate power was with the person who handled the final editing of the production.

As editor, Helen could take a story about the tragic famine in Somalia, a famine which the President visited, falling to his knees in prayer, weeping with the awareness of the helplessness, then reshape what happened. First would come the images of the dead and dying. Then would come a voice over about how deeply moved the President had been upon arrival in Air Force One. And then she would segue to another visual of a party later that night where the President is shown laughing at a joke made by the U.S. ambassador. It did not matter that the joke was the only light hearted moment on a trip that saw the President dedicate every American resource to save the lives of the people. The message Helen would give the viewer was that the President was unfeeling in the midst of horror, exactly the opposite of the reality. Yet if someone just listened to the sound track, did not see the carefully planned juxtaposition of unrelated images, he or she would think the story was an objective reporting of the President's deep sadness.

Not that Helen would do such vicious editing. She was simply fascinated with the morality play that was unfolding with each choice she could make while working behind the scenes on longer pieces.

Editing meant power. Being in production meant power. Being the person on camera, interpreting the news, meant power.

For someone who had felt that her life was out of control, the job with WNN was exciting. She could not make her parents come alive again, or restore youth to the old woman who had raised her with such love and faith. But she could produce something structured to her desires, something that could possibly outlast her time on earth, and that fact brought her pleasure. She was at last being "paid to be nosy" as well as in charge of at least some of the news segments. She realized she could not have asked for a better job.

If there was any problem with her life, it was Bronson. Love meant giving up control, being vulnerable to the pain of loss, too much of which she had already experienced. She remembered when her parents died, Pastor Holmes talking about death being another part of life. He tried to tell her that her parents had passed over, though she did not find his words particularly comforting. In her grief, she was convinced that he was expressing ideas meant to bring her a degree of comfort and hope, and while she knew he believed what he said, she found his words empty for her. Maybe when she was older she'd share such faith, she told herself, anxious to please her grandmother and the kind men and women from her grandmother's church. But for now she could only feel sad, saying nothing. As an adult, she still had mixed feelings, though she knew she did not want to get involved with a man only to have him taken when she committed herself.

It was easier to stay focused on work these days. The dangers the world was facing, the nightmares already experienced, were unlike any that had ever been recorded before. The Los Angeles earthquake, though a major disaster in its own right, had triggered even worse catastrophes. There was a volcanic eruption in Hawaii, a tidal wave off the coast of Japan, and a looming crisis in several agricultural regions due to unexpected climate changes accompanying hurricane force wind currents in normally placid areas. WNN reporters were at all the scenes, including providing on-going coverage of the evacuation of a small Pacific Island nation about to be completely submerged by the rising ocean water.

Then there were the growing terrorist activities that had led the European Union, the United Nations, the U.S. Government, and a host of other countries and organizations to begin shifting their military personnel around the world. Rapid deployment forces were being heavily reinforced. The American military had quietly reinstated the draft, and National Guard units were being mobilized for retraining before being shipped to one or another global hot spots.

APOCALYPSE

All of the stories were colorful by television news standards. There was violence and despair as people were forced to evacuate their homes, leave their jobs, and journey to make-shift camps in officially neutral territories. There were also occasional stories of hope in individual acts of heroism and compassion that revealed the triumph of the human spirit in even the worst of days. Many of the stories were being recorded by WNN crews, and each was being brought to the world by Helen and the others who worked the news desk.

*

For those whose job it was to stop and analyze world events, the actions taking place in the Middle East made little sense. It was like the time of Pharaoh when Moses demonstrated that the power of the one true God was far greater than the tricks of the Egyptian magicians. He would intimidate Pharaoh, showing him again and again that the leader was helpless in the face of the Lord above in whom Pharaoh refused to believe. Then Pharaoh's heart would be hardened and Moses would have to plead the people's cause anew. Finally, when Pharaoh was beyond all reasoning, every first born son in homes not protected by the blood of the Passover lamb was taken by the Angel of Death.

Perhaps the Egyptian people who had witnessed the argument between Moses and Pharaoh wondered how their leader could let matters go to such an extreme that death ruled the land. They probably wondered how, even after this example of the might of Moses' Lord, Pharaoh could send his troops to drown in pursuit of people he had no reason to continue holding in bondage against their wills.

No one knew exactly what caused Pharaoh to act as he had, yet astute observers of the Middle East saw a similar crisis arising. Multi-national troops were being drawn into a series of conflicts that were increasingly focused on the area of Megiddo. Alliances that had been formed months or years earlier based on special needs — oil, food, weapons — were suddenly called upon to act in a manner no one ever thought would happen. Russian troops, American troops, French forces, Germans, Chinese, Syrian, Lebanese, Jordanians, Iraqis, Iranians, and others were deploying in an ever tightening knot around Israel. Missiles were being retargeted. Nuclear and biological weapons were being quietly placed in armed warheads. Conventional troops were positioned for maximum first strike capability. Former enemies were acting in consort. Former friends sometimes found themselves with conflicting alliances. And no single issue seemed great enough to warrant the increasingly dangerous power plays.

"The world has become an elementary school playground where immature children are playing a dangerous game of chicken, none of them willing to back off," said Hogarth Chapman, commentator on WNN's Nightly Update. A former high official with the United States State Department, he had been involved with other periods of confrontation. He had been in college during the Suez Canal Crisis under the Eisenhower administration. He had witnessed the Berlin Airlift, the Cuban Missile Crisis, the tension between India and Pakistan, the rise of the Islamic fundamentalists in Iran, and similar events.

"The weapons of mass destruction have changed. The fear used to be of the bombs that were dropped on Hiroshima and Nagasaki. Masses of people were killed in a matter of seconds. Far more were killed slowly or were genetically altered so their children suffered after birth. The effects of just those two small bombs lasted for two generations, yet the actual destructive force was not as great as the fire storm bombing of Dresden, Germany.

"We 'improved' our atomic and thermonuclear weapons during the Cold War. We made them bigger and more powerful, and we made them smaller, tactical. We found ways to destroy entire cities or to eradicate 50,000 soldiers massed on a battlefield in seconds. We also began working on neutron bombs which would only destroy human life, allowing us to eliminate every resident of Moscow without damaging the office buildings, museums, and churches.

"Although the major powers gradually amassed an arsenal of perhaps 60,000 atomic bombs, perhaps more, they controlled access to the means of production, limiting how fast other nations could gain such power. Yet some small nations surrounded by enemies, such as Israel and Pakistan, used spies, double agents, bribery, and theft to acquire atomic secrets and the equipment needed to turn the knowledge into bombs. Others, such as Iraq, simultaneously began developing the biological equivalent of the neutron bomb — chemicals and biological substances that could kill large numbers of people.

"Anthrax, Bubonic Plague, and other deadly diseases that are quick to kill were obtained from legitimate research labs. Most people do not realize how readily available vials of these killer diseases can be. While there are antidotes known, since the diseases were mostly eliminated from the world, such antidotes are available only in very limited quantities. The small stockpiles would be depleted within hours if a widespread assault with germ warfare occurred.

"Chemical weapons are even worse. Countries such as Iraq have manufactured tons of chemicals so deadly, one drop can kill a human within moments of its coming into contact with someone's skin. The quantity of such chemicals manufactured by Iraq, even when under United Nations' sanctions against having such weapons, was enough to kill every man, woman, and child in the world. And it can be transported in vials or even in a child's squirt gun, a weapon simpler, deadlier, and harder to stop than even the largest of thermonuclear weapons."

Helen Hannah, acting as narrator for the taped program, explained that the current international crisis was one once thought impossible. When the early authorization was given for the manufacture of such weapons, the belief was that they were so horrible, no one would use them. It was like hiring the biggest, toughest, meanest martial artist available to act as a body guard.

"The statistics were chilling," she said. "The United States had missiles targeted against 16,000 sites, mostly in the Soviet Union. This was not our nuclear arsenal. This just represented the number of missiles that could be launched simultaneously should war break out."

"We believed in victory," said Hogarth Chapman. "Our deterrent policy involved our enemies knowing we were prepared to destroy them if they attacked us. It was insane, of course. No one ever believed we would make such a launch. And even when we downsized to approximately 2,000 missiles by the end of the century, we still had the capacity to destroy the world."

Helen Hannah explained to the viewers what nuclear destruction would actually mean. "We're not just talking about eliminating a city with perhaps a million deaths. That would happen, of course. But it is the long term effect that is truly a concern.

"Radiation would poison the water and effect crops throughout the world. The food we need for life would be the means of our death.

"The explosions would also create atmospheric changes that would reduce growing seasons and alter the temperatures of the world. This may mean colder weather that creates widespread famine. This may mean hotter weather which melts some portion of the polar ice caps, causing oceans and rivers to rise, flooding fertile land essential to farmers. No one is certain exactly what would happen, though all scientists interviewed agree that epidemics of illness, mass starvation, and similar catastrophes would destroy life as we know it."

Helen explained that, in the past, countries always managed to restrain their use of force. They planned their battles with a specific victory in mind.

"There is no precedent in the history of the world for what is taking place in the region that surrounds Megiddo," said former State Department Envoy Melissa Hargrove, a commentator heard over WNN's radio division. "There is no monster determined to control the world. There is no Alexander the Great. There is no Attila the Hun. There is no hate filled madman like Adolf Hitler.

"Past wars have always had an evil force behind which the enemy rallied and against which the people of goodness could do battle. This time there is no single leader seeking to dominate the world and subjugate the people. There is no one against whom the nations of the world seem focused.

"I fear that war is inevitable. I fear that the nations of the world are not going to back off, to say 'Enough,' to let good judgment overcome ill conceived and foolishly followed treaties. God help us, I fear that the war we have so long made a seemingly impossible Bogeyman, a war in which civilization itself will be the ultimate loser, has already begun. We just don't realize it yet."

*

Many people agreed with what they heard. Some began praying that what seemed so certain would pass without eruption. Others wrote letters to their government leaders, pleading for cool heads and reasoned judgment. Still others found themselves angered by what they were witnessing, demanding the United States use whatever force was necessary to restore order in the Middle East.

And a few, like Edna Williams, read their Bibles, went about their business, praising the Lord for each new headline of even greater tension, yet always having compassion for those who were suffering. "Let the time of trial be short, oh Lord," prayed Edna, both during her daily devotionals and at church. "I see your hand in all the suffering, but I see the suffering as well. If this is taking place as you have planned, I accept that those who are in pain and sorrow will be comforted by the love of your Son who also was innocent and hurting. And let me always remember the words our Lord Jesus taught us, Thy will, not mine.'"

*

"I meant what I said at the airport," said Bronson Pearl. He was sitting with Helen in the back seat of the large Lincoln the network had hired to transport him back into the city. His eyes were closed, his left hand holding hers. It was the first time he had been able to truly relax in days.

"About killing me?" said Helen. "I knew that. You'd do anything to boost the ratings for WNN. Of course, it would have to be done as a special with plenty of advance promotion. The promotion department would want to have a viewer contest to see if you should use poison, suffocation, or a gun. They'd use a 900 number so they'd also make money each time someone voted. And they'd want to get Dr. Kevorkian to do play-by-play, and..."

"About marrying you," he interrupted.

"I knew that, too," she said, her voice growing softer. "But it wouldn't do a thing for the ratings. You might even lose your status as the most trusted man in broadcasting. Geraldo Rivera would have me on his show and ask whether you really take out the garbage, squeeze the toothpaste from the bottom of the tube, and leave the toilet seat down when you're done..."

"You can't hide behind jokes all your life, Helen. I love you, and as much as you don't want to deal with the fact, you love me, too."

"I know I love you, Bronson. You just said so, and you're the most trusted man in..."

Bronson took her face in his hand, kissing her into silence. "Helen, just once will you please shut-up and take me seriously? I want you for my wife. No matter how much time we spend together, it's not enough. No matter how devoted we feel to each other, it's not the same commitment as marriage."

"Bronson, I..."

"And don't tell me that the world is going to hell, that it's no time to be raising children, that our jobs are so consuming we'd never be happy. I've heard all your excuses and I know they're all lies. Even your grandmother says so. The only thing wrong with you is that you're afraid of commitment."

"No I'm not. I'm afraid of what commitment might bring."

"It's certainly not going to be the little suburban home with the picket fence, rose bushes, a swing set, a slide, a dog named Fido, and 2.3 children, or whatever number people are supposed to be having these days. We're not that type. But love without marriage is hollow. It's a denial of what love truly means.

"We're not kids, Helen. We've each got almost twenty years in this business. We've both been through bad relationships. We've both seen as much failure in our professional lives as we have our recent success. And we both have experienced enough human tragedy to know that you need to embrace that which is good in life because nothing is forever."

"That's the problem, Bronson. Everyone I've ever loved has failed me. As a little kid, my teachers taught me about Jesus, about how when I was in the depths of despair, He would wrap me in His arms. Then my parents left me when I needed them most, and when I tried reaching out to Jesus, all I could feel was a pillow damp with a teenager's endless tears.

"I've told you about losing Jeff. And you know the humiliation with Norman...."

"Your parents were killed in a plane crash. They didn't abandon you. They experienced what you, I, and every frequent flyer fears.

They were locked in a slender tube thousands of miles in the air with no way to survive if anything unforeseen happened. You've seen the report. It may have been a bomb. It may have been mechanical failure. But if it was a bomb, your parents didn't construct it. They didn't plant it. They didn't trigger it.

"And if it was mechanical failure, they weren't the technicians who worked on it. They were passengers. Helpless passengers. They could neither have predicted what occurred nor prevented it.

"As for Jeff, it seems like every time you tell me that story it grows in importance in your mind. You were seventeen years old. He took you to the Senior Prom. You had a summer romance. Then he went in the Army and you went on to college, and by your own admission you were so caught up with being a freshman and enjoying the campus that you thought nothing more about him until you learned he was killed in a training accident. In all those months, he never called you, never wrote you a letter, and you never tried to reach him. Let's face it, Helen, you've exaggerated a summer fling that went nowhere into some great lost love that's proof of the Hannah cloud of doom."

"What about Norman? He was certainly a serious part of my life. We were engaged to be married."

"And you discovered he got your best friend pregnant because he hated the idea that you were saving yourself for marriage.

"Helen, he was a rotten human being. You said yourself he lived on schemes and pipe dreams, a guy who was going to end up going to jail.

"We won't even discuss the character of this so-called 'best friend' who had an affair with him. They were both losers without a shred of morality.

"From what you've said, the guy was handsome, with a good line. You were what...23? 24? lonely, vulnerable, and convinced you were worthless. He fed on your ego so you never looked beneath the surface."

"But we were engaged to be married. I loved him. I was willing to commit myself to him for life."

"With all the wisdom of a kid just coming out of adolescence. It was a terrible blow, Helen. I don't question that. But let's face it, if you met a guy like that today, you wouldn't look at him twice.

"Everybody experiences pain and loss. Everybody makes mistakes. And everybody questions God at some time in their lives. But that doesn't mean you have to be held back by the past. It's time to get over it."

"It's just been too many losses. I feel like I've done something so terribly wrong that God's determined to keep me from being truly happy."

"You're the only one stopping happiness. I'm not Jeff. I'm not Norman." He paused, touching her cheek. "Helen, I'm Bronson Pearl, the most trusted journalist in America. Time magazine said so. I even have theme music. And I'm telling you I love you. I want to marry you and spend my life with you even if your ratings slip and they demote you to Weather Girl in Fargo, North Dakota, where you will have to look perpetually perky in a parka while telling everyone how cold it is."

"You'd love me if I was Weather Girl in Fargo?"

"How much more devoted could I be?" he said, yawning. The intensity of his final hours before leaving Europe and the Middle East were catching up with him. He closed his eyes as they talked.

"You could try saying 'perpetually perky in a parka' three more times without screwing up."

"So maybe I'm not that devoted." He yawned again and shifted to a more comfortable position on the seat, never letting go of Helen's hand. "Now will you marry me?"

*

"Don't ask," said Helen Hannah as she entered the Production Department to work on the editing of what WNN top brass were calling The Macalusso Project. It was a rush-to-air biography of the newly elected President of the European Union and it was being handled by Helen and Kathy Tamagachi, chief of production for the Special Projects Division of WNN. Kathy was delighted with the assignment. Helen was frustrated that in a matter of weeks after she had teased Bronson for running a series of three 5-minute Special Reports, she was the one who had agreed to help produce a two hour biography of the man. She tried to tell herself she hadn't compromised, tried to say that the depth made the difference because the truth could be revealed. However, she realized that, like Bronson, she liked the job too much to balk. There were many wars to fight in a career, but this was not one of them. At least she could work with Kathy whose skills and integrity as a journalist she respected.

Tamagachi was jokingly called a part of the "New World Order." Her father was Asian, her mother a red headed Irish woman. The two of them met while students at the Sorbonne in France, married while on a holiday in Berlin, and conceived Kathy after moving to Chicago where her father was a college professor and her mother worked for the art museum. She had originally planned to go into publishing, then became fascinated with the possibilities of electronic journalism as a medium for telling stories. She worked in Boston for Public Broadcasting, spent three years with a private video production company, and then moved to WNN. She was considered the top producer/editor in network headquarters, the reason she was assigned to Helen. Unfortunately her office remained the one she had used when her responsibilities were far less. In order for Helen to be there, she had to clear file folders, stacks of tapes, and other items from a section of the floor. Shelves that reached the ceiling and required a small step ladder for the highest levels were crammed with tapes, film cans, still photographs, and books. File cabinets were crammed with papers. Her massive desk, equipped with multi-line telephone, in-line recording device, and two computers was so covered with stacks of file folders that it had been weeks since she had last seen the surface. Only the editing bays, monitors, and related equipment that filled the rest of the room were clean and well maintained, but that was because they were easily damaged.

The floor had become the sorting area for much of the material being edited into the documentary on Franco Macalusso. It was littered with stacked tapes and film cans that had been gathered for weeks from throughout the world. Some of the editors in the news department wanted to take credit for having anticipated the change in world events, but the truth was they had no idea what was happening. What they did know was that Franco Macalusso had seemingly come out of nowhere to be the most influential leader in the world. They knew he had briefly contemplated some sort of religious life which he abandoned while in his very early twenties. They knew he had made a fortune in the communications industry through a series of companies the ownership of which was carefully hidden. They knew he had gone to work with the United Nations. His public rise to a position of influence everywhere in the world had seemed a logical future when the biography was first assigned. What no one anticipated were the serious changes in world affairs that had brought so many nations to the brink of war.

Kathy was running a tape of Macalusso when Helen arrived with sandwiches, coleslaw, and coffee from a nearby delicatessen. Both of them were working on the editing and voice overs when their other duties did not interfere. With time pressures mounting, they had begun working through lunch. "Don't say one word about Bronson Pearl to me. If you have any questions, you can ask him whenever he's rested enough to come in to work."

"That serious, huh?" said Kathy. Then laughingly holding up her hands as though defending herself against a possible attack, she added, "I didn't say his name. My question was purely rhetorical."

Helen scowled, then glanced at the monitor. "Forgive my disrespect, but sometimes I feel like I'm watching that old television series 'Charlie's Angels' when I see some of the footage of Macalusso and the Women Who Watch. The way he's been courting them, it's like he's building a cult following."

"My, you are cynical," said Kathy, taking a bite from a corned beef sandwich. "Watch the interviews I've been assembling. He doesn't come across as *that* much of a saint."

Helen switched on the monitor speakers instead of putting on the headphones Kathy had been using. Kathy had seen the tapes made at the United Nations appearance several times during the editing process and could quote the speeches and interviews almost word for word. Helen had only viewed the two minutes of material aired as part of one of her newscasts.

"I firmly believe that these women are in the vanguard of those who understand what is needed for the return of the Messiah," Macalusso was recorded as saying when introducing the Women Who Witness during a press conference held just prior to their appearance before the U.N. General Assembly. "The Middle East is a land where too many people of all religions are content to look to the Heavens for the peace only they can bring. The false faithful say that God holds the power of life and death, peace and war, justice and injustice. Some endure bombings, sniper attacks, and the desecration of all they hold sacred, claiming God wants them to suffer so they can not stand against what is happening. Others feel they are called to commit acts of terrorism to cleanse the region of those they consider evil.

"But if God's hand is in every rock thrown, every grenade exploded, every rifle shot fired, then each of us is God. It is not to the Heavens we should be looking but inside ourselves. Your mouths spout the hate that fuels the flames of hatred between brothers and sisters. Your hands make the bombs, launch the rockets, fly the fighter planes. Your feet take you to confrontations easily avoided if you so choose.

"And if the God in you can do unspeakable violence while blaming some invisible being in the Heavens, so can the God in you know and give boundless joy. Only the God in you can love. Only the God in you can heal another. Only the God in you can nurture the weak and helpless. Women Who Witness are among the outward and visible signs of the God in each of us.

"These anonymous women have chosen to accept the responsibility so many of us avoid. They have homes. They have families. They have tended the sick and the dying, made love and given birth, nurtured the weak and helpless into the full bloom of adulthood. They radiate the best of the God within and they stand as witnesses against those whose choices cause only pain, suffering, and ill-will. It is right that they should have formed in the Holy Land, though their message is one that matters in all the countries of the world. They speak from where the Messiah will appear, their witness certain to grace the pages of any Holy book yet to be written."

"How can you argue with that?" asked Kathy.

Helen said nothing, watching a series of private interviews with one of the WNN field reporters who had taken several of them aside at the United Nations. The women who spoke in this way seemed somewhat embarrassed by Macalusso's comments. One, a Jew who had been raised in Brooklyn, New York, not moving to Israel until she was in her thirties, said that Macalusso sounded a bit like one of those New Age motivational speakers. "They tell you that good people deserve to be rich. They tell you that you don't need a college education, a good job, or an inheritance from a wealthy parent. They tell you to embrace the God of greed who is inside you, buy their motivational tapes, buy their books, and spend a few hundred dollars at a time attending their seminars. Then you will get very rich, and if you don't, at least you know where your money went... into their pockets."

One of the others, a Christian, thought her Jewish sister was being too dubious. "I think he meant that we are partners with God, not gods ourselves. Did not the Lord above give us free will? We all know that we can nurture His creation or we can harm it. I think he's talking personal responsibility as Jesus taught us. I don't think he really means we should blaspheme by denying our Lord and Savior."

"It does not matter what he said or what he meant," said a third. "He is a very powerful man who has enabled us to keep Witness to the world. We are all of different faiths, different backgrounds. We stand together solely as sisters determined to bring peace. If this man, who is not of my country, not of my religion, not of my culture, can end the violence that has brought us all such personal sorrow, I will follow him anywhere."

"A cult," snorted Helen. "Next thing you know they'll be wearing uniforms. I still don't see what makes Macalusso so important that the powers that be want you to spend so much of all our time putting this biography together. Bronson did a series on him when he first was with the United Nations. He didn't seem to be that big a deal then, and I keep feeling that he isn't that important now. He's been lucky with his peace initiatives, but maybe no more so than Henry Kissinger was when he developed shuttle diplomacy for Richard Nixon. There were people talking of running Kissinger for President because he was more popular than his boss in the White House."

"He couldn't run," said Kathy. "He wasn't a natural born citizen."

"That's not the point. There were people who probably would have agreed to a change in the law to let him run, so popular did he become. And who remembers him now? I keep thinking that maybe Macalusso's like that. He's center stage as the world's in crisis, but maybe things will work out and he'll be next year's game show trivia question. So what makes the man so important to WNN that we have to do this?"

"Besides the fact that he is one of our employers, Helen?" Kathy laughed.

"Are you serious?"

"Fifteen percent share in the company, at least. Maybe more. Gordon found it along with a whole lot of other properties that would surprise you. I'll show you the print out when I'm working with that file.

"Macalusso's business days were *very* successful. Whenever he wanted to acquire ownership in a company, he would create a number of straw operations seemingly independent of Macalusso Enterprises and have them each take a stake in what he wanted to buy. Unless you spent weeks tracing the ultimate owners as Gordon did, you'd never know what he was doing."

"Is that legal?" asked Helen, surprised by how much she did not know despite having run periodic stories about him on the news.

"Good business. You don't get to be a billionaire in the communication field by making mistakes that can get you in trouble. Remember this is the guy who put together the most powerful satellite link of formerly third rate independent television stations in the world. He's also the man who coordinated the development of the two-way miniature voice pager that allows multi-national companies to keep track of their employees no matter where in the world they're traveling."

"And now he's President of the European Union. What's his next career move going to be, becoming Pope without first being Catholic?"

"He's the type who'd see being Pope as a stepping stone to a higher calling," laughed Kathy. "He's into everything, and he seems to thrive on a pace that would kill the average person."

"And now he's our boss," said Helen.

"He's a stockholder. I don't really know if he could control our paychecks."

"I hope you treat him nicely in the final cut of our documentary."

"It's not hard. This is the kind of guy who helps Boy Scouts cross the street so they don't get hit by little old ladies driving too fast in their high powered BMWs. If they ever erect a statue to the guy, the pigeons will probably fly past in order to deface icons of lesser mortals. And the worst part about him, his features never seem to age. If anything, the bags, sags, and wrinkles he started to get earlier in life seem to have smoothed out in recent years."

"Plastic surgery?" asked Helen, delighted that Mr. Perfect might at least have a streak of vanity.

"I don't think so. This guy seems to thrive on challenge. Give him a two week vacation and he'd probably shrivel up and die."

"His wife must hate him."

"He isn't married. No wife. No secret cache of kids. Just a few billion dollars in the bank, the respect of the United Nations, and the leadership of the European Union. The most powerful man in the world and this is the first time anyone's done anything on him other than *Time*. Even they just focused on his peace keeping methods which were quite similar to Henry Kissinger's Mid-East 'shuttle diplomacy' of a few years back. The only difference is that Macalusso's efforts have been working in ways no one else has achieved. That was why the members of the European Union unanimously voted to bring him in to fill their presidency even though his recent history has been with the United Nations, not any member government."

"So why has this taken you so long?" asked Helen. "This seems like the kind of story you've done a zillion times before. Go to WNN files, pull up old video clips, piece together his history, let Research fill in the holes, then work with me on the writing of the voice over. Two, three weeks tops, and that's if you're interrupted by some world calamity. You've been at this for more than a month. What makes this guy so different?"

"You've seen much of the background material. There's almost nothing on him. He was born in a small village where the only person who could read and write was the local priest. He was tutored along with other local kids, but he was the only one who seems to have left the area. He was in the seminary for a while, began drifting, taking jobs in one field or another while attending several different colleges to study business, electronics, political science, and psychology, never being particularly outstanding.

"You have to look at his career in hindsight to see how brilliant he's been. Everything he's done has been too minor to matter much to the big money players at the time he was doing it. He took what no one else wanted, then linked it together into a global business. Macalusso Enterprises is headquartered in Rome in a non-descript building in the wrong part of the city to impress anyone. He has key operations people in every major city of the world, but it takes work to realize what he's done. His communication network can reach perhaps three-fourths of the people in the world. His investments in both countries like the United

States and emerging nations has given him influence with every government that matters. His success with the United Nations comes in part from his being able to get the ear of the leaders. Through his interlocking businesses, he can adversely effect the economies of more nations than want to admit it."

"I'd have thought he would have left that behind when he went with the United Nations. Don't they have some rule about blind trusts or divestitures like our government?"

"I don't know about that, Helen. I think they wanted him to keep active in his businesses so he would have an economic influence that might mean more than weapons. Certainly he's gotten the results people have wanted.

"That's probably the same with the European Union. Who better than someone who has a real economic stake in world peace and stability to lead them?"

"So what's the problem? I still don't see why the guy doesn't show up everywhere in our files with all he's done."

"He's not like that, Helen. It's like... like... I guess Anissa, our new editor, put it best. She's been going through more than a hundred hours of videos related to his projects, pulling two minutes of Macalusso here, three minutes there, and thirty seconds somewhere else. Then suddenly he goes from being a minor league player in an enterprise to the leading authority in the world. Everybody's quoting him. Everybody's paying him big bucks to speak somewhere. Everybody's got him in the news. And then he disappears again. The media loses track of him. Past business associates interviewed about what he's doing talk of rumors, but nothing they can confirm.

"And then Macalusso does it all over again. Suddenly he's cornered some other industry.

"Many men would sell their souls for the success he's had in just a single field. This guy's done it over and over again until he's the least well known power player in the world."

"And now they're saying peace in the Middle East is dependent solely upon his skills. It just makes no sense to me."

"Me, neither, though that's not our problem. I've asked to have Bronson do the final interview with Macalusso to wrap up the documentary. Len Parker is arranging access, and it will be Bronson's job to get answers to all those questions. He did tell you he'll be leaving again in a few days, and then I can do the final edit."

"He didn't say anything about it. But aside from my personal life, I wonder if it's fair to put such a burden on him. He's just back after being away for... what was it this time? A couple of months? It seemed like an eternity to me. But what matters is the poor guy's exhausted. He'll just be getting over jet lag when..."

"He knew what he was getting into when he signed his contract. The real question is, what's your problem? Why not just marry the guy, then ask to be reassigned so you can work together. You could be like those television wrestlers, only you'd be doing tag team tradeoffs with your tougher interview subjects. Bronson and Helen Pearl going ten rounds with the worst scoundrels in the world.

"I can just see the WNN lead-in for your segments. Some announcer with a rich baritone voice will intone, 'World Network News will now cast its Pearls before swine.'"

THREE

Growing Turmoil

Franco Macalusso was angry. It was an emotion few people ever saw in the man. Not even United Nations Special Agent Len Parker, a man who continued to work as his assistant now that Macalusso was President of the European Union, had witnessed the rage of which he was capable. Self-control had been too important to him all his adult life. Anger, appropriately directed, could be a strength. But in allowing yourself to be aroused to anger, you could also show your weakness. You could reveal those things that truly mattered to you, and with such knowledge came power.

Not that this anger was fully appropriate. It was not Bronson Pearl's fault that Franco's rise to ultimate power required behind the scenes manipulation for so long, a major story on the world's most important network was critical to the transition.

Bronson Pearl was not the enemy. The journalist was famous, in many ways still better known than Macalusso himself. But the influence of the Bronson Pearls of the world was fleeting. Their time in the public eye was based on ratings, not the ability to wield real power.

Len Parker had been right. The interview was important, the timing of its airing coming within days, perhaps hours of the events that would change the world in ways that had long been written yet rarely believed.

The airing of the documentary would serve as a clarion call for the fulfilment of Franco Macalusso's destiny. With the words and images Bronson Pearl and the WNN staff would broadcast to the farthest reaches of the world, Macalusso would be welcomed as no other leader in history. Global television with satellite down links had replaced the drawings on cave walls, the scrolls of Bible times, the newspapers of today. The WNN staff would shape the lie of his existence while he took control, then be prevented from freely operating except as Len Parker allowed when they at last knew the truth.

He understood all that, yet the anger lingered. With each passing day, it grew in intensity like the festering green mold on leftover meat left far too long in the darkest corners of a bachelor's rarely used refrigerator. He was as impatient as a child anticipating Christmas. He felt he had waited long enough. He wanted to be in full control now, not dependent upon anyone else any longer. To have come as far as he had, to have left a village where wealth was measured in the number of sheep a family could graze and now control not only one of the world's largest communication businesses but also the economies of the members of the European Union.... He should not have to use a man like Bronson Pearl to further a destiny for which he had been working his entire adult lifetime.

Macalusso took a deep breath, exhaling slowly. The window of his penthouse apartment overlooked a lush public garden where butterflies flitted among the blooming flowers and mothers strolled with their children. Nearby was a park, a gathering place for families to picnic, lovers to stroll, and the homeless to clothe themselves in nature's beauty before sunset forced their return to the steam grates, doorways, and shelters whose grayness marked their cold, bleak, and lonely nights.

How different life would soon become for all of them.

Soon, no later than hours or days after the scheduled airing of the WNN biography, he would assume his rightful place in the world. Then he would have the power he had long ago chosen to seek to determine his destiny. Then he would know peace from the anger that felt so close to overwhelming him.

*

"You didn't give him an answer?"

"Grandmother, he fell asleep in the car."

"Fell asleep? What do you mean?" asked Edna Williams. She and her granddaughter were sipping coffee at a table in a corner of the WNN commissary. It was a quiet period, the handful of employees in the large room reviewing scripts, reading one or another of the 50 different newspapers that daily arrived at headquarters, or listening to music on their Walkmans'.

"He had been awake almost 27 hours by the time he landed. Between the stories he had to cover, jet lag, and a talkative seat mate, he had no sleep. One minute he was proposing marriage. The next minute he was snoring so loudly, the startled driver almost crashed the car. I had the driver take him to my apartment, help me drag him inside, and lay him on the couch. He didn't wake up until three the next afternoon when he called me here at the network."

"So why couldn't you have told him you'd marry him when he called?"

"I was in the middle of a planning meeting for the night's broadcast. We were placing stories, preparing all but the last minute copy, and..."

"Bronson Pearl has been chasing you for three years? Four years? And suddenly he finally decides it's time to make a commitment, and you don't say yes just because you're in a meeting about a show that will last an hour and then be forgotten? Helen Hannah, I thought I raised you better than that. Don't you know what is important in life?

"I can still remember the first moment your grandfather touched me on our wedding night. I can remember the gentleness and the passion. I thought no one could be loved so fiercely by another human being, and I knew that God had to be present in our union to bring me to such ecstasy. And Helen, years later, when his body was as familiar to me as my own, when we had known financial reverses, illness, and all the calamities of life, when we had experienced children and grandchildren, when his life was ebbing from his body, I also remember the passion with which he kissed me still. What had seemed an unsurpassable joy that first night was as nothing compared with the feelings honed by a life together experiencing the Lord's plan.

"Marriage may not be possible for everyone. But when you have the opportunity with a man you love and who loves you in return, no other commitment we humans can make to one another is so important."

Helen set down her coffee cup, took her grandmother's hand, and said, "Yours was a very special relationship with Grandfather. Few people are ever so lucky as you were." Her voice was soft, gentle, expressing the love and wonderment she had known with this woman all her life. That was why her grandmother's reaction was so shocking.

"Utter nonsense, young lady!" said the older woman, irate at her granddaughter's misunderstanding. "What your grandfather and I experienced was *normal*, the way all marriages are when you share your life with the Lord. You put down what you know nothing about because you're afraid you will somehow be different. You're so sure that love and loss are all of a one, you won't reach out to the joy that is the greatest part of the human condition.

"I buried my daughter, Helen Hannah! She was your mother, yes. But to bury a parent, even one who dies too soon for our wishes, is the way of life. It is an abomination of all we desire to have to bury a child.

"I railed at God for that. I wept bitterly at the sudden burden He had thrust upon me. I even reminded him that Jesus was a bachelor. What did He know about child care or the stress of trying to grieve, raise kids when your own were grown and you thought you'd finally have some peace and quiet, and working a job where you were under paid just because you were an older single woman who should be 'grateful' for any employment?

"Oh, I tell you I gave our Lord and Savior a piece of my mind."

"But you never told us any of that. You were as loving as any parent, even when we must have been driving you crazy with our rebellion."

"I have a right to say anything I want to God. His gift of His son proved how much he loves us, and when you have that kind of love, there is understanding. But to argue with our Savior in front of you? I would never do that because deep in my heart I never meant it.

"But you are changing the subject, young lady. The point is that Bronson Pearl finally got around to asking you to marry him and you let him fall asleep without an answer."

"I didn't let him fall asleep. The man was exhausted. I don't know how he could look so good in the airport when he must have been asleep on his feet. He was snoring before I could..."

"Could what? Say no? Tell him you're afraid of commitment? Tell him you're afraid of joy? Tell him you're afraid to love and experience the full range of emotions our Father has blessed us with in marriage?"

"Not exactly."

"What then? These may be the end times before the Rapture as the Good Book says, but Jesus himself said we will not know what time He will return. It's not like you're on a mission devoting yourself to the starving, oppressed people of some isolated jungle. You're a journalist and a very successful one. I don't know when our Lord will return. I don't know when we will experience the time of the Rapture. I only know that we would not have been given the joy of commitment if we were expected to avoid commitment until He comes again. The Lord does not work that way. If Bronson finally has gotten around to asking you to marry him, say yes."

Helen looked down at her coffee cup, embarrassed. "It isn't the first time he's asked me. Bronson told me there would be no one else for him six months after we met. I'm the one who..."

"Good! I knew I liked that young man for something other than his looks. So he's been faithful from at least the moment he told you, hasn't he?"

Helen nodded.

"And you're worried about the future? Here's a man with no strings attached. He travels the globe, meeting women who are probably smarter and more beautiful than you are. Yet he never strays. He is faithful to my idiot of a granddaughter who I love dearly but sometimes would like to strangle with my bare hands for being such a mule."

"Grandmother...."

"Helen...."

"Grandmother...."

"Just say yes, Helen. Trust me on this. I've been through everything life can bring to people like us. I didn't always like your grandfather. There were times when I wanted to walk out of the house or send him packing. We fought. He was stubborn. I was stubborn. In fact, there were days when, if we had been one of those couples who vow never to go to bed mad, we would have had to stay awake for a week. But ultimately we worked through our differences. Ultimately we found compromise. Ultimately we kept going back to the love that is our gift if we will only accept it. And I can tell you this. If the Good Lord had seen fit to extend the time your grandfather and I could live together by a hundred-fold, it would still not have been enough.

"That's what love can do for you. That's what commitment can do for you. That's why you're going right back to your office and tell Bronson Pearl you will marry him."

"He's gone, Grandmother," whispered Helen, tears forming at her eyes. "He's back in the Middle East, in Megiddo, the place you call Armageddon. It looks like at least some of the countries gathered there are no longer going to back off. It looks like there's going to be a war, and Bronson is..."

Edna Williams stood up from her chair, walked around the table, and took her granddaughter in her arms. She held the younger woman's head against her chest as Helen wept deeply, oblivious to her surroundings, oblivious to anything other than the comforting touch of the grandmother who had given her so much love.

*

The change, when it occurred, was subtle. Sporadic gunfire had been heard for days. Snipers, tactical units, civilian patrols.... So many men with weapons, it was impossible to tell who was shooting at whom or why. Yet it was neither the volume of gunfire nor the closeness of the weapons that was different. Each armed group seemed to have staked out its own territory, targeting its own enemies, not moving from its entrenched position.

Instead, the change was in the sound of the weapons.

The early shooting had been mostly small arms fire — hand guns, automatic rifles, even an occasional shotgun or hand grenade. The weapons were the type many civilians maintained, especially the Israelis since they were subject to instant call-up for full military duty in the event of war.

Now the sounds were louder, deeper. Higher powered weapons had been brought to the front. Lightweight anti-tank weapons, machine guns, shoulder fired rocket launchers, and the like could now be heard. Where people had been individually targeted during the first few days of the shooting, the distant sounds made clear that buildings were being destroyed as well.

Aircraft seemed to be flying around the clock. Aerial reconnaissance planes, armored helicopters, fighter planes and bombers were in the sky. Most were meant to serve as a show of force, though occasionally a plane for one or another country would engage in a dangerous game of aerial "chicken," at least three crashes taking place over Libya and Jordan.

All of the journalists assigned to the area were being equipped for whatever might happen. They were given injections to protect them against the more common biological weapons believed to have been stockpiled by several of the potential combatants. They were carrying gas masks, and many wore bullet resistant vests and helmets. A few kept handguns in their equipment bags, though most preferred to work unarmed. There had been too many times when spies and assassins had pretended to be journalists, going so far as to carry counterfeit credentials for major networks, newspapers, and magazines. Any journalist caught with a weapon was instantly suspect and likely to be killed. As a result, only the more inexperienced travelled armed. The rest felt they had a better chance of staying alive if captured if they had no way to defend themselves.

Bronson Pearl had flown directly to Israel following his

interview with Franco Macalusso in Paris. It was Bronson's understanding that the European Union President would also be coming to the Middle East within 24 to 48 hours in order to continue his previously successful peace negotiations. However, from the sounds of the explosions, someone was going to fire one shell too many in the direction of an encampment of soldiers from another nation. There would be retaliation, a call for allies to join together, and then an escalation into full scale warfare well before Macalusso could repeat the type of success he had experienced in the past.

Judith Shimowitz, the Tel Aviv based videographer, had been assigned by WNN to accompany Bronson Pearl as he interviewed Israeli General Moishe Alizar. They were standing by a large tactical table on which maps had been spread. The positions of dozens of different armed forces totalling more than two million men and women had been charted. Of greatest concern was that segment of Megiddo where the largest battle was likely to erupt. Only one section allowed ground movement through a pass that had been used for centuries. The other sides were blocked by water and mountains. Depending upon which side was speaking, where their forces were located, and how they were armed, the impending battle would be either a tactician's dream or a tactician's nightmare.

"General Alizar, to many of our American viewers, the name of the site where we are standing has deep significance," said Bronson Pearl. "They believe that the final battle between good and evil will begin here in Armageddon."

"Is that what you believe, Mr. Pearl?"

"I believe that when people are convinced that something is going to happen in life, they try to find a way to make their belief come true. If they believe that what we are hearing is the start of the war to end all wars, then it may be true."

"From a purely personal level, such talk is not important to me or the state of Israel. I am a Jew and this is my land.

"Your country is large, Mr. Pearl. Your neighbors are your friends. Your flanks are protected by two oceans. When people hate someone in your country, either party can move hundreds or thousands of miles away and still be in the United States.

"For two thousand years we Jews have been a hated people. If we try to live among ourselves in a village, raising our own food, making our own clothing, building our own homes, practicing our faith within our own territory, we have been attacked. We have been declared a blight on the face of the country in which the small village has existed. Or our rituals have been blamed for problems one ruler or another can not solve, the scapegoat used to keep him in power. Or our land is coveted because we have made it lush with crops. Or as the Kibbutz here in Megiddo has learned, the danger can come because we are simply in the way, a people too near roads that are the pathways for conquest by warring nations.

"We have been despised, dispersed, and reviled for trying to live in harmony with God, the Father of us all. We have been tortured and murdered by people who have never tried to get to know us.

"When we try to assimilate into a large city, we frequently face restrictions. We may not own a home, though all around us there are those of different faiths who may buy as much property as they desire. We have been forbidden an education except as the elders can pass their knowledge to the young, often at night, by candle light, in secret. We have been told what jobs we may work, then been vilified for being too lazy to do anything else. We have been systematically extermi-nated, often with the 'good' people who had been our neighbors either hiding their eyes or tacitly approving with a wink and a nod.

"Yet always God has been with us. He has let us survive. He

has reminded us that He is faithful, chastised us when we turned away from Him, and ultimately brought us to this land. It is a place of refuge, a place of opportunity, a reminder of what can happen if we keep the faith.

"This land of ours is a tiny sliver of no importance to anyone. Others have the oil, the gold, the mineral wealth that men of all nationalities covet. There is no reason to come here, to mass against us in such numbers, except to destroy those whose ancestors managed to survive the pogroms, the concentration camps, the inquisitions, and the Diaspora.

"We will fight because we can do nothing else. We are not people who can hope for a better day. What we face is what we have always faced in one form or another. The names change. The alliances are different. Yet always we have known that we must live as one and die as one."

"The history of your people and this land is a tragic one," said Bronson. "But isn't this somehow different? Yes, there are armies of nations who have viewed you as the enemy. But there seem to also be dozens of heavily armed fringe groups, suicide bombers, and others not connected with any single nation. If one of these extremist groups acts irresponsibly, they will be like a match lit too near a fuse. They could start a full scale world war before cooler heads might prevail."

"That is true, Mr. Pearl. That is also why our Defence Minister has insisted that you and your network have unlimited access to the front. We are a people of the Torah, the scroll. The early scribes wrote the word of God, preserving it on scrolls. They were collected into what we now call the Bible and made available in all the tongues of the world when the printing press was created. Our great rabbis commented on this blessed book and how it applies to life in their own writings which we call the Talmud. And it is to the Word that we have always returned for unity, tradition, and righteousness in times of prosperity and times of adversity.

"You are an electronic scribe. What you say reaches more people in an instant than the scrolls first reached in a thousand years. Your words, your insight, the truth the Lord gives you to speak to the people may be the only hope we have.

"I am convinced that whatever happens in the coming days will be determined by how you, Mr. Pearl, are heard by our friends and by our enemies. We generals know how to destroy. You have the capability of bringing the truth. It is a special gift and I know you have been honored for it. We will see how God uses it in the days ahead."

*

The designer of the WNN headquarters broadcast studio had created what he called an "environment for the twenty-first century." The lines of the brushed aluminum trim of the desks curved gracefully into a sculpture that was meant to mimic the anatomy of the human heart. "The newsroom is the heartbeat of your communication empire. The anchors are like the valves that control the flow of blood, only instead of blood, they issue information to all the extremities. That is why the metal sculpture, when seen from above, will mimic the view a thoracic surgeon sees when opening a chest," the designer had gushed in his over-written, rather pretentious proposal. He probably would not have been hired except for three points in his favor. First, the sketches and mock-up of the proposed design were both more visually interesting and more practical than the written document indicated. Second, he was inexpensive, arranging for much of the equipment seen during broadcasts to be donated in exchange for a regular credit rolled at the end of the news. And third, he was the younger brother of the founder's fourth wife.

On the wall behind the anchor desk was a bank of monitors

showing satellite feeds from throughout the world. Each was carefully labelled with the country of origin (along with the name of the set's manufacturer as agreed). And each was supposed to reinforce the idea that WNN provided breaking news from everywhere in the world every minute of the day. Instead the set looked more like a discount television store where some bored clerk had taken the time to turn each television to a different channel.

But none of this mattered to Helen Hannah and the rest of the people who worked both on and off camera. WNN was their home. The sights, the sounds, the smells, the coffee and pizza stains were like images in a family album. They recalled old stories, good times, sad times, shared losses and shared triumphs. The world might be falling apart, but within the news set everything was familiar. Everything was under control.

Except Bronson.

There had been a time when the live feed was enough for Helen to feel the man she loved to be close at hand. His voice was transmitted to the tiny receiver in her ear. His image was on a dozen monitors positioned around the set. She could close her eyes and almost feel his touch as he spoke.

It was a false intimacy, of course. And when he was again back in her arms she felt like a fool. But during his absences she had long used the surroundings to maintain a semblance of closeness.

Until he returned to Armageddon.

The relationship had been a foolish one from the start. Both she and Bronson had planned never to get involved with anyone in the industry.

Bronson's father was a newsman from the days of print. He was a crusader who lived in a small Midwest town, publishing a weekly newspaper that provided the lone dissenting voice against the state political machine. The daily newspaper editor knew which issues to champion and which could lead to his dismissal if he honestly told what was taking place in the community. The paper's owner was a major contributor to the most corrupt politicians to ever steal from the people. There were rumors that he had political ambitions of his own, though he never did run for office.

Bronson's father had endured the wrath of the community, especially when he championed an unpopular Hispanic store owner's cause after the man had been jailed for murder. Conviction was never in question, but truth seemed to have gotten lost during the trial. Many of the quotes run in the daily newspaper did not match the transcript of the trial. And the better suspect among the possibilities was from what passed for society in the community.

Eventually the weekly newspaper stories resulted in an outside investigation that freed the falsely convicted man. However, the triumph could not be fully savored because Bronson's father was dealing with both an advertising boycott that almost put him out of business and an unsuccessful firebomb attempt.

Bronson knew that he had broken his father's heart when he went into the field of broadcast journalism. "Nothing but blow dried pretty boys trying to read what real newsmen have written for them. They know how to read, I'll give them that. Or are those ear piece things telling them what to say while they pretend to mouth the moving type on the Teleprompter?"

Bronson's dues paying early jobs didn't help him change his father's mind about the potential value of electronics. For example, there was that station in Nebraska where he co-anchored the six o'clock news. He was hired to be a "Ken Doll", sitting with a blond "Barbie", exchanging light hearted banter and sexual innuendo between stories about plane crashes, babies dying in their cribs, and the latest shooting.

Staff meetings inevitably were about whether to open with a cute kid story or a little gore, and the conclusion was always the cliched, "If it bleeds, it leads." "Barbie" worried about her hair, her make-up, and her wardrobe. Bronson was criticized if he seemed to be wearing the same sports jacket more than once a week.

There were other cities, greater responsibilities, and enough other "Barbie Dolls" (not to mention "Ken Dolls" who would never dream of giving up the anchor opportunity to actually go in the field and be a reporter) that Bronson knew he'd have to go outside the industry. He dated a journalist for a regional magazine, and two or three other women he met when pursuing stories. All were fun to be with. All were intelligent. Yet there was no spark until Hannah, a woman who was both in the same business as he was and an anchor at that.

Helen was different, of course. She had a background with news magazines and some award winning smaller television stations when she was approached by WNN. She handled all phases of production for a number of major documentaries as well as being both an on and off camera reporter prior to her being offered the anchor position. And when they had worked together on various major stories, Bronson had been impressed with her dedication, willingness to seek the story beneath the obvious story, and her unquenchable desire for knowledge about the world. They were two of a kind, and though his career was keeping him separated from her for long periods of time, he grudgingly admitted that he would rather have a long distance marriage with Helen Hannah for some portion of each year than a more stable 8 to 5 life with any other woman he had ever known. What he had not expected was her irrational fears that would keep them apart during the most tumultuous period the world had ever endured.

It was 6:23 Eastern Time, and though the picture feed was beginning to be relayed, there was not yet sound, not yet a chance to speak to him. Instead the director had instructed Helen to switch to Yuri Breedlaff at the Pentagon where Richard Stanfield, Pentagon spokesperson, was announcing that the President was leaving Washington.

"Mr. Stanfield, it is my understanding that the President and his family are boarding the aerial command center in preparation for surviving a possible first strike attack against Washington, D.C. Is that true?" asked Yuri.

"I must argue with your choice of words, Mr. Breedlaff. As you well know, Air Force One is always a mobile command center. It is equipped with all the military codes and special equipment the President needs to conduct a war or run the country. Unlike you or me, he can never be out of touch, never fully relax on his flights around the world. There is nothing special about this trip."

"That is not my understanding, Mr. Stanfield," the reporter persisted. "I have heard from some well placed sources within your own agency that key personnel are being evacuated to the Colorado Springs area."

"Colorado Springs was a favorite vacation spot of the President long before he entered politics. He has traveled there at least a dozen times since he has been in office. There is nothing special about this trip."

"Except that it is not a vacation, is it?" Breedlaff said. "I've checked and the President is not staying in any of the hotels, nor will he be staying with any of the friends with whom he's stayed before. My understanding is that he is going to be living in the old Strategic Air Command bunker that was created for his use in the event the United States was faced with an enemy strike. The WNN research staff has also determined that key members of Congress, the Senate, and the cabinet will be joining him."

"Are you deliberately trying to panic the American people with your innuendoes?" asked an angry Stanfield. "Are you trying to make more of the Middle East situation than is truly happening? Are you..."

"Please answer the question, Mr. Stanfield."

"I won't dignify it with an answer. This interview is now over."

The camera followed the Pentagon spokesman as he left the room. A second camera picked up on Helen, sitting at the news desk, her right hand lightly cupping her ear so she could better hear what was happening. "Yuri? Yuri, this is Helen Hannah in New York. What can you tell us about the President and his family?"

"You just heard the official version, Helen. The President is travelling to Colorado Springs where he has gone many times in the past. There is nothing special about this trip."

"But you said he is staying in the bunker."

"Yes, and while I can not give you my source, a few members of Congress have been confirmed to be present. Officially they are on a fact finding tour. Unofficially this is the start of an evacuation to assure the smooth running of the country should full scale war break out. The situation is perceived as extremely grave despite official denials."

The camera focused back on Helen. "Thank you, Yuri, and for a front line perspective, we now bring you Bronson Pearl in Armageddon. Are you there, Bronson?" Her voice was calm, professional, betraying nothing of the inner turmoil she was experiencing.

"The situation becomes more tense by the moment, Helen. A few minutes ago it was obvious that the violence was escalating. Now there are reports of troop movements in a manner General Alizar considers highly aggressive. What we have not been able to determine is which country is taking advantage of the tension in order to make a first strike and dominate the territory."

"What will that mean, Bronson? Will the war be limited to Armageddon?"

"There are too many alliances. The generals have told me that if one country makes a serious power grab here in Israel, the retaliation will be global. Cities have been targeted throughout the world in the way they were during the Cold War. Unless a miracle happens in this tiny strip of land, we could be seeing a World War of unprecedented proportions."

Helen broke for a commercial, the satellite feed from Megiddo still on one of the monitors. She signalled to the engineers to keep her mike open to Bronson and said, "Can't you get out of there?"

"This is where the story is, Helen."

"I don't care about the story. I care about you. If you're in ground zero for the war zone..."

"Helen, you're in a city that's as much a target as Megiddo, maybe more so. This is our job. Whatever happens, we've got to record it."

"You can't report a story if you're dead. Bronson... I love you."

"Helen...."

Suddenly the picture began to shake. The videographer was moving and there was noise breaking up the satellite feed. Helen could see someone rushing over with gas masks, handing one to Bronson, pointing. The camera was set on the ground, still running, presumably so the videographer could put on her gas mask. Then Bronson said something unintelligible into the camera, the picture went out, and the only sound was an explosion before all connection with Armageddon was cut off.

"On in 5, 4, 3..." The floor director signalled Helen that they had come out of the commercial break and were about to air images of Franco Macalusso getting into a limousine in Rome as a motorcycle escort raced him to the airport. A crawl at the bottom of the screen read: "Film shot earlier today."

"In Rome, European Union President Franco Macalusso announced he was travelling to the Middle East in a last minute attempt to defuse the tensions. The only man respected by all sides, Macalusso has been instrumental in negotiating settlements among factions fighting in several Eastern European countries."

Helen's voice caught. Her mind kept returning to the last few seconds in which she had seen Bronson. Something was happening. Something serious. She wanted to scream, cry, race to the engineers and see if they could find a way to restore contact with Armageddon. But showing such emotion was unprofessional.

Now she wished she had said yes to marrying Bronson Pearl. Her grandmother was right. What had she been waiting for? The end of the world? And now the world just might...

*

The aircraft was a simple one, a light pleasure craft with no military value. Propeller driven, slow flying, and unable to perform sophisticated maneuvers, it was the perfect plane for the mission.

The pilot was young, not yet eighteen, the son of fanatical extremists who felt that neither Jews nor Christians nor Moslems were practicing the will of God. The youth's father was in jail for his part in the bombing of a marketplace in East Jerusalem. One brother had been killed by an Israeli commando unit trying to arrest him for his part in the assassination of three senior members of the Likud Party. Another brother was in training in Libya, hoping to return with a suicide squad. His mother operated a safe house, a concealed basement serving as a hiding place for fanatics travelling to and from their objectives. Yet none were a part of a specific organization. They believed that God worked only after violent change, and they associated with any group working to enact such violence. Ultimately they believed that people like themselves would be elevated to positions of authority. For the moment, their concerns were solely about death.

The bombs had been loaded on the aircraft in such a way that they could be hand dropped by the pilot. A special remote control would trigger the explosions when they were just a few hundred feet above Tel Aviv. As the designers of the weapons had explained, the detonation would send the chemical stored in the heads of the explosive devices both outward and downward. The wind currents would then carry the chemicals for several miles until the entire city had been blanketed by an almost invisible mist of death.

The pilot checked his fuel gauge, his radio, and the other controls of the light plane. He was wearing casual clothes, an Uzi Machine Pistol, a gas mask, and a small first aid kit containing an additional dose of the antidote were placed in the type of backpack tourists his age routinely carried while exploring the Middle East. He planned to land the plane after his mission, walking away as though oblivious to the devastation he would have started. Everything in readiness, he turned on the ignition.

*

Chung Kwan Wong was a rebel, a military leader of the New China yet a student of history who viewed himself as carrying on a tradition of the emperors of the past. For centuries the Chinese, one of the largest civilizations on earth, had been less technologically advanced than the armies of other nations. They were constantly getting overrun by invading armies, sometimes being conquered, sometimes enduring the violence of bloodthirsty warriors practicing battle tactics as they passed through the land on their way to their true targets.

The cohesiveness of the Chinese society was caused, in part, by the people recognizing their unusual situation and adapting to it. The civil service involved extensive memorization of the laws so that each time a conquering nation was repelled or conquered in turn by yet another country, the people could return to the same system they had known for centuries. Thus they could keep their identity, never assimilating, always knowing that eventually they would regain control of their vast territory.

Now China was recognizing that its land mass, the number of its people, the unity of their thinking, and the emerging reforms improving education and lifestyle could make them the major power in the world. There were thoughts of a quite different future, a giant finally roused to action after being bullied for most of its life.

Chung Kwan Wong understood all this, but he also understood that the precarious situation in the Middle East that had brought him and a handful of fellow Navy submarine officers to the coastal waters could be used for China's advantage. If they could target a ship of one of the super powers, if they could use one of the tactical nuclear weapons they secretly had loaded, they could trigger violence that would destroy the lives of millions. Given the relations among the different allied nations, a war of the type Wong envisioned would devastate the United States, Britain, France, Russia, Germany, India, and several other powerful nations. People and second strike weapons would survive, but the demoralization of such violence would prevent the survivors from continuing the war. Perhaps only one in ten would be left alive in some countries, and with those numbers, a true second strike would be foolish.

Not that China would escape some of the violence. The difference was in pure numbers. Take out every major city in China and there would still be a people several billion strong. More important, they would be seeking the leadership of the younger military officers, men like Wong who were not yet in their mid-thirties. Such men had been trained to understand the past and the future, and in Wong's case, at least, they had the self-declared wisdom to act in the present.

It was at 3 p.m. that Wong made his move. Trained in all aspects of the missile system, he ordered the loading of one of the tactical nuclear warheads as a "training exercise." He had the men target the American troop ship, a massive vessel as large as a small city almost 5,000 men and women on board. He joked with the men as the lights flashed and a digital counter prepared the firing. No one knew he had changed the computer codes controlling launch. No one knew that instead of the system stopping itself as it had done so many times before during training missions, this time the launch would occur. No one understood just what he had done until they heard the muffled whoosh and felt the sub-rocking response to the missile suddenly moving from the vessel through the water.

*

Franco Macalusso's plane touched down on the tarmac of a military runway. There were no throngs of admirers, no special escort, no reporters shouting questions. The area was under full wartime security as he and two aides clambered down the staircase and hurried to a waiting armored staff car. It was a converted four wheel drive vehicle, capable of travelling over any terrain. The tires were designed to stay inflated even if shot by a bullet from a high powered weapon. The under carriage was reinforced against land mines. And the passenger compartment was built to sustain a direct hit from one of the small, tactical rockets that had been developed for close combat. Nothing was going to stop the President of the European Union from reaching his objective.

Helen Hannah was resting on a small couch in the break room. She should have gone home, should have called her grandmother, should have done something other than stay in the WNN Studios. Her news-cast was over, and though the on-air staff was on 24 hour alert, all that meant was that they were instructed to never be away from their beep-ers and cellular telephones. Most had gone home to their families. A few, who commuted from New Jersey, took hotel rooms close to the studio. Only Helen decided to stay, knowing that if Bronson Pearl was still alive, his most likely link to the States would be through WNN.

It was 2:30 in the morning when Bud Johnson tapped her on the shoulder. He was one of the engineers for Helen's newscast. He was also a bachelor who had agreed to cover for some of the other employees. He had brought a sleeping bag and several changes of cloth-ing and set up camp in a corner of one of the engineering equipment storage areas. The network had bathrooms, showers, and food. "I've got more space than in my Upper West Side studio apartment," he had laughed. "Let the guys with wives and kids go home."

"Helen?" said Bud. "Helen?"

Helen murmured something only barely intelligible. It had to do with a refusal to eat oatmeal, whether or not she would wear her ugly yellow raincoat to school even though it had been raining all morning, and something about her homework.

"Helen, you're dreaming. Wake up," said Bud.

"You're not Grandma..." Helen said, groggily. She had not thought she could sleep, had not thought she would sleep again until matters were resolved and Bronson's whereabouts were known. Now she was being awakened, and from the look on Bud's face, she was frightened something was wrong.

"Bud? What is it? Is it Bronson?"

"We've got the feed up again. There was a sniper attack, then a counter. Judy's Ikigami got hit, but she and Bronson are fine. A spare camera was rushed to her while a technician began field repairs.

Everyone had to go to a shelter. Look, he's on the line. Ask him yourself. You'll feel better about it."

Helen rushed to a small broadcast booth where a monitor would let her see Bronson as they talked. The staff switched the satellite signal directly to her, knowing how worried she had been.

"So this time *you* fell asleep," laughed Bronson. "Now we're even for the other night."

"Bronson, what's happening?"

"Macalusso's here but I don't think he can do anything. I don't think anyone but God can do anything now."

"What do you mean? Has the war begun?"

"Not here. Not around Megiddo. It's like we're in the eye of the hurricane for the moment, but you can feel the wind shifting and know we'll soon feel the full force of the violence."

"I don't understand."

"General Alizar said it in that interview I sent Production. The people of Israel have to fight. They have no choice because they believe they have no choice. It is as though everything in their history, everything in the Bible is being acted out at this time in this place. Men, women, and children are dying, and more are going to die. Nothing makes sense except survival right now."

"I can't believe all this is happening and we're so far apart. I want to hold you, Bronson. I feel like we're married to microphones when we should be ...."

"Married to each other? Is that what you're thinking, Helen?"

"Yes. Yes, even though I know I'm going to lose you like I've lost everyone else who's ever mattered to me."

"This isn't the time for that, Helen. I love you and I'm going to marry you whenever I get back. It's the only revenge I'll ever get for the theme music stunt at the airport."

As Helen watched in horror on the monitor, Bronson looked off in the distance, a frightened look on his face. There was a loud explosion, the picture jumping as though Bronson had been dropped from a great height onto a trampoline. Then the screen faded to black.

"Bronson!" yelled Helen.

"Don't break my ear drums," she heard over her ear phone. "The explosion just knocked out the camera. We've still got voice."

"Are you all right?"

"It's happening, Helen. It's getting worse. There's troop movement starting. One of the planes just dropped a bomb on the road ahead of one of the ground forces. I don't know which yet. I may have to change position. Let Bud know to get ready to tape a report when I can see what's going on."

Helen heard another explosion. Then Bronson's voice said, "That's it. I'm moving. I love you, Helen."

There was nothing but silence as Helen whispered, "And I love you, my darling. God keep you safe."

FOUR

The First Fullfilment

It was early afternoon in New York when Helen Hannah sat at the anchor desk, having interrupted WNN's scheduled programming for an emergency report from the Middle East. An exhausted Bronson Pearl, his face shadowed by a two day growth of beard, his eyes showing the exhaustion of too little sleep, came on to the screen. "We have now confirmed that Tel Aviv, Israel's largest city, has been struck by one or more chemical weapons. The exact nature of the poison has not been reported, though it appears to be a fast acting nerve gas absorbed through the pores of the skin. Dr. Shimon Lipkowitz of Mt. Sinai Hospital has stated that the chemical is a familiar one, a staple of several of the illegal biological stockpiles hidden in a number of different countries. But while an antidote is known, the unexpected nature of the attack has been such that woefully inadequate supplies are in the city. Thousands are believed dead already, and...." He paused, looking at someone just off camera. Then he continued.

"I have just been told that Ben Cohen, a spokesman for the Israeli Defense Department, is making a statement at this time. We will be switching to the Knesset Building for that, Helen."

The television image returned to the WNN broadcast studio in Manhattan. "That was Bronson Pearl," said Helen, speaking to the camera. She saw the signal from the floor engineer that they were ready to go to the live broadcast from the Israeli Defense Department. "We take you now to Israeli Knesset building where a press conference is in progress."

The scene switched to a somber faced man, standing at a microphone covered podium, angrily speaking to the press. "....an act both heinous and cowardly. The poison gas knows neither combatant nor civilian, man nor woman, newborn nor elderly. It is a weapon of genocide, a cloud of death meant to eradicate all human life."

He paused, composing himself. What he was not saying was that his own family lived in Tel Aviv. His wife, Rachel, their three daughters and two sons, all were at home when the attack occurred. He had no idea if they were dead or alive, but word from an observation craft sent over the area indicated that their home was in the path of the prevailing winds, no more than a few hundred yards from the flash point of the bombs.

"The enemies of peace have accomplished nothing of a military nature. The Tel Aviv defense emplacements have not been touched. All buildings are standing. All communication links remain open. Airfields, missile emplacements, army barracks, weapons storage units.....all are untouched. It is as though a new city full of people could walk in and take over. Except for the air befouled with poison. Except for the corpses that litter the ground."

One of the reporters listening to the speech asked a question to which Cohen responded, "It is one of a half dozen nerve gasses absorbed through the pores of the skin. One drop can kill hundreds of people, which is why it is mixed with liquid, then sprayed in an outward direction when used tactically. It's active life is only a few days, and there is protective equipment that can be worn when entering the area. We have a team of specially trained soldiers driving to the city right now, all of them wearing full body suits that do not allow the gas to pass through the material.

"But this attack came without warning. This attack had only one purpose, to kill as many people as possible as quickly as possible. And that is what it is doing. We are estimating one hundred percent casualties among those who were caught outside when the bombs exploded. Those who can not stay in their homes or do not realize the danger and venture outside will also die. As for the rest of Tel Aviv residents, we just do not know."

"Is this the same substance used in the blackmail of several upscale apartment houses throughout the world a few months ago?" asked the foreign correspondent for the *Chicago Tribune*.

"Yes, or at least from the same chemical family. Those cases remain unsolved so we can not tell if the same people are involved. We also have not had a sampling of the substances found in those buildings for comparison. But they are quite similar in their effect."

"Mr. Cohen," shouted a reporter for the *Los Angeles Times*. "Isn't your family living in Tel Aviv."

"That is true," said Cohen, his face suddenly tense. Several of the other reporters glared at the man who had asked the question. Israel had long been a land joyously celebrating life because the people knew how precious and fleeting it could be. No citizen who had been in the country more than five years was untouched by death. Family members, lovers, a neighbor's children, co-workers... Someone you knew had been killed or injured in a marketplace, while at the beach, on the way to or from work, or riding the bus. It was a fact of existence in a land chosen by God, then made fertile by flowing waters, endless sunshine, sweat, blood, and hope. The reporters knew Ben Cohen's family was in Tel Aviv. The reporters knew that only Cohen's job kept him from being by their side at this time. And they also knew that it would be a miracle if any of them were alive.

"Have you been in touch with them? Do you know if they survived the gas attack?"

Naomi Prado of *Le Monde* stomped on the reporter's instep, making certain her action would not be seen by the camera. He turned and glared at her, not understanding her outrage. He was only doing his duty, bringing the full story to the American public.

"I have not heard from my family since the attack. I have called them, but the lines are so crowded, no one can get through. I do not know if they are alive. I do not know if anyone is alive. Our weapons experts tell me that the wind currents were ideal for the enemies of civilization today. Depending upon the chemical agent used, how it was diluted, and the exact altitude at which it was released, the wind would spread it so that as many two-thirds of the people of Tel Aviv may be dead right now. My family may be among them." His speech was clipped, his jaw set, his eyes filled with tears. Several photographers moved in for close-ups of his face. It was the type of poignant personal drama that sold the newspapers.

*

It was dusk, the time of transition for Edna Williams' neighborhood. Sadea Vadalia was rolling down the steel shading that protected the display windows and entrance to her specialty clothing shop. Herman Waring's diner had closed two hours earlier, but he sat in a back booth, reading a racing form, planning his food orders, and relaxing from a busy day. The coffee he was sipping had been made to service what he jokingly called the "afternoon rush of night shift workers." Mostly they were the pimps and prostitutes who were eating what, for them, was breakfast before going on the streets to sell their bodies and souls. Now the coffee was dark and bitter, a reminder of how the neighborhood had changed since he was a boy. Back then families would stroll the streets after dinner, stopping to share the day's news while their children safely played unattended. Today... Well... He was glad his children were all grown and living elsewhere.

James Misanno's Pizza Heaven was gradually filling with the usual assortment of gang members, drug abusers, drifters staying in cheap area motels, and teens whose working parents had long since given up on trying to supervise their children. Pizza Heaven was neutral territory, though the outside back wall was covered with graffiti announcing the latest death — "R.I.P. Little Tone" "We loved you, Antoine" — and the latest challenge — "Kill the 83rd Street Rolling Gangsta's."

No one caused trouble for Misanno inside his establishment. Rival gangsters knew better than to throw signs or show their colors until they were down the block. James Misanno owned the last pizza shop within a two mile radius. A drive-by shooting at one chain restaurant, and the kidnapping of a delivery girl at another had resulted in the area being blacklisted. Misanno, an independent running a store that had served the area for three generations, remained. If he closed down, the food staple of street people would be history.

Several Mom and Pop "delicatessens" were open, but the stores were not what they were in nicer areas. These were not locations where you could buy a corned beef sandwich, roast beef on rye, and cole slaw, though some carried package goods so short dated for freshness you had to check to see if the filling had started to turn bad. The main sources of income were cigarettes, forty ounce bottles of malt liquor, condoms, and in a few of the delis, if you knew the owner, cheap handguns.

APOCALYPSE

The cars that moved slowly through the neighborhood contained a mix of suburbanites looking for action, local drug dealers settling accounts with "employees" who worked from the shadows of abandoned buildings, and seekers of cheap motels with a reputation for renting by the hour when asked. Most of the trouble makers lived elsewhere, coming into the area after dark to take advantage of the disreputable image they were actually creating. Most of the "good" people stayed inside, their shades drawn, their curtains closed, their eyes and ears focused on anything other than the sounds of the street. What you don't know can't hurt you, they told each other. Don't get involved and you won't get in trouble.

The elderly, like Edna Williams, sometimes joked that they were living in the waiting room. Some would leave the area by death. Some would leave to enter nursing homes. And some would one day have a son or daughter come by to move them to a spare bedroom in a safe suburb where they could be free from fear in exchange for acting as live-in sitter for their grandchildren.

Yet where others found despair, Edna Williams found only hope each night as she took to streets most law enforcement officers would never use alone. "No one is open to the Lord's message when everything is going well," she had told Pastor Holmes during one of the afternoon visits he routinely made to his elderly parishioners. "Look at those boys over there," she had said, taking him to her apartment window and showing him a half dozen youths standing in the doorway of an abandoned, boarded up building. They were wearing identical outfits of white T-shirts, pants pulled low to show their underwear, and expensive basketball shoes. They each had the same colored bandanas hanging out of their back pockets, and from time to time they would raise a fist to a passing friend, their fingers carefully positioned in the recognition sign used by every member of their gang. "See the tall one? That's Jo-Jo.

His mother is a drug addict who spent the money his older sister saved for a prom dress in order to buy cocaine. The one with the cap is Angelo. His father used to beat him so badly, he has permanent nerve damage and walks with a limp. LeMar's had so many different mothers and fathers, he doesn't know who really gave birth to him. Philip..."

"You know all these young men by name?" asked the astonished minister.

"Of course. They're my neighbors."

"But aren't they dangerous?"

"Perhaps the way you're thinking. I've visited two of them in the workhouse, and all of them have been in trouble with the law. But don't you see? By coming together like this, they're searching for something better than themselves. They want love, structure, a family. They have a spiritual hunger that is awesome to witness.

"The gang has filled that gap for them. There are rules. Demands of loyalty. Mutual support...

"I find them a wonderful challenge. If we can bring them the Word, they will turn their passions to the Lord. They are in the wrong place with their lives, but their hearts are reaching out to Jesus. They just don't know it yet. That's why I talk with them whenever I see them. I want them to know who they're really searching for and how He's with them even in the depths of their despair."

"And they listen?"

"Of course not. They laugh at me. They think I'm a crazy old lady. They try to shock me with their stories of sex and violence. But they don't turn away when I come. They don't mock me while I'm speaking. They listen, and I know that in God's time their hearts will be reached by the Holy Spirit. Until then I just love them."

That was why she found her evening walks so joyous. It was a time to accept unconditionally, to share the Word, to bring them her peace in Jesus when their lives were so often in turmoil.

It was well after the evening news should have been over when Edna returned to her apartment and turned on WNN. She had not heard about the attack in Tel Aviv, about the announcement that Israel was planning retaliation despite the impending arrival of Franco Macalusso.

There was a commercial about a luxury car, and as Edna sat in her favorite reading chair, planning to read from the Bible while keeping one ear open in case her granddaughter came back on the air, the image was that of the European Union President arriving in the desert. His face was grim, as were the faces of all in the picture. Key leaders of the various factions had agreed to this meeting, but the events in the world had probably escalated beyond healing.

Edna's Bible was open to Paul's writing of Second Thessalonians. Ignoring the reporter talking about the arrival of Macalusso, she silently read from the second chapter, "Now we beseech you brethren, by the coming of our Lord Jesus Christ and by our gathering together unto him, that ye be not soon shaken in mind, or be troubled, neither by spirit, nor by word, nor by letter as from us, as that the day of Christ is at hand." Paul was talking about the Rapture and the Second Coming. It was a familiar passage, one her Bible study class had discussed a few weeks ago. She wondered why it seemed so important to her now.

"Let no man deceive you by any means, for that day shall not come, except there come a falling away first, and that man of sin be revealed, the son of perdition...."

She glanced at the screen, saw a close-up of Macalusso. He was saying something about a test of the new world order to handle the crisis. He was talking of negotiations. But the words seemed to fade into meaninglessness. There was something troubling about the man, something both more and less than he seemed. She would have to ask Helen or that nice young man of hers, Bronson Pearl. They would know.

"And now ye know what withholdeth that he might be revealed in his time. For the mystery of iniquity doth already work, only he who now letteth will let, until he be taken out of the way. And then shall that Wicked be revealed, whom the Lord shall consume with the spirit of his mouth, and shall destroy with the brightness of his coming."

Edna set down the Bible. Something was happening, something she had somehow known would be a part of her lifetime, yet nothing she could ever have imagined. For reasons she did not understand, she felt compelled to write a note to her granddaughter. Hurriedly she took up pen and paper. There seemed so little time, though she did not know why.

The soldier was frightened as he ran to Bronson Pearl who was still broadcasting live from Megiddo. The soldier's face was pale, his stomach churning. He had vomited when he read the message as it came over the computer, terror gripping his heart. This was a time all the men and women had known was coming, yet prayed they were misinterpreting the escalation of violence over the last few days.

He had no illusions that God would necessarily spare his life. His family had lived in Eastern Europe when Hitler came to power. One grandmother had survived by being used as a prostitute by the SS, a captain of which later claimed her as his personal mistress. Her food ration was increased enough to prevent starvation, but the trauma had stayed with her and she had eventually been overwhelmed by guilt, not only because of what she had been forced to do but also because she had survived. Most of his relatives had died, some being worked to death, their food allotment assuring gradual starvation within 12 to 18 months of their capture. Others had gone directly to the death camps.

His grandfather's family had been saved by a righteous Christian who hid them in a back building on his farm. Another righteous Christian had lost his own life hiding a handful of other relatives who eventually were captured in January, 1945. Fortunately they were shipped to a work camp, the war ending before they could meet the fate that befell so many others.

He understood that God's covenants with Abraham, Noah, Moses, and others assured his people would survive. But he also knew that he was as likely to be one of those who died in this new Holocaust, a distant memory, if that, for some family member as yet unborn.

He did not want to die, did not want to go through the horror of war. He feared a lingering death, feared having to face God, knowing how many of his failings had been written in the Book of Life. And now, the message...

The soldier said nothing as he passed the printout to Bronson who stopped in the middle of the broadcast, scanned it quickly, then looked into the camera and said, "I have just been handed a report saying that the U.S. Aircraft Carrier Nebraska has been struck by a tactical nuclear torpedo fired from a Chinese submarine. Aircraft in the area say that the vessel exploded with such force, no one is believed to have survived. The water is filled with debris and the bodies of what are believed to be 5,000 men and women. Other ships have launched search and rescue efforts, but helicopters flying over the scene with searchlights report no sign of life.

"The 90,000 ton ship was destroyed by a single torpedo. My understanding is that the U.S. Government is planning an immediate and overwhelming retaliatory strike against key targets on mainland China. However, the Pentagon has not yet issued an official statement.

"We have unconfirmed information that the President of the United States is staying in Air Force One, using it as a flying command post, rather than landing in Colorado Springs. He is making a declaration of war which is expected to be endorsed by Congress."

As Bronson spoke, his words were drowned out by the din of low flying, high speed fighter planes.

"Bronson... Bronson..." Helen Hannah called out from the anchor desk at WNN. "Can you hear me?"

Bronson watched the low flying aircraft, then looked back into the camera, cupping his hand around the ear piece receiving Helen's voice. "I'm sorry. There's a lot of chaos here."

"Bronson, is there any word about how widespread the fighting is?"

"My understanding is that approximately three-million troops are deployed within 100 square miles of where I'm standing now. Another two million men and women are reported to be less than three hours away and under full mobilization. There is..."

Several explosions shook the ground. There was the sound of automatic weapons being fired. Bronson grabbed his helmet and put it on. He reached for his gas mask, then said, "This is Bronson Pearl, WNN News near Armageddon, Israel."

The picture was cut as Bronson and his videographer grabbed their equipment and raced for a shelter. The military leaders had told them to run in a zig-zag pattern to prevent being targeted by snipers. However, with the explosions taking place all around them, they just ran in a straight line, wanting to get out of the line of fire as fast as they could. They managed to leap into one of the protective trenches, dropping and rolling just as the shrapnel struck the sand bag barriers above their heads.

The black bag had always been a joke for the President. He had come to power in the most incredible period in the last century of United States history. The Cold War was long over. The once mighty

Soviet Union had been disbanded, its military decimated by factionalization, alcoholism, budget cuts, and a lack of clear objectives. China was an emerging industrial giant, and any warfare seemed likely to be economic, a battle among international corporations, not soldiers in the field. Even the trouble spots such as Korea had originally seemed like problems geographically contained.

It was only a few weeks earlier that the President and a handful of Secret Service agents had jokingly played catch with the little black bag. Another time, on the night of his thirtieth wedding anniversary, when he and the First Lady were in a celebratory mood, rekindling one of the few monogamous love affairs to grace the White House, he had picked up the bag and jokingly said, "If you don't go to bed with me, I'll start a nuclear war."

She had pushed it aside, laughing. Then she lowered her eyes and playfully commented, "If I must sacrifice myself for the sake of the western world, then let history record my selflessness at this moment."

The idea that he had all the special codes and keys needed to start a nuclear holocaust was beyond something which he could take seriously. He had served in the military. He had trained to kill others and once thought briefly of a career in the Marines rather than returning to law school and then entering politics. But taking a life one on one in the midst of a conflagration where the enemy was real, the violence all around, and survival meant doing the otherwise unthinkable was quite different than what he was facing. To use the codes as he knew he must meant horrors beyond past experience. Whole cities would be destroyed. The innocent would die with the guilty, and many of the living would curse their fate, referring to those who had passed before them as blessed.

The luckiest ones, including the world's leaders surviving in specially prepared shelters, would be left with a land so radioactive that deaths by cancer, birth abnormalities, and possible slow starvation would be inevitable. Triumph would mean facing a bleak existence that would make Adam and Eve's expulsion from the Garden of Eden seem like an inconvenience. Yet he knew he had to act.

The President opened his wallet and looked at the pictures of his family. The First Lady was with him, but he did not know if even their close marriage would survive what he had to do. Their daughter, Cara, was a commercial artist living in New York, a first strike target for retaliating countries. Their son, Zachary, was in Los Angeles, a fledgling maker of documentaries in a city that was also a first strike target. And their other son, Brad, was on a tour of England. He had just called from London, a city within a country that would probably disappear entirely from the map.

To do his duty meant to be responsible for the deaths of the children he loved, the grandchildren yet to be conceived. His heart ached and tears came down his face as he ordered the courier to bring him the bag. Then he opened it, at the same time using a secured telephone to make certain the previously selected targets had missiles locked in to those sites. What he did not know but would not have been surprised to learn was that similar actions were being taken in Israel, China, India, England, North Korea, France, Germany, Italy, Iraq, Egypt, and elsewhere. So many warheads were about to be released that it no longer mattered who was an enemy and who was a friend. All would suffer unprecedented agony.

Helen Hannah's dress was rumpled, her shoulders slightly hunched, her hair mildly disheveled. There was redness in the corners of her eyes, and she had obviously had little sleep. The floor director had suggested she send out for something else to wear, perhaps let make-up touch-up her appearance.

"We are at the start of World War III," Helen had snapped. "We've all been working around the clock to bring our viewers the news. Nobody wants to see Suzy Sunshine. They want hard news from professionals who have not let them down. If the missiles are launched, no one's going to care if our ratings suffer because I didn't qualify for the Newscasters' Best Dressed List today."

"Helen, I just meant..."

"You just meant that I look like hell, and I suppose I do. But if anyone cares more about what I look like than what we all have to say, they're bigger fools than ...." She stopped herself before she could turn nasty. The floor director didn't mean any harm. Like Helen, she was using the routine of her job to keep from thinking too much about what else was taking place. The young woman's boyfriend had been in the National Guard and was now on active duty in the Middle East. She was as scared as Helen, and from the looks of her face, she too had been grieving for what might already be her boyfriend's fate.

"Look, I'm sorry, Patty. You're just trying to do your job. I'll brush my teeth and put on extra deodorant during the commercial breaks so I'm not so offensive that people have to sit too far back from their television sets when watching me at home. Is that okay?"

Patty smiled at the weak joke. "Okay, Helen. And I'll have Bob use a long lens on the camera during broadcast. Maybe we'll substitute Demi Moore's head for yours. We can do Elliott with computer graphics."

The two women paused when a voice from the control room told them that the WNN Los Angeles Bureau had Dr. Stephen Horne in their studio for a live interview. He was a professor at UCLA and the leading expert on nuclear research and development.

"Thank you for taking time to speak to us," said Helen after returning to the set. Dr. Horne's face was on the monitor. He was a heavy-set man with a rather jolly round face, rapidly receding hair line, and bushy white beard. He looked like the type of man everyone would ask to play Santa Claus at their office Christmas parties.

"Always a pleasure, Ms. Hannah."

"Dr. Horne, we have heard that the Chinese have used a tactical nuclear weapon against one of our ships in the Mideast. The President has been silent about his planned response, but military experts are saying that a nuclear strike against one or more cities is a possibility. This is a frightening thought, especially when so many of us thought that with the fall of the Soviet Union, the world would have less concern with such possibilities. Just what are we facing?"

"First, the obvious question is whether the President of the United States is willing to commit nuclear weapons to the escalating tension. There have been a number of treaties signed in recent years and a large number of missiles removed from launch bunkers. But most of those were aging and of little value. Others were simply removed from their position locked on to long time targets in the Soviet Union and elsewhere. These can be retargeted in fifteen minutes, and most of us feel that the remaining nuclear arsenal includes approximately 60,000 weapons internationally."

"That number was used by Hogarth Chapman during our Nightly Update program," said Helen. "But it was my understanding that these are under the control of the United States and the former Soviet Union. These nations have used great constraint over the years. What has changed that makes us all so fearful?"

"Most of the publicity has been about the biological weapons and away from the nuclear arsenal. The numbers have been so large, the bombs we talk about so devastating, we tend to overlook the miniaturization of what is still the most likely weapon we all face. There are tactical nuclear weapons, some of which can fit inside a suitcase and be transported anywhere in the world without discovery. There have been rumors that one or more were smuggled into New York City by the Bulgarians who worked for the Soviet KGB back in the late 1960s. And certainly countries such as Iraq and Pakistan are likely to be able to launch a limited nuclear strike.

"If just the known nuclear weapons are launched, they have an explosive power somewhere in the area of 9,700 megatons. That's the equivalent of 10 billion tons of TNT. By contrast, the bombs we dropped on Hiroshima and Nagasaki look like harmless fire crackers. The current world arsenal is such that there is an explosive force equal to four tons of TNT for every man, woman, and child on earth.

"Do you remember the truck bomb that destroyed the Oklahoma City Federal Building?"

"Yes, Dr. Horne. I was out there after it happened. The loss of life was horrible, and the building was unusable rubble."

"Picture the equivalent of that explosive force striking every person on this planet. That's the potential for destruction if the nuclear stockpiles are used.

*

Richard Stanfield stood in a corner of his office, holding Eleanor Lansing, a Washington lawyer whom he had been dating for the past year. He touched her cheek, gently caressing the side of her face with his hand. He felt her tears, felt the quiver of her lips as she tried to speak, then realized there was nothing to say.

They kissed again, long, lingering. Then she pushed him back, looking into his eyes as though she was trying to see the depths of his heart, then retain that image for eternity.

"What... What next?"

"For us?"

"That's over. At least in this life, isn't it?"

"I don't know. Washington has excellent air defenses, but it's always been a first strike target. That's why the President left."

"We're still here."

"So you know where I stand in importance in government."

"Do you believe in God?"

"Does it matter?"

"You're calm. I assume something's giving you peace."

"I'm not calm. I've given up. The President has had me working night and day, and now..."

She kissed him again. "I want to make love to you. My one regret is that we never did that. Do you think we can be lovers in Heaven?"

"I think I'd better go out there and talk with the press. The President..."

"Safe on Air Force One. We're the ones left to be statistics when the missiles strike."

"You'll be a beautiful statistic."

"And you'll be fired before we can be vaporized. Go out there. If by chance there's a miracle, you'll need a job. I'm not going to support a husband."

*

The camera was running, showing the face of the President of the United States sitting behind a small desk in the office area of Air Force One. Behind him was the Presidential Seal. The image was supposed to be reassuring.

"....Approximately eleven minutes ago, we received confirmation that fifty-one ICBM's, each containing multiple nuclear warheads, have been launched against us and our allies by the enemies of world peace. The exact targets are not known.

"The attack on the U.S.S. Nebraska was intended to reduce

our ability to respond. That was a mistake in thinking. We have long had a policy of mutually assured destruction in order to deter an event such as this one. We have missiles capable of massive death and destruction in roving submarines, in underground bunkers, and in other locations throughout the world. They can be targeted towards any city necessary in no more than fifteen minutes. The loss of even three-quarters of our defensive emplacements will still enable us to destroy any enemy anywhere in the world.

"Now we are faced with the most frightening concern of this century. We are experiencing nuclear attack and must decide if we should follow through on our long stated policy. The answer, I am deeply saddened to say, is that we must. If we have any chance of surviving as a nation, as a people, it will come from being true to our word. As a result, just before this broadcast I have ordered the launch of a retaliatory strike which will stop those who would rather destroy the planet than negotiate a just peace. I do this with the knowledge that I am responsible to the people of America and the people of the world. I am deeply saddened by the loss of life we are about to incur, yet feel that to do less would be to deny our obligation as the leader of the free world."

*

The WNN news set looked like a montage from a series of horror movies. One monitor carried live feed from the increased fighting in the Middle East. Another showed the firing of anti-aircraft missiles from a coastal military position. A third had a tape of the President leaving the White House grounds which was being used as lead-in for the address from Air Force One. Others showed various world leaders, some being evacuated, some addressing their countries' citizens, and some meeting with Franco Macalusso. There were images of refugees from advancing armies, children sitting by the side of the road, crying. Old people staring vacantly in the distance. But Helen and the others on the set focused solely on the monitor of the broadcast going over the air. It was coming from Calvin Smith and videographer Charles Tafe of the Denver Bureau. Calvin was reporting from a major intersection in Denver, providing local color from the largest city near where the heads of the American government were taking refuge.

"I am standing on a street in downtown Denver where many people are in shock. For years Colorado has been the command post for the Strategic Air Command. The headquarters built into a mountainside was designed to take a direct hit from a nuclear weapon. Many of the people in this city worked for the military over the years. They grew up with the idea of the threat of nuclear war, but as the years passed, the fears lessened. The likelihood seemed increasingly remote — until today.

"Now there is a grim determination to the way people are making their way on the streets. The nature of the missile warheads is such that none of us know if we are in a targeted city. Yet what is certain is that..."

Suddenly there was a deafening crash, the camera dropped to the ground, still broadcasting. "Charley?" shouted Calvin. "Charley?"

Only Calvin's feet were visible, though in the distance the monitor seemed to be showing cars run up against a fire hydrant, telephone pole, building walls, and other vehicles. There were screams in the distance, a sense of panic even in the low, limited view.

Helen swiveled in her chair and picked up a head set. Holding the microphone near her mouth, she told the engineer to patch her through. There was no answer. She looked up at the control booth and saw that it was almost empty. The only person remaining was Alan Ditmar, a college age intern. Although the room was soundproof, she could see his mouth was contorted into what would have been a scream of terror.

FIVE

The Rapture

"Far be it from me to gossip, Lilly, but I would not be surprised if that new girl in Cosmetics is.... Well, you know," said Ethel Bosley, standing behind the check-out counter in Ladies' Blouses. The department store was quiet, the lunch hour crowd having dissipated, and the after school rush of mothers and their children still an hour away.

"In a family way? I've thought that myself. She's put on five, ten pounds since she's been here and you never see her eating much," said Lilly Nelson. She worked in Accessories, but there were no shoppers browsing in her department.

"What you do see is her mooning about that Proctor boy in Electronics. They take their breaks together. They leave work together. They..."

"....browse in lingerie together," said Lilly, finishing her friend's sentence.

"Really?" laughed a delighted Ethel, looking again at the young woman. "Do they know they can also get a discount on maternity clothes?"

"I was just joking," said Lilly. "But I wouldn't be surprised if while we're having lunch, they're looking at some unmentionables he can take from her willing...."

Lord, give me strength, thought Enid Farkas, a retired school teacher who had been trying to buy a blouse for the last ten minutes. The display area had only one in her size and that was a color she hated. But the blouse was perfect for the fiftieth wedding celebration of her church pastor and his wife and she really wanted to buy it if she could get the right color. "Excuse me. I hate to interrupt, but..."

The women glanced in her direction, then continued their conversation. "You know, her mother used to work here in personnel. I met her when I first started here. She handled my orientation, though what I needed orientation for, I'll never know. Been working in one department store or another since I was sixteen. And I know for a fact that either this girl or one of her brothers or sisters was one of those six months babies."

"The apple never falls far from the tree," sniffed Lilly. "You'd think in this day and time..."

"Excuse me," said the customer. "I realize you're busy, but I'm wondering if..."

"Yes, we *are* busy," said Ethel. "But if you want me to ring this up..."

Lord, I know this is why you gave us patience, but must you test me so frequently? thought the woman. "Not exactly," she said. "The blouse will fit perfectly, but I'm afraid it's the wrong color."

"Nothing wrong with that color," said Lilly. "I wear it myself all the time. Perhaps if you learned to accessorize..."

"On you the color would look lovely. I'm afraid that my complexion is different, though. This shade of green always makes my children worry that they're about to get their inheritance. Perhaps a pale pink if you have it."

"That's her department," said Lilly, pointing to Ethel. "I'm in Accessories."

"And I'm still with my quandary. Do you have the blouse in back?'

"I suppose I could look. You are buying it, aren't you?" she said, appraising the clothing of the old woman. There was nothing fancy about her, obviously a pensioner or one of those crazies with a hundred cats living in too small a house, squirreling away all her money. She didn't want someone wasting her time, having her run all over the back room just so she could change her mind.

"It's to wear for a special event at my church," she started to explain. "This is perfect except for the color."

Lilly looked away, disgusted. Church people seldom spent their money on accessories. "Too frivolous," they told her. Too cheap was more like it, she thought.

"Back in a sec...." sighed Ethel, walking with enough deliberate slowness to show the customer she did not approve of the intrusion. There was nothing wrong with the color of the blouse she was holding. Some people were so...

The scream caught Ethel by surprise. High, piercing, the sound of terror. She was certain the store was being robbed. One of the clerks must be facing a gunman. She turned, expecting to see one of the security guards summoned by the silent alarm system hidden by every cash register. Instead she saw Lilly pointing to where the customer had been.

For a moment Ethel's former annoyance took over. She as-

127

sumed the woman had just walked out, probably taking the blouse with her. Just another time wasting, lying shoplifter. Then she realized that a shoplifter would not cause the kind of fear she could see on Lilly's face.

"Gone...." said Lilly, pointing. "She..."

"Lilly Nelson, why are you making such a big deal out of a customer walking out? I knew when I turned my back she would..."

"N...no...Vanished."

Ethel looked at the floor where Lilly was pointing. The blouse the woman had been holding had fallen in a heap. But what was scaring Lilly were the clothes, the old woman's clothes, neatly folded in a small pile, the glasses she had worn resting on top.

"The old woman was a stripper?" laughed Ethel, not yet understanding. "We've got some naked old lady walking through the store, sagging and bagging, and..."

"She's gone, Ethel. One minute she was there. The next she was gone. Only her clothes were left. It was like something in the movies. Just...vanished..."

Easton Blakely McNamara sat in the large motor home that served as rolling office for his New Millennium Televival Ministry. The tent had been set-up for several hours, the cameras positioned, the satellite up link made operational. Key staff members had unloaded the wheelchairs from the equipment truck, and the two way radios used for communication during the show had been tested.

McNamara had been on the road for more than a month now, his headquarters staff saying that contributions were running 12 percent ahead of early projections. And that was just the American returns. They were still finishing the language dubs for China, Italy, Germany, France, and several Eastern European nations. The financial returns from those countries would not be known for at least another three weeks. Only then would he know the full financial impact of what he called "the only television tent revival in the nation." What was certain was that Ellie Mae would be able to have that Italian sports car she had been hinting about and the kids could have the swimming pool they wanted him to add to their Florida vacation home.

"We have the people from the Hinson Home in the wheel-chairs," said Freddie Renford, an attractive blond who had interned at his Texas broadcast studio before proving herself loyal enough to work with the road team. She coordinated the seating, making certain that elderly, rather frail looking but otherwise quite healthy men and women sat in wheelchairs during the broadcast. They were met at the bus by Freddie and her staff, and those who could be induced to ride inside were photographed as they were being pushed by several ushers. During the healing call, they would be encouraged to leave their chairs and walk down the aisles. The tape made as they were wheeled in would be played just before they began moving to the front under their own power. People watching the show at home would think they were watching a healing ministry, as would many in the audience. If anyone attending the event knew the people were able bodied when they arrived, they would be told there was no effort to trick anyone. The wheelchairs were more comfortable than the folding wooden seats available to the people coming by car, church van, and chartered bus.

"Have you taken information cards from the people?"

"As many as we can before you start. Murray's running them through the computer right now to see which problems are the most often reported. He'll radio you before you start working the crowd."

"You've tested this thing you've given me?" he asked, checking the radio receiver he kept in his pocket. A thin wire went under his shirt and into a tiny ear piece the lighting people kept in shadows so it would not be detected.

"Several times, and we're keeping the cards as back-up. Leland likes the idea that you will seem to be getting a personal message from God rather than just reading names from cards before offering prayers. If there's any problems, and we don't anticipate any, Kathy will bring you the cards after her second solo."

McNamara removed one of the silk sports jackets he purchased by the dozen during his London travels. They were custom made, the tailor he used updating his measurements each trip in case his weight fluctuations also changed the line of the jacket. They were also inappropriate for these broadcasts, the reason he kept a couple of conservative looking polyester jackets he bought off the rack from Sears and into which he changed before going to work.

He checked his hair piece to be certain it was properly in place. He removed his Rolex watch and the gold signet ring he had had made by a brilliant goldsmith in the Middle East during his 1987 trip to the Holy Land. Then he drank the six ounces of orange juice laced with vodka Freddie left him in a coffee cup before each performance, picked up his Bible, and left the trailer.

It was exactly two o'clock when the theme music was played and McNamara ran down the aisle, bounded onto the stage, and shouted his standard opening line: "Do you have the faith of a mustard seed?"

"Yes!" the audience yelled back, prompted by Gene Gibbons who held a variety of reaction signs used to cue the audience what was expected when the cameras were panning them.

"Then let's move some mountains!" replied the preacher, breaking into a song about faith, hope, and the constancy of the Lord. He had a rich, lustrous tenor which he once tried to parlay into a career in musical theater. He was also blessed with the handsome appearance of a man who seemed at once powerful, deserving of respect, yet approachable enough that men did not resent their wives and girlfriends making fools of themselves at the stage door. Unfortunately, he was far from unique both on Broadway where he was only occasionally cast in supporting roles, and in Chicago where he had more leads but never reached the level of income he desired. It was when he learned to combine the earning power of television with the show business appeal of old time tent revivals that he found his success. Now he was one of the highest grossing preachers on cable and satellite television, a Christian recording star, and the head of a video distribution company that made millions from both tapes of his shows and special productions available only by mail. "Not bad for a Baptist drop-out who hasn't been in a real church since we were married," he proudly told Ellie Mae who stood by him through the opening number, looking adoringly into his eyes.

The show followed a formula the marketing staff found gained the most response. The opening gospel song would be followed by Praise Time Testimony — taped interviews with people who felt McNamara had changed their lives for the better. "I know it was God, but if He didn't have you for His holy vessel, I doubt I ever would have been reached," said one old man whose wizened body, heavily lined face, rheumy eyes, misshapen nose, and mottled teeth indicated a hard drinking, hard fighting past.

It was during the appeal for contributions for McNamara's forthcoming pilgrimage to Bible Land that he heard the sounds. There were horns blaring and cars crashing, the noise surprisingly loud since the tent was several hundred yards from the nearest road. Startled, McNamara glanced up at the engineer's booth to see if there was a problem, then had to look away, his eyes partially blinded by one of the spotlights.

For a moment McNamara's vision was blurred. Then, as it cleared, he was startled to hear Freddie cry out, "Easton!" She was standing in the back, surrounded by mostly empty wheelchairs. As he spun around, he realized that the majority of the people who had come to hear him were gone. Here and there sat a confused, frightened man or woman, a staff member from his ministry, or a hired security guard. But the majority of the people, almost 500 he would learn later, were gone. In their places, neatly folded and occasionally topped with eye glasses, hearing aids, pacemakers, or crutches, were their clothes.

"What's happening....?" asked McNamara, shocked.

"I don't know," said the engineer from the control room. "One minute they were there, then came that loud sound, and suddenly they were gone. Neal pulled one of the tapes for replay, but we can't see anything there either. One minute the place was packed, the next..." His voice was calm. He had been a career military man prior to joining the ministry. Electronics had been his specialty and he had set-up forward reconnaissance listening and viewing devices in a number of combat zones throughout the world. He was used to pressure, used to the unexpected, used to dealing with life and death issues as he worked. This was unlike anything he had ever experienced, but he remained calm, certain there was an explanation.

McNamara also tried to remain calm, thinking there had to be a logical explanation for the almost empty building, an empiness that happened in a flash. That was when he remembered what other ministers had tried to discuss with him in recent years. He had dismissed their words, of course. They saw television as a means to expand God's words to all the corners of the world. They saw their fund-raising efforts as being a vehicle for God's work, limiting their salaries to what was actually less than many of them would have made pastoring a regular church within their denominations. The rest was spent on teaching, medical/spiritual missionary work, and establishing transitional centers to help the hard-core unemployed gain job skills, parenting skills, release from addiction, and to ultimately become productive citizens and nurturing fathers or mothers.

For years he had thought they were jealous of his success. His ratings were often higher than theirs. His weekly take was often much greater. And though he lived modestly, he had invested substantial sums of money in a number of enterprises from which his name was hidden.

Lately he had realized they were serious. They saw him as a sinner to be saved, as an influential leader who had strayed from the fold. They had given him books and videotapes. They had addressed long letters to him, trying to show him how the events of the day had been prophesied long ago. They talked of the Rapture, of the time of trial, of the reign of the Anti-Christ and the return of Jesus.

As he stared in wonder at the emptiness before him, McNamara thought for a moment that the other clergy had been right, that the Rapture had, indeed, come. Yet even as he thought about it, his heart seemed hardened to the idea. He would have to make a few telephone calls when the show was off the air. He would have to find out how widespread whatever was happening might be. He would have to talk with the other clergy who used the media, certain that they were still conducting their shows, perhaps as bewildered as he was. He would...

And then he realized that there was a chance the others were gone, that he was alone among the religious broadcasters still... still not raptured, if that was truly what this was.

But the Rapture could not be real. It would mean that God had looked into his heart and found... Found what? And for the first time in his adult life, Easton McNamara stared into one of the cameras, not knowing what to say.

*

The eighteen wheeler with the double load was barreling along a highway in the middle of Wyoming. The sun was just beginning to move to the west and the glare was such that sun glasses were essential. It was a perfect day for driving, a perfect day to be anywhere but cooped up in an office. At least that was how the driver, Dan Mansfield, saw it. Kevin Orr was in the passenger seat. "What say come around six we pull off at some motel that's got a big enough lot to park this rig," said Kevin. "Here it is just the start of the afternoon and already I'm too tired and achy to sleep in the cab another night. Saving fifty bucks just isn't worth it a third night in a row."

"You been driving as long as I have, it's all second nature. First few months are the roughest. After your first year, you get so you feel funny when you have a couple days off and those aches disappear. It's like not hurting a bit seems abnormal."

"Then you want to just go to a truck stop?"

"I didn't say that. I think you're wasting your money, especially the way they're changing the miles we get and the way we're paid, but I'll share a room with you. You don't smell too bad and you don't snore. Besides, if I'm still alert enough, I think I'll go see if I can have a little fun."

"You're going to get a girl? I didn't think you were the type. All the pictures of the wife and kids you got in this rig... Or is that just for show?"

"I said fun. Adultery's a lot of things, but fun isn't one of them. No, I noticed in these small towns there's usually one church or another's got a Bible study group meeting. We get to the motel, I'll check their church directory and call around. If I find one, those meetings usually only last a couple of hours. Plenty of time left to get enough sleep. Besides, they refresh me more than if I just sat in front of the tube to relax. Want to come along if I can find one?"

"Not my style. You know that. I got nothing against religion. I just don't see the point of it. Life's what you make it. You do good to people, they do good right back. What goes around comes around. I don't need some preacher reminding me when I screw up. I'll just watch TV. You think they'll have cable out here?" Kevin stared out the window at the rugged terrain. Traffic was sparse in some of these states. The biggest cities would only pass for small towns back in Pennsylvania where he was from. Dan seemed to like the small town life, even said he might settle there. Kevin thought he'd be bored to tears if he stayed in any of those places more than a week. Still, it was fun to see them from the cab of the rig, especially since he planned to drive only a few years, saving his money, then go looking for some business to invest in back home in Philadelphia.

The rig began slowing and Kevin looked out the front. The road was straight, no accident or other hazards in sight.

Kevin glanced at the speedometer, saw it had dropped from 75 to 70 to 65. He looked at the visor mounted radar detector, but it was not giving a warning. "Something wrong, Dan?" he asked, for the first time looking at where his partner had been. Dan had disappeared. Only his clothing, neatly folded, was on the seat.

Before he could think, the rig began moving slightly towards the side of the road. At the same time, a driverless car heading west flipped the median and spun out in a gully. Another driverless car, this time going in the same direction as Kevin's rig, slowed a hundred yards in front of him. All he could do was take the steering wheel and try to move into the driver's seat without getting himself impaled on the shift lever. He needed to regain control of the truck before he did anything else. When he was done he could look for his partner.

*

They walked him to the small, rather sterile room between the hall to the exercise yard and the prison infirmary. His hands were cuffed in front of him, a chain wrapped around his body through the belt loops of his prison jump suit as an extra restriction of movement. His ankles also were cuffed, the chain long enough for him to take comfortable steps yet too limiting to run.

Not that he was offering any resistance. Johnny Amsterdam had caused the warden no trouble in the last year and a half he had lived on Death Row. He had even been one of the intermediaries during the prison riot that, for a tense several hours, threatened to become a violent conflagration with heavy loss of life. Instead, Johnny had kept the ring leader from hurting a school teacher who regularly volunteered at the prison and who had become their hostage during a failed break-out attempt. He had also disarmed another inmate who was planning to kill a guard with a makeshift knife he had fashioned from a spoon stolen from the kitchen.

But unlike so many men who try to parlay a handful of good deeds in prison into a reduction of sentence, Johnny was a reluctant hero. He refused to talk with the media. He refused to see himself as special. More than a dozen years earlier he had murdered three people during a botched hold-up. It was the worst crime of a lifetime spent stealing what other people worked hard to achieve. And the circumstances of the crime coupled with his history of recidivism and incorrigible behavior led to his receiving the death sentence.

Two years ago, for want of anything better to do, Johnny had begun assisting the prison chaplain when he came to the ultra high security unit where death row inmates were housed. He began reading some of the books the chaplain brought him, as well as tackling a study guide on the Bible. He had learned about Jesus, learned about His love for the lowest of society. He realized that Jesus had been a death row inmate like himself. And like himself, Jesus had been classed as incorrigible by the Romans.

Not that he thought of himself as Jesus. Johnny had spent a lifetime being a punk, a jerk, a two-bit criminal who had gotten way over his head during one horrible crime spree. But Johnny also knew that if this was ancient times, his punishment would also have been the cross. He might have been placed next to Jesus, might have been the one to whom Jesus promised a room in His father's house.

Johnny never talked of his change. The chaplain knew, and some of the guards. But Johnny felt that if the Lord wanted him to spread the Word, it would happen whether he was on death row or a big shot in the free world. That was why he studied, prayed, and talked quietly to anyone both troubled and near where he spent his final days.

There was a glass partition leading to a viewing room. Several of his victims' family members had chosen to watch the execution and he took a moment to look into the eyes of each one. Some of the witnesses saw only a blank look which they took as being the eyes of a remorseless killer. But others saw a deep sadness and regret, and they wept as the cuffs were removed while he lay on a gurney, then was strapped to the sides.

Johnny heard the chaplain recite the Twenty-Third Psalm. He was asked if he had anything he wanted to say, but only thanked the chaplain and the guards for their kindnesses. "This isn't easy for you, I know," he said quietly. "But it's what is necessary and I understand that. The Lord God has brought us all to this place, just as He brought His Son to that hill so long ago. May we all know the peace of the Lord in Jesus' name." And then he was silent.

The doctor assigned to administer the drugs attached an intravenous line and began dripping liquid into his arm. It was dextrose in normal saline — sugar water — into which a sedative would be added through a shuttle cock. Then, as he fell asleep, another drug would be administered, slowing his respiration, then stopping his heart from beating. It was a peaceful way to die, as executions go. Twelve minutes from start to finish. Yet it was an execution and when it was over, Johnny would be dead.

"I'm starting the pentathol drip," said the doctor, quietly. He opened the valve, first a little to make certain it was mixing properly with the harmless first solution, then more. He glanced at the IV bottle, then was startled to see the line suddenly dangling, the liquid dripping onto the floor. The straps were still in place, but they no longer encircled wrists and ankle. All that was on the gurney was the prison uniform of Johnny Amsterdam. The condemned killer had vanished.

It was not a weapon. Of that Judith Shimowitz was certain. Despite her grief for what she was certain was the loss of her family in Tel Aviv, despite the shock of the reports Bronson was preparing to report, despite the nightmare of falling aircraft and out of control ground transport units, this was not war. At least not as humans controlled their fate.

Judith had gone to college in New York City, had spent a few years living in Cleveland, Chicago, and Atlanta, working for a number of broadcasting companies before returning home to Tel Aviv and the

WNN Mideast Bureau. She had been an old science fiction movie buff, an "addiction" aided by her proximity to enough large video rental stores that she was able to watch dozens of films from the 1950s. There was "Earth vs. The Flying Saucers," "Them," and so many others, almost all of them having scenes where death rays would vaporize people, creatures, and buildings. There would be the saucer-like shape coming down from the sky, emitting what looked like a flashlight beam but was supposed to be a type of laser. And there would be the response, an equally deadly laser-like ray coming from a device that looked like a parabolic microphone. Parents of friends had said the movies were scary in their day, but she just thought they were good for a laugh, so naively simplistic and paranoid were they.

She knew of President Ronald Reagan's Star Wars initiative from one of her history classes, but that sounded like a man who had also seen too many of those movies. Real lasers could not be aimed with such accuracy, nor would they vaporize without a trace. Besides, no one had reported any unusual lights. One moment the people were there, the next all that remained were neatly piled uniforms and weapons. The men and women had just disappeared. Some aircraft crashed. Tanks, troop carriers, Jeeps, and the like had also either suddenly ground to a stop or crashed into buildings, military emplacements, and each other.

She was scared for the first time since the war began. She had lived too many years in Israel to be frightened of war, of terrorist bombings, and the like. The violence over the years had affected her, of course. She was cynical, pessimistic, believing in living for the moment for no one knew who or what would be around tomorrow. There had been times when she drank too much, said yes to things where no would have been the better answer. But actual fear... This was the first time. It was as though the world was out of control.

No. It was worse. It was as though the world was in someone's control and she no longer could be certain who that might be.

SIX

Those Left Behind

"There isn't any right answer about this business," Bronson Pearl told Bill Farkas the last time they had a chance to have lunch together. It was weeks earlier, before Bronson began his shuttling back and forth between the Middle East and New York. "Those of us who make careers in broadcast journalism have an unquenchable thirst for knowledge. I often joke that we're paid to be nosy, but it's more than that. Even the worst, most opinionated news people, still seek the truth. It's just that some of them don't know it when they see it."

"I can relate to that. When Lainie and I were first married, I worked for one of those small town stations where the owner was the richest man in town. He kept wanting us to broadcast his opinions as if they were news, and he hired a number of people who went along with it. He had so many kooky stories on the air, when we had some serious issues we tried to report objectively, no one believed us.

"But it's not the business. It's.... Well, Lainie wants me to leave

WNN for a job that won't force me to travel so much. We've been trying to start a family, and though she hasn't said anything to me yet, I think she's pregnant. I think she's waiting to tell me because she wants me to make a decision without the pressure of knowing there will be another mouth to feed."

"Do you want to leave broadcasting?" Bronson had asked.

"Not now. Not when there are so many stories breaking and I'm getting a chance to be in the midst of some of them. It's all I ever wanted to do growing up. I'm not comfortable with the public relations industry, and the only other career where I could use my skills would be teaching. I've had offers in both fields, but I'm not ready to make the change."

"Is your job worth your marriage? What if Lainie wanted you to choose between the network and her?" Bronson had asked.

"She wouldn't do that. That's why I love her. She married me just after I got the job here in New York. I missed an engagement party because of a California earthquake. We switched honeymoon plans because it looked as though there might be a Libyan terrorist story in Texas and I needed to be near the border if it broke. She's never had any illusions about the pressures of the industry nor about the fact that she comes first."

"Your wife's a writer, isn't she? Doesn't she get the same demands with print journalism?"

"She's a writer of children's books. It would be easier if she was in the industry like Helen."

"Maybe. But Lainie married you, and Helen and I remain what they used to call 'an item.' You have no idea how I envy your being able to go home to the woman you love each night."

"Except when a story is breaking."

"Yes, but you're only working stateside. You're never more than five hours from home. If something happened to Helen, I might be miles from where I could learn about it and miles more from where I could get transportation to an airport."

"I'll trade jobs, Bronson. If there is a baby coming, I could use the extra pay."

"If you're going to be a father, you need to be home. Helen will tell you how much a child misses when both parents aren't there to raise him."

"Is that why she won't marry you, because your careers keep you apart too much?"

"I wish that was the case. You'd see me moving to some small town and getting a job on a paper like my father used to run. That woman means everything to me, and the way the world seems to be going, I don't know how much more time we'll have to truly be together. Now go kiss Lainie for me. Tell her how lucky you are to have her, and don't do anything that will make her regret supporting your career."

Bill had agreed with Bronson. He also knew he wasn't going to quit his job with the network. He wouldn't try to move up in the business, not unless he could move into an editorial position coordinating coverage. The international travel both Helen and Bronson had had to do to achieve their present level of success would put too much pressure on Lainie.

Not that he was the husband he thought he should be right then. Lainie had wanted him to stay at home that day. "Call in sick," she had urged. "Take a personal day. You've got enough personal time coming that no one would say there's a problem."

"To do what?" he had said, putting on his necktie.

"Take a walk in the park. Go to a coffee shop for lunch and just talk. Make love to me. I don't care what we do so much as that we do it together. I want to feel you, experience your voice, remind myself of all the reasons I married you."

"We can do that this weekend. You told me you have a deadline for that series of underwater adventures you've been writing. And I'm supposed to do one of those man on the street interviews about the Middle East crisis. Tell you what. On Friday night I'll unplug the telephone, take the batteries out of my pager, turn off the cellular phone, and refuse to answer the doorbell. We'll have all weekend, just the two of us."

Lainie had smiled resignedly. "That sounds wonderful," she had told him. "If there is a weekend."

The comment had made him pause. "You're really scared about all this, aren't you, Lainie?" he had asked, not really wanting to hear her answer, not knowing what he might do about it.

"Of course I am. Neither one of us is thirty yet. We're just at the start of our adult lives. I don't want to miss the joy of knowing you when you're old, fat, bald, and crotchety every time the grandchildren come to visit."

"Lainie, you're a writer of novels and children's books. You live in fantasy. You create worlds that never existed, people them with characters you come to love or hate, put them through a crisis or two, and everything comes out all right in the end. You may scare yourself along the way, but you're always in control."

"My world is the news. It's facts, figures, reality. I have to report what's happening, but I also have to put it in perspective. This planet's been through this kind of brinkmanship before and nothing's ever happened. Millions were supposed to die from biological warfare during Desert Storm. The North Koreans were supposed to overrun the South and start a nuclear war. The Chinese were...

"But you know all this. What I'm trying to tell you is that people always seem to throw themselves to the brink of disaster, then get better sense at the last minute. It's not as clear cut as your novels There's usually no one person acting as savior, but something always happens to keep countries from going too far. It's one of those cases where real life can have coincidences and an end to terrible problems that would seem unnatural in fiction."

Lainie had been adamant. "This is different. This is something.... I don't know. This is not a time for a husband and wife to be separated. This is a time for closeness. This is a time we may never have again."

He had kissed her then, tender, lovingly. He loved her and she loved him. That wasn't the issue.

Bill Farkas's work had convinced him that the worst was going to happen, and he had become too frightened to stay home.

Bill Farkas had been in the news business since he was fourteen and began volunteering on weekends at his local public television station. He had been a "go-fer" for the weekend staff. He had learned lighting and sound. When he had some experience, he was allowed to go out with one of the videographers, learning to record public service programming. He had also tried his hand on camera, being the "anchor" for a kids news program the station instituted on Saturday mornings.

By the time Bill was sixteen, he had a part-time paying job at the local UHF commercial station. Before he went on to college, he had participated in the production of several feature shows, one of which resulted in his sharing in an Emmy award. His part had been minor, but it was critical enough that he was given credit at the ceremony.

Bill Farkas had been in the radio business since he was 16 and working at a small station doing off-hours announcing and general "gofer" work nobody wanted The microphone and camera were familiar to him. When he was working, whether in the midst of a violent prison riot, a political rally turned hostile, a major fire, or any other event where there was a serious chance of getting hurt, he felt no fear. He had a job to do and knew how to do it. Instead of being brave, he ignored the reality, as though he was watching television instead of broadcasting it. He became the dispassionate observer, protected, he had once joked, by the journalist's impenetrable protective shield.

Marriage had changed all that, or it should have. He knew he needed to think about his wife's feelings, not just his own. He knew he needed to compromise for Lainie. Yet he could not. He was too scared, too certain that she was right. Their city was probably a first strike target. Even if there were no efforts to hit it with a missile, he knew that the wind currents would cause deadly radiation to drift over their area inside of a few days. Death for them would be slower that way, yet just as certain.

Bronson Pearl had been right about Lainie, about their marriage. He just wished he had been brave enough to admit he was weak. He wished he had the courage to admit to his own feelings instead of reporting on everyone else.

It was ten minutes before Bill was scheduled to go live when it happened. He had been pre-interviewing passers-by for their reactions, taping all of them, then asking the more colorful ones to remain long enough to go on air. A few agreed. Others signed permission forms so that the tapes of their comments could be edited and broadcast later.

Suddenly it was as though the world had gone mad. Cars went out of control, smashing into light poles, jumping curbs, breaking department store display windows. A police officer directing traffic suddenly vanished, only his uniform, shoes, and equipment belt, complete with gun, remaining piled neatly in the center of the street.

Two men washing windows on the thirty-second floor of a nearby building were startled when an extremely attractive young secretary suddenly vanished from the desk where she was sitting. A bus traveling down Main Street turned a corner with approximately half the passengers it had been carrying, the driver striking an out of control bus whose driver had disappeared.

Broken fire hydrants spewed geysers of water into the air. Car alarms began sounding their alert. Ambulance and police sirens wailed in the distance. Fire stations stopped answering calls, the men and women going from one crisis to another as they moved along the streets. And everywhere there were people in such shock and fear that the stress brought on violent chest pains, the first symptom of a heart attack.

Inside the Auttiden Bank And Trust, a man with a gun and a note demanding money fled in terror when the teller, the branch manager, and three of the customers suddenly disappeared, only their clothing remaining piled neatly on the floor.

And then, in the midst of the cacophony of crashes, screams, wailing sirens, and mass confusion, Bill Farkas was told to stand-by for broadcast.

"Helen!" shouted Nino Gibraldi who was acting as floor director when several of the WNN staff vanished. "Helen, where are you? What is going on around here?"

He was livid. He felt as though he was principal of a high school instead of directing a group of news professionals. One minute he has everyone in place — lighting people, sound, the camera operators, writers.... Then there's this... this sound which he should never have heard on the floor of a studio about to go live. And then everyone was.... So where was everyone?

"Helen? At least tell me where you are, Helen."

There was a scream, and that's when Nino looked closer and saw that Helen Hannah was on the floor by her desk. The scream had come from Angela Flowers, an intern who had been typing last minute text into the prompter. A light pole one of the technicians had been setting into place had dropped when he disappeared. It had smashed the computer terminal the intern was using, then struck Helen a glancing blow at the side of her head.

"Somebody call 9-1-1," Angela shouted, grabbing some tissues to dab at the blood on Helen's face.

"Is she hurt badly?" asked Nino, running over to look.

"Two minutes, Nino," he heard in his ear piece. The engineer's countdown to their return to the air.

"Helen's been hurt," he shouted, and the engineer strained to look.

"Should I throw in a commercial or do you want to keep the camera on Helen?"

"Throw in a commercial, and if Helen's not okay, go back to Bill for more reactions until we can get this mess straightened up," said Nino.

"I'm not a mess, I'm a person," said Helen, shakily. She kept her eyes tightly closed against the light. She felt as though she had been struck in the head by a twenty pound weight, a feeling fairly close to the truth.

"Stay still, Helen. The paramedics are coming," said Angela.

"To do what?" she asked, raising her hand to touch the spot where Angela was dabbing at the wound, then opening her eyes enough to see that her fingers were lightly covered with blood. Wincing, she said, "Does this have something to do with Nino's pep talk about trying to boost the ratings?"

"Helen, please don't joke. Are you all right?"

"I'm not going to die," she said, trying to sit up, then having to pause when a wave of nausea overwhelmed her. "I'm also not going to be able to talk on the air for a few minutes." She closed her eyes again, bracing herself in the half sitting position while Angela held one arm, Nino the other, in order to give her support.

"You'll go to the hospital."

"I'll go to the lounge and lay down for a minute. Is Ellie still around?"

"I think I saw her near the control booth, Nino."

"Before or after this... This whatever that just happened."

"After. It was when I looked up to see what fell."

"Then let Ellie cover. You only need a talking head right now, and Ellie's subbed for me before."

"Are you sure you should walk, Helen? A few of us could lock our arms together and carry you."

"First my head and now you're implying I'm too heavy for one man to carry me off. This is too cruel," she said, bracing her hand against the top of the desk as Nino and Angela supported her back. She pulled herself up, paused, then started moving unsteadily. She winced with every step, and for a moment thought she might have to vomit. But she also sensed that she was all right. The paramedics wouldn't have much more to do than bandage the cut and tell her to get a tetanus shot because of possible infection. She had been through a similar injury before, while covering a story about guerrilla insurgency in Sao Paulo. But then she had seen her assailant, known she was in trouble, known he wanted to kill her. She had survived that blow, which was worse than this one, and she knew she would be okay.

As Helen left the studio, she glanced up at the catwalk from which the lighting technician must have been working when the pole dropped. That was when she realized that the lighting man was gone. All that remained on the catwalk were his neatly piled clothing and the small two-way radio he used to communicate with the control booth.

"Please clear the set. We're on in 10, 9, 8, 7..." boomed a voice over the loudspeaker system. Then it was cut off and the floor director silently continued the countdown by holding his fingers where Helen could see them, mouthing the seconds.

"This is Ellie McPherson of WNN News substituting for Helen Hannah. While our bureaus in Washington, London, Moscow, and the other capitals of the world try to get official statements from the heads of the various governments, we will continue our broadcasts from the streets. Right now we're live with Bill Farkas who has been talking with passers-by in downtown Houston.

"Bill, what's happening out there?"

"Ellie, it's unlike anything I've ever seen. It's not a bomb, or if it is, it's not..." He paused as a hysterical woman running past, shouting the names of her missing children. Ned Wharton turned his camera away from Bill in order to follow the woman as she hurried to the front of a toy store where she had last seen the two boys and a girl. As the woman fell to her knees, wailing, Ned zoomed in on three small piles of neatly folded clothing just below the window of a toy store. The television screen was filled with the image of the woman, her eyes wide yet almost sightless, obviously overwhelmed by shock, clutching the clothing to her chest, moaning as though she was holding a corpse.

"Was it a bomb, Bill?" asked Ellie, her voice shaky. She was clearly moved by what she was witnessing. "Have we been struck by a rocket of some kind?"

"This is unlike any weapon I've ever seen," said Farkas as the camera was turned back to where he was standing. "There was a sound like an explosion. At least I think there was. What I remember for certain was talking to people and then having them just disappear. Driverless cars and trucks crashing out of control. Piles of clothing where some man or woman had been standing a moment earlier.

"You saw the clothing that woman was clutching. Her children must have been standing there when... when whatever it was happened."

"But is this some weapon, some death ray?"

"I was hoping you could tell me, Ellie. From where we are, I don't know what to think. I learned a lot about biochemical warfare when we did that backgrounder on Gulf War Syndrome. But everything I know about would not cause the human body to vanish. We should have people writhing on the ground in agony. Chemical and biological warfare is meant to attack the nervous system, the respiratory system, anything that would cause great pain, horrible illness, or rapid death.

"This....Well, surely you must be experiencing whatever is happening in the studio."

"It's happening all over the world, Bill. We have several who have disappeared here in the building." Then, turning to the camera, she said, "We'll have reports from other cities." Then the broadcast switched to a commercial break while Helen, refusing to rest any longer, came back on the now off the air set and anxiously asked, "Has anyone heard from Bronson?"

Franco Macalusso stared out the window of the helicopter transporting him to the Mount of Olives near the Western Wall of the city of Jerusalem. It was the last stop, the moment he would ascend to his rightful place.

This is the land where The One Who Came Before Me walked

and taught and healed the people, he thought. Parlor tricks. He had no power. He has no power. His time was then and they murdered him. My time is now and those who oppose me will be swayed when they see I am the bringer of peace. That is the difference between us. That is what they will have to understand if they are to find the true happiness that will only come through living with my will.

Oddly, he felt uneasy about the Rapture. It had to come, of course. He understood the Word at least as well as The One Who Came Before Me. The Rapture had been predicted, and what was predicted would be fulfilled. But what of those who were left behind?

Macalusso knew that all believers in The One Who Came Before Me would be taken. Otherwise he would face an army of believers who would recognize his heart for what it was, whose opposition would be unstoppable.

He also knew that those who rejected The One Who Came Before Me, "who believed not the love of the truth," as the Bible stated, would be his most ardent supporters. It was they who would be moved by his actions. It was they who would be his strongest allies. It was they who would be blinded by his powers and the fact that he was at last bringing peace to the world.

It was the others, the people who had never heard the gospel before the Rapture, who worried him. He would need to keep such people from seeing or hearing the body of work that told the story of The One Who Came Before Him. Len Parker assured him that the homes of the raptured would be sealed by law. Then, over time, there would be a house to house search to locate and destroy videotapes, books, and of course the Bible. They could use troops or his civilian supporters.

Certainly some might be missed or family members might have already discovered them. However, holding facilities had been prepared throughout the world for those who were hearing the Word for the first time. Many would be football stadiums, large areas where tents could be quickly erected, the buildings ringed with razor wire and land mines. There would be adequate water and toilets for those who they would re-educate or use for propaganda purposes.

"I have read the prophecies, too, President Macalusso," Len had said. "And I know you are more powerful than all who can come against you. The Rapture eliminates your enemies. It does not give them strength."

But Len did not understand what the disappearances would mean. Len did not understand that though many people would seek a new leader who could make them safe, doing whatever was asked in the face of his awesome power and seeming compassion, others might not. They might find what they had not previously known to seek. They might read what they had previously not known about. They might change in ways he might not be able to influence, though the peace that would be at hand would hopefully assure their inability to influence others.

But such thinking was counter-productive as he came into his glory. Peace would soon be at hand. He needed to relax, to feel the inner peace of triumph.

It would take a while for some of those who were left behind to understand where the disappeared had gone. By then he would have solidified his control over the media and the major cities. By then any opposition could be countered, not just by the law enforcement and military he would command, but also by the others, his new followers.

They were the ones who had not believed the Word, would not believe it now. They were the ones who likened the life of The One Who Came Before Me to mythology. A nice story with good moral values, they would tell themselves. But we need to be following someone living and real, they would say. Franco Macalusso has brought a lasting peace, they would say. We owe him our total loyalty.

Macalusso inhaled deeply, then exhaled slowly, calming himself and smiling as the helicopter touched down. He knew that overhead were missiles ready to strike their targets. He knew that every military force in the world was aware that massive devastation was just moments away. He knew that every radar monitor was following the trajectories of horrors that many people said should never have been built. He knew that everyone aware of what was taking place was in panic over what might be their last moments.

And he was pleased.

The first missile was seconds before the instant of detonation when Macalusso stepped to the ground, faced the waiting camera crews, raised his hands above his head, and shouted, "ENOUGH! WE WILL HAVE PEACE!"

The words were broadcast to satellites, and from there transmitted to receptors throughout the world. Millions of television screens were capturing the same image. Franco Macalusso, arms out, a sorcerer unleashing his most powerful spell.

"ENOUGH!"

And that was when the first air traffic controller noticed that several fast moving blips had disappeared from his screen. That was when military observers began to realize that their weapons of mass destruction had vanished. Pilots of long range bombers were calling in to say that their bombs had disappeared from the drop bay. Their air-to-air and air-to-ground missiles had vanished. Their controls no longer worked except to allow them to safely fly their aircraft back to base.

The unthinkable horror that had been unleashed on the world no longer was possible. It was not that the hearts of the commanders and world leaders had been changed. It was not that old enemies had become friends. Instead, the nuclear bombs, the missiles, the chemical agents meant to maim, kill, and demoralize those who lived in what would become a life-long agony had all vanished. The storage facilities remained. The launch sites were untouched. But the world's most powerful weapons might as well not have been invented or deployed.

SEVEN

Day Two

Helen paced the production area like a caged animal so angered by hunger and isolation, it was ready to strike at the slightest provocation. She had asked permission to fly to the Middle East, to join Bronson and report together, live.

"There's no way, Helen. The network's not going to pay for you to have some passionate love fest in a Jerusalem hotel."

"I'm not talking romance. I'm talking ratings," Helen said. It was a lie, of course. Overseas communications were down on a regular basis. Too many people disappeared. Too many critical jobs waiting in line for the remaining people who knew how to correct the problems that were arising. The New York operation was holding together and Helen was skilled enough to work among the reporters as one or another region temporarily lost the ability to broadcast. She had the knowledge of global political interactions necessary to explain breaking stories so the viewers would understand them. What she didn't have was the assurance that Bronson was safe.

"You let Bronson and me broadcast together, we'll wipe out the competition. Never mind our personal lives. If we were at one of the other networks, if we barely spoke to each other off the set, I'd be sent overseas to cover what's taking place. It's a natural. It's..."

"It's a waste of time and money. You want to see if Bronson's all right because we're having so much trouble with our satellite link. But if you went over there and the problems continued, then we'd be out two key people, not just one. We'd be in worse shape than we are now. You can't have people tuning in to watch something that's not on the air."

"But..."

"No, Helen. I sympathize with what you're going through just like I sympathize with Bill Farkas' desire to take some time off to be with his wife. But I told him no and I'm telling you no. We need all our remaining reporters available for the field, and we need you at the anchor desk. I'm sure Bronson's okay. Now get back to work."

"Work?" said Helen, angrily. What she wanted to do was cry, to bury her head on the desk and sob until the tears would come no more. But she wasn't going to give this nitwit the satisfaction of knowing he was almost a hundred percent right about her motivation. "This isn't work. This is the stuff of tabloid television."

"This is what millions of Americans are talking about, and it's our job to explore it. Effective reporting will let the viewer come to the same conclusion that we have about these people. We're not pandering."

"Then why do you want me to interview the same woman who was on that afternoon talk show where they're always featuring stories about sex, violence, and pigeons being agents of an extra terrestrial power because thousands are seen everywhere in the world, yet no one has ever seen one die?"

"Constance Cathcart-Brown happens to be an articulate, extremely well educated member of one of the wealthiest families in America. She owns prime commercial property in a half dozen cities and is so socially prominent, she probably has Martha Stewart personally cater her parties. Both *Town & Country* and *Architecture Digest* have devoted entire issues to her lifestyle, and..."

"If the woman didn't have millions or billions or zillions of dollars, she'd be locked away as a hopeless crazy. The idea that she was one of the earliest people to be part of an alien scientific study of Earthlings, and that the disappeared are the fulfilment of what they had discussed when first testing us.... I mean, this is not a news story. This is the plot for one of those summer movie releases aimed at adolescents."

"Maybe before the disappeared. Maybe before we came to experience the power of Franco Macalusso in the Middle East. Now the idea of aliens making a mass culture study of a broad range of the earth's citizens doesn't seem so strange. It's as plausible as anything else that can be said about this cockamamie world. We've had missiles vanish from the air, bombs disappearing from planes moving in for the kill, clothing piled where once men and women had been... The UFO enthusiasts have as much right to be heard as those few religious leaders who we can still locate. And who's to say the woman is wrong?"

"You did a year ago when that ditzy intern you fired after two weeks kept lobbying to have her on Bronson's show. You said that the only difference between her and a hopeless psychotic living in a Thorazine straight jacket in the back ward of some high security mental hospital was all her money and powerful friends."

"I would have said the same thing about someone predicting the events we've been seeing in the last few hours.

"Look, Helen, things have changed. A lot of people are on the

UFO kick and I want you to look into it. Assign some people from our various bureaus, get a local expert, then pull it all together. Kathy can help you in production. She's good at that."

Fuming, Helen walked back to her office, hoping there would be a note that Bronson had found a way to again make contact.

Hours later, with seemingly no hope that she would make contact with anyone in the Middle East for a while, Helen again tried to telephone her grandmother's apartment. There were eight rings, nine, ten...

Helen Hannah replaced the receiver. There was still no answer, just Edna Williams' voice on her machine, requesting that a message be left for her. She had tried a half dozen times that day, always without success. She had also tried the office of the church her grandmother attended, hoping someone would know where she might be. With all her grandmother's volunteer activities, anything was possible during a world crisis such as they were facing. But the church telephone also went unanswered.

She had to see her grandmother, had to make certain the old woman was safe. Things were still too hectic at the network for her to go to the old woman's apartment. Tomorrow. She had been promised some time off tomorrow. She could stop on her way home.

They gathered in the woods in Framingland, a small, rural Wyoming community too tiny to be on the map. The only business in town was a combination gas station, bar, short order restaurant and general store that sold a few clothes — jeans, shirts, socks, underwear, and jackets, mostly — food staples, ammunition, fishing gear, freeze dried food for camping, and other basics. When anything more was needed, it usually fell on Joe and Ellen Cartwright or Nelson and Cheryl Lynn Aston to get it. They were the only area residents who owned all terrain vehicles large enough to hold a lot of groceries. Any time they were going to the "big city" — a town of 3,500 almost forty miles away — they'd check with the other long time residents about anything they needed. Then they'd take money and a list, loading their cars with boxes and bags before returning home to deliver whatever was ordered.

Some people lived totally off the land, their only concession to modern society being an occasional solar panel to operate a television or a hydraulic pump to bring the well water into the kitchen. Other people were city dwellers who came to the area on weekends, bringing coolers filled with expensive food and wine to enjoy throughout their stay.

And a few, like the True Patriot Protectors, gathered whenever they felt themselves threatened by one or another of the conspirators working to take control of the world. They would dress for war, come equipped to survive off the land, and use generator powered short wave Ham radio to keep in contact with the rest of the world.

The men, women, and children of the Patriot group had begun to arrive within hours of the Rapture. Some reported seeing black helicopters in the sky with special high intensity lights just before people around them disappeared. Others blamed the Mormon Church, the Jehovah's Witnesses, Avon Cosmetics and/or Tupperware Party salespeople for what had taken place. They had long known that among the missionaries, proselytizers, and salespeople, there was a concerted effort to gain access to the homes of average Americans. What they could not decide was whether the disappeared were the enemy, secretly being called to be part of a Communist military force ("Who needs clothing when you're changing into uniform?"), or if they were innocents now being held prisoner. No ransom demands had been made, but a terrorist might bide his time before revealing the real meaning of his actions.

APOCALYPSE

None of them had heard the news after the event. None of them had listened to President Macalusso's speech. They were convinced that the media was controlled by the other side. And though they could not be certain just who comprised the other side, they were certain listening to or reading the writing of such people could be dangerous. That was why they avoided all aspects of the media. That was why they gathered together in the woods as planned many months earlier. That was why they were deploying guards to protect the camp they were erecting.

The work had been intense, not only because of world events but also because all the bureaus were unexpectedly short handed. She had eaten lunch at her desk, the one block trip to the deli being the only escape she had from work. Even now, when she realized she was dozing over some computer print-outs related to the UFO story she was supposed to produce, write, and air as she could, she was interrupted by the telephone.

One of the medical news stories the network had run recently discussed the importance of napping in the workplace. There had been some statistic about how a five minute nap could refresh you enough to do an hour or two of work at peak energy level. According to Helen's watch she had been asleep at least five minutes and all she felt like was finding a bed and crawling between the sheets. That was why the shrill cry of the phone was so annoying, her groggy state of mind so numbing that she almost missed what she had been waiting to hear.

The news director was calling to tell her that they were going to cut into the documentary on the life of Franco Macalusso they were rerunning in order to present a report from the Mount of Olives. He wondered if she wanted to handle the anchor duties.

"Who's filing the report?" asked Helen, suddenly excited by

the news. Both the uplink and downlink systems were working again. And if they could broadcast from there, perhaps....

"Bronson Pearl. He's been asking about you, Helen. Said he's called your apartment and only gotten your answering machine. I told him you've been pretty much staying here because of all the pressure."

"Bronson's all right? He wasn't hurt in all this?"

"Bronson's fine. You know we've had technical trouble out of the Middle East. This is the first time we've been able to re-establish our link."

"Oh, Harry, I love you. I'll be right there." She put down the telephone and ran down the hall to the broadcast studio. She took her position, attached the lapel microphone, said a few words for a sound level, then looked into the camera lens as she heard the countdown to going live.

"Ladies and gentlemen, as you know there have been several hours without contact in the Middle East," Hannah began. "My understanding is that there has been some sort of technical failure unrelated to the events of recent days. However, we have restored communication and now have a direct link-up with Bronson Pearl who is standing near the Western Wall in Old Jerusalem. Bronson?"

As Helen watched the monitor, Bronson Pearl could be seen in the midst of a small crowd of people gathered around the illuminated white stone of the Western Wall.

"Helen, it's hard to know what to say about the events of the past few hours. Throughout the past half century, people have been remembering where they were when news of a catastrophic event first reached them. The elderly mark time by the day Pearl Harbor was attacked or the announcement of V-J Day. Younger Americans remember where they were when they first learned that John Kennedy was shot or the Vietnam War officially came to an end. But no one alive today will ever forget where they were when they realized that seemingly imminent nuclear destruction was just moments away.

"I was a short distance from here, near the valley of Armageddon, surrounded by other reporters, photographers, and videographers, pretending we were somehow invulnerable. It was as though if we went through the motions of broadcasting the news, we would make it through a time when millions of people would die. We hid our fear, somehow thinking that we had to stay alive in order to record whatever was going to happen. The world could not come to an end unless we documented it's demise, and somehow that would save us.

"Then, as we have seen, European Union President Franco Macalusso arrived at what we thought were just a few minutes too late. We had been told he was coming to broker a comprehensive peace agreement. Yet while his helicopter was hovering to land, hundreds or perhaps thousands of missiles were being fired from bunkers throughout the world. The imminent devastation would have been massive and unstoppable.

"Even before President Macalusso could step from his helicopter, the unforgettable, currently unexplainable event took place. Sirens wailed, cars crashed, planes fell from the sky, people screamed, and everywhere there were the missing. Sometimes one or two disappeared. Sometimes dozens seemed to vanish from the same spot at the same time. Only their clothing and whatever else they were wearing remained. There was no smell of gunpowder, no burn marks from some sort of sophisticated laser. They just... vanished.

"Then, in the midst of this incredible event, President Macalusso raised his arms and commanded it all to stop. He raised his arms, shouted to the winds, and suddenly there was peace. The missiles just vanished. Vanished. They did not explode in mid flight. They were not called back to the launch sites. They vanished as though their launch, which many of us witnessed first hand, never happened.

"A short time later, President Macalusso requested time to speak to the nations of the world. Although we broadcast his speech at the time, in the terror and confusion we know that many may not have heard what he had to say. We also know that many may not have understood the full import of what he was telling us. Now, with several hours having passed, we can see the truth in his statements, and it is for this reason that we are replaying the talk he gave."

"Cut to the video," said the WNN engineer. Helen continued watching the monitor, hoping there would be a break when she could speak directly to Bronson.

The tape began with footage of the arrival of Macalusso's helicopter, his stepping from the whirling craft, his raising his arms and shouting into the wind. Then he could be heard to say,

"Citizens of the world. We are living at what, for you, is an extraordinary moment in history. This is the time when I have come to this place to fulfill what is written.

"Until today I have been known for my work with the United Nations, working to bring about a new world order of peace and justice. When I became President of the great union of Europe, a union larger than the Roman Empire of days past, I continued to keep a low profile. I worked among the leaders of the world to stop the fighting, but I also refrained from bringing the truth to the world until the appropriate time. Now you are at last seeing who I am, seeing the power I bring to lead you into your destiny. The people of the world will become one as we walk together towards the light of truth, a light that has been repressed for more than 2,000 years.

"You stood today on the brink of self-destruction. You have revealed the depths of your souls. You have shown a measure of foolish pride and hate which would allow you to tolerate the devastation of everything you have built, nurtured, and held dear. Parents were ready to kill their children, neighbors were ready to kill neighbors, leaders of nations were willing to subject their people to lingering death in order to triumph over other people just like themselves. There were no restraints. There was no self-control.

"Your actions formed my signal that my time had come. I came to this spot, so sacred for so many, to take my rightful place in eternity.

"I have spoken the word and the nuclear weapons have been vaporized. I have spoken the word and the chemical clouds have harmlessly dissipated into air made clean. I have spoken the word and armed factions have set aside their weapons. And most importantly, because I understand your fears and worries, I have spoken the word and anyone whose mind was not open to the truth has been removed. Those who are now being called the disappeared were actually the hate filled, the people of closed minds. Their continued presence would have slowed or prevented the growth of those of you who remain. Like a weed removed from a garden, like a cancer excised from the skin, you have been freed by their departure so you can grow into the beings I created you to be.

"Your destiny is greatness beyond anything you ever imagined possible. My promise is that you will achieve that destiny. I have the power to do it! I have the power!"

EIGHT

Day Three

The walk to her grandmother's apartment was stranger than usual for Hannah Williams. The near cataclysmic destruction that had been averted was of no concern. Too many people had lived too long in their own form of Hell for them to fear death. Some felt their lives could only get better if they passed on. Some felt death would be like a long nap you get to enjoy to the end, not one from which you get rousted by the cops because your bed is made of cardboard placed over a heating grate and the Mayor thinks you look bad to tourists. Still others believed they had no chance for Heaven yet did not fear Hell for that is where they felt they had been living most of their adult lives.

A woman known locally as Crazy Connie was dancing down the sidewalk while pushing a shopping cart stolen from an uptown A&P. The cart was piled high with clothing, eye glasses, hearing aids, and, most important for her, wallets and purses. Not that she showed anybody the wallets. You could still find yourself in an alley with your throat slit and blood pouring down a sewer if you showed you had more money than sense. No, she had hidden the money in the clothes she was wearing and in the pile of clothing in her cart. The rest of her new possessions — the eyeglasses, hearing aids, cheap watches, and various items of jewelry — would be pawned.

Some of the clothing was cheap and soiled, often smelling of one of those fake designer perfumes you could buy for a dollar from a street vendor. Other clothing was more expensive, though in the neighborhoods she traveled, still second hand. Usually it came from one of the wealthy ladies on Park or Fifth Avenues. They would give it to one of the resale shops, taking a tax deduction exceeding what they had paid for the garment, at the same time greatly helping the poor. Crazy Connie had it all, a blessing from the streets.

A man who smelled of his own urine, several teeth missing, his face in need of a shave, lunged at Helen, grasping her jacket sleeve with a filthy hand. "Pray to Dugas," he said. His breath was as foul as his appearance and it caused her to cringe. "Dugas is coming. Dugas brought us this, sisters and brothers, and we love you. Or are you not? Are you not? Are you..." He became distracted for a moment, letting go of Helen's sleeve and wandering towards another passer-by, delivering the same message in a sing-song voice. He never did explain who Dugas might be.

The street people who lived in her grandmother's neighborhood were handling whatever had occurred very differently from the more affluent areas. Some were nodding in doorways, having consumed anything they thought might be intoxicating enough to blur the memory of what they had seen. They had never been able to cope with life, their minds fragile under the best of circumstances. To witness people disappearing before their eyes had been overwhelming.

Others were babbling incoherently, no longer able to grasp the difference between reality and fantasy.

Most of the street people did not recognize Hannah, cable television being a luxury rarely seen in the neighborhood. A few knew her as Edna's granddaughter and greeted her accordingly.

Helen stopped at the apartment entrance, ringing the buzzer for her grandmother's suite. There was no response.

Helen reached in her purse and removed the keys her grandmother had insisted she carry. "I'm an old woman. I don't know when the Lord will call me home. You may need to get inside my apartment. Take the key."

The first key opened the outer door. She went to her grandmother's suite, knocked, listened, then used the other key to get inside. As she entered the front hallway, her eye was caught by the flashing red message light on her grandmother's answering machine. There were 17 unchecked calls according to the digital counter display. She pressed the play button, listening to the first few messages.

"Edna? It's me, Doris. Have you been watching the news? It's just like Pastor Holmes was talking about last week. I really think this may be it. I think the day of the Lord could be...Well, it could be today."

"Grandma, are you there?" Helen heard her own voice. "It's me. Helen. Please call me as soon as you get this message."

"Grandma. It's Helen again. Please call me. I need to talk with you."

"Grandma, it's Helen. Are you all right? Grandma?"

"Good evening, Ms. Williams. This is Warton Insurance. I'm sure you've been seeing about the disappeared. If they have Carter Insurance, their loved ones will be provided for if they don't return. Are your loved ones protected? Call me at 1-800...."

"This is Dr. Hurley's office. Just a reminder that your dental appointment is for Thursday afternoon at 1 o'clock..."

"Grandma. I know I haven't been reachable if you've tried me in the last few hours. This story has taken all my time. Please call me at the network. I'll leave word for them to have me paged. Are you all right?"

"Edna, I can't reach Pastor. I wanted to talk with him about the bake sale. I know he pretends there are more important responsibilities and that our youth group usually has the meeting room, but I think making us set-up outside, even with this nice weather..."

"Grandma?" said Helen's voice on the machine.

"Grandma?" whispered Helen as she stopped the answering device and nervously started down the hall. "Oh, God, let her be safe. Please let her be safe. I love that woman..."

For a moment Helen thought she heard the old woman. Then she realized it was only the television. Her grandmother had left the set turned on, WNN's Round-The-Clock News playing softly.

Helen moved to the kitchen where she found a half prepared cup of tea. A pot was on the stove, some of the water having been used to fill a cup sitting on the counter next to the burner. A tea bag had been opened and was resting to the right of the cup as though it had been set down just before it could be placed in the water. And on the floor in front of the stove was a dress, a pair of shoes, a hearing aid, and earrings, all in a neat pile. Helen also noticed a long gold chain she had seen her grandmother wear around her neck. What she had not realized was that attached to it was a key with a small piece of paper wrapped around it, then held in place with a rubber band.

Frightened, Helen worked the rubber band from the key, took the note and opened it. "My dear Helen," the note read. "I will be gone when you read this, but do not worry. I'm with the Lord now.

"I told you about the Rapture. I told you that I felt it would come in my lifetime. Since you are reading this note, then you, too, have become aware of this fact.

"What I've been reading in the Bible is true, Helen, and though you have been left behind, it's not too late for you. God will help you and all those who ask. That is all you have to do. Just ask.

"The key is for a small box in which you will find some information you may want to see. Know that I love you even as we are apart.

"Grandma."

Helen stared at the paper, uncomprehending. This was not a suicide note. This wasn't left as the last contact of an elderly, lonely woman about to commit suicide. This was a note left by someone who knew she was going to be.... Be what...?

"Grandma...." whispered Helen. She touched the clothing, tentatively at first, then lifting it to her face. She felt the familiar fabric, inhaled the aroma of laundry soap mixed with a hint of perfume. She closed her eyes and tried to imagine that she was once again embracing the gentle Christian soul who had given her so much, comforted her so often, loved her unconditionally. It was through her grandmother's selfless actions that she had first begun to understand the love of God. And it was the loss of her parents that had somehow deepened her grandmother's spirituality while robbing her of the faith she wished she could have retained, if only for her grandmother's sake.

And now.... Now.... Now what?

The note. The key. It was as though her grandmother was reaching out to her from.... From where? She had to find whatever was her legacy, whatever might give her answers to questions she suddenly realized were far more personal for far more people than she had understood when the events of the past few days began.

Helen took the clothing to the table, lovingly setting it down as though her grandmother might any moment come in and praise her for finally learning how to fold blouses and dresses properly. Then she returned to the living room, to the book shelves and drawers. For an instant she was a little girl again, fearful that she would be scolded for exploring in her grandmother's drawers, looking for whatever secrets they might reveal. She was scared of being caught, scared she would be scolded for not respecting other people's property.

This was different, she reminded herself. She wasn't a little girl. She was a grown woman, a professional journalist, and she was looking for something her grandmother wanted her to find.

Tears filled Helen's eyes. Now she understood how the families of men listed as Missing In Action in the Vietnam War could continue their search for concrete evidence more than 30 years later. The finality of what was happening was evident. Yet each time she touched one of her grandmother's treasures, she expected the woman to enter the room and scold her.

It was all so confusing. It was all so... She began weeping again. She did not want to think about yet another loss, yet another loved one taken from her in an instant. There needed to be more time to talk, to ask the questions which needed answers based on the wisdom of her grandmother's years of richly living life. She had not shared the old woman's spirituality, yet now she felt that to not at least be able to discuss it with her was to miss something vital in the events of the last few days.

She wanted to yell at her grandmother for leaving her, an irrational anger at once shameful and embarrassing. Yet she knew it was human, knew that it was a part of the grieving process that would never be complete because she was certain she would never truly know where her grandmother had gone.

It was time to stop thinking so much. She returned to the search for whatever it was she might find, whatever might make some sense of the moment.

As Helen searched, the television in the living room continued to broadcast WNN commentaries from around the world. Sid Felix was on the anchor desk. Bronson Pearl was shown in taped segments, he, too, having been given time to get some rest.

The first image was that of a tired General Alizar who had found himself on the front lines with the Israeli defense forces just seconds before the vanishing. "I have never seen anything like it," said a somber, wonder-filled Alizar. "It was just like the '73 war, you know." He paused, looking away, dazed, as though living the experience all over again.

"They were all over us. We have the best trained fighting force in the world. Our people are all skilled at doing battle against over-whelming odds. We are a nation of citizen soldiers. Yet we are still small. We are few in number and our enemies... Our enemies are many. As prepared as we were for their coming, their numbers were simply so vast that there was almost nothing we could do.

"Our front lines were overrun in less than two minutes. We were deafened by clouds of warplanes and missiles flying over our heads. We knew that Jerusalem and Tel Aviv would be rubble within minutes. There was nothing we could do but fight and pray. It all seemed so futile, so horrible, so..."

The program segued to Ben Cohen, explaining the events that had been planned. "We knew what we would lose, knew that the brav-est of our fighting men and women would die in the next few minutes or hours. It was then that we sent word to Bersheba, our nuclear site.

"For years we have thought about and prayed about when or if we should use our nuclear weapons. The Bible tells us that the punish-ment should never exceed the crime, an eye for an eye. A few days before....before all this, we talked of Samson. We made the decision that we were not going to go down alone. Just as he used his strength to bring the walls down upon his enemies, so we were going to do the same. The Prime Minister gave the order to counter attack with every weapon in our arsenal."

The scene returned to General Alizar. He was sitting wearily. As the lens moved for a close-up, he seemed to have aged ten years from when Bronson Pearl had talked with him prior to the battle.

"It all stopped. I know no other way to describe what happened.

"How do you explain the unexplainable? What took place was impossible.

"I...I remember in my youth, reading the Bible, reading the stories of God's intervention in the lives of my people. I read of his staying the hand of an overwhelming enemy when my people were following His word, and I read of my people being defeated by a smaller, weaker force, when they had broken their covenant.

"But I thought...I thought they were maybe just stories. Exaggerations. Like my history professor in college who said that everything is written from the viewpoint of the victors.

"Now...It was the hand of God. Only God himself, directly intervening in all our lives, could have accomplished the miracle that happened.

"Warplanes turned in their flight and returned to their bases. No orders were given. No pilots remember consciously taking such action. They all said... They all just had to return.

"And the missiles... The missiles can not be recalled when in flight. The missiles can still reach their targets when our nation is destroyed, our computers but rubble, our people all dead. For the missiles to just...

"They were gone. Vanished. One moment they were in the sky, the next moment they were not.

"My eyes were not deceived. My mind was not clouded with drink. They were real and they were vanished, all thanks be to God.

"And the ground troops. The thousands upon thousands of men who were advancing on my people suddenly stopped as one. There was a silence, a serenity. It was as though a glorious peace descended upon the region. My fear had vanished. My anger was gone. I could embrace my enemy or my brother with the same joy and wonder."

The general's voice became broken, tears filling his eyes. "Only later did we learn that the Messiah himself had returned to Jerusalem at that very moment."

Helen, looking through her grandmother's papers, heard the word "Messiah" and glanced over at the set to hear more. This was not part of a story she had been covering and she was curious. But as she looked at the screen, a NATO officer was speaking.

"I am not a religious man. I am not an emotional man. I deal with link analysis, counter-intelligence, strategic planning....I know fact from fantasy. I know....

"So there we were. There were more missiles in the air than any of our people could keep track of. It was as though every nation in the world had decided to make a first strike its only form of attack. Win at all cost because there would be no reserve forces.

"You should have heard this place. Every light was blinking, every siren was blaring. There were flashing lights, code reds, alarms sounding. In war time you might hear one, two, maybe three of those signals. You learn to watch for them, listen for them, responding in kind or with slight escalation. The idea that they would all be on maximum, all going off simultaneously.... It was impossible. None of us had ever conceived of such a possibility.

"Then silence came so suddenly I thought I was either deaf or driven mad. Everything just stopped. The missiles were gone. The spotters could not find them. The radar could not track them. Nothing.

"One minute it was a war, not just to end all wars, but to end all life. Then next minute there was a peace such as the world has never known. I saw it with my own eyes and I still do not believe it."

Helen moved to her grandmother's bedroom. A well worn Bible was on the night stand beside the bed. A note attached to it read, "In the event of my disappearance, I want my granddaughter, Helen Hannah, to have the comfort that this book has brought me through so many trials. The notes in the margins are my thoughts and prayers as I read it. The underlined passages will help her better know what I am certain has happened. I only wish I could be with her when she reads them, to talk, to explain, to show her how they bring comfort."

Again Helen cried. She took the book, then continued looking for what her grandmother had specifically wanted her to see. Finally she found it on the floor of the closet, an old fashioned strong box. Helen used the key to open it, finding a videotape and some books inside.

WNN was broadcasting from Jordan. The name General Assad flashed on the screen under the face of a man in his forties, lean, hard, weathered. He was a powerful figure, an obvious leader, a man who seemed to expect violence from all quarters yet was ready to handle any challenge.

Behind the general were tanks and men. Some seemed to be trying to fix their rifles and automatic weapons. Some were packing equipment. Everyone was preparing to leave the area, to return home.

"We knew the Israeli defense forces. We had studied them for many years, knew their strengths and weaknesses, knew the land.

"This time it was a textbook battle. They were in perfect defensive posture assuring many, many deaths. We had planned our attack so we could overwhelm them, which we did. We passed through their front lines quite easily, though casualties were heavy as we expected.

"We thought the price would be worth the effort. We were on our way to victory. We were...

"The change started with our radio communication. Everything was scrambled. No, not scrambled. It was as though none of us could speak to each other. Our own language became impossible to understand. We would speak in Arabic. I am certain we spoke in Arabic. Yet what came from our mouths was a language none of us could understand. We brought our interpreters to listen, but they could do nothing. It was as though we came to the Tower of Babel.

"Then our tanks stopped. Our trucks stopped. It was as though someone had taken the engines.

"Our mechanics checked the equipment and found it all to be working perfectly. But nothing would move.

"And our guns. We tried to shoot, to kill, yet bullets would not fire. The triggers pulled. The firing pins could be heard. The bullets were in place. Yet nothing. Our handguns were useless. Our rifles.

"We did not think, could not know in the midst of such panic and violence that Allah had returned. He had gone to the Mount of Olives to make his message known. And though we did not hear it until later, we felt his presence in the way he stopped the war.

"Allah delivered us from our enemies. Allah delivered our enemies from our weapons. And Allah delivered all of us from our foolishness. Praise be to Allah."

APOCALYPSE

The stories of the generals were quick cut to tell what was happening. General Alizar described the firing of the missiles as WNN showed previously secret clips of what had occurred. In the past 24 hours, the world had become more open, leaders sharing information while trying to gain a perspective on what was taking place.

"Samson's fist was ready to slam down on our Arab brothers. The missiles had been fired. All our weapons of mass destruction were in the air. But thanks to the Messiah, not one missile struck its target. The nuclear holocaust we unleashed had disappeared like the morning dew. God saved us all from ourselves."

The final clip was that of the Pentagon briefing room. Richard Stanfield was speaking.

"I am speaking only for myself when I say I am not a religious man. I had a baby brother who suffocated in his crib when he was just three months old. I watched how his death affected my mother, my father, all of us in the family. I decided then, a child of seven, that God, if there was a God, would not allow such a thing to happen. Despite my parents still taking me to Sunday School, I became an atheist and stayed an atheist. Until now.

"I have come before these cameras to officially tell you that what has happened in the world is the direct intervention of God. There can be no other explanation.

"The first strike launch of 300 missiles each containing nuclear warheads a hundred times more powerful than the bomb we dropped on Hiroshima would have eliminated an estimated two-thirds of the world's population. There would have been climate changes. Growing seasons would be altered and many crops would be unsafe to eat. Animals would die of starvation or be so badly irradiated that eating them would cause a lingering death. Water would be contaminated. Festering corpses would foul the air, the soil, and the oceans. Disease would be rampant, and once mild illnesses would be deadly because of the reduction in all our immune systems.

"There was no power on earth that could stop what we all had unleashed. No nation was innocent. No people were protected. We had launched forces from all sides that should have ended life as we know it.

"That I am here today to speak to you proves the hand of God in the affairs of men. It is God who lets me speak. It is God who I thank. It is God in whom I now believe with a faith that can not be shaken."

Helen turned on the VCR and inserted the tape her grandmother had left her. The room was orderly by Helen's standards, in shambles by those of her grandmother. Everything had been pulled from drawers, shelves, and tables, checked, then put back less neatly than before. She would straighten better later, after watching the tape. That was what she had told herself. That was what she told herself when she was a little girl after having explored in her grandmother's possessions.

This is different, she had to remind herself. This time Grandma isn't coming back. This time...

No, no more tears. Her grandmother had wanted her to see something entitled Jack Van Impe's *Left Behind* so that would be her next chore. She pushed the tape in the VCR and watched as the image came on the set.

Jack and Rexella Van Impe were talking about the Rapture, Armageddon, and the last days. The tape had been left part way through a viewing instead of being rewound to the beginning. For a moment Helen thought about rewinding it. Then she realized that her grandmother probably wanted her to view the specific passage. She decided to look at what was on the screen, then go back to the beginning when it was over.

"Well, Jack, we've talked about all these signs of the times," said Rexella. "But what is the next thing that the Bible says we should be looking for on the prophetic calendar?"

"Rexella, what we're watching for now is something called the Rapture of the Church," said Jack. "Any day now every one of us who has accepted Jesus as our Lord and Savior is going to vanish off the face of the earth. It'll happen according to the Bible, in a moment, in the twinkling of an eye. First Corinthians 15:52."

Helen listened, intrigued, as they talked. She opened the Bible she had found in her grandmother's bedroom, looking for the passages they were describing. As she listened and read, she felt both amazement and calm. It was as though the words of her grandmother's final days were being repeated, validated, and taught to her anew.

"Oh, Jack, it is so exciting," said Rexella on the screen. "It's something that every Christian is so looking forward to. But what about those who are left behind? We all have friends and loved ones who aren't going to know what's happened. So what happens to them after we all vanish?"

"Well, Rexella, the Bible tells us that after the Rapture a great world leader is going to arise on the scene and he's going to try to explain the whole thing away. Not only that, but he's going to take credit for saving the world from destruction. In fact, he's going to try to make those left behind believe that he is actually the Messiah, but the truth is that he's nothing but an impostor empowered by Satan himself."

Helen, wanting to deny what she was hearing yet knowing words of truth were being spoken, began reading the passages the Van Impes had been quoting. She took other tapes her grandmother had obtained through her church, placed them in the VCR, and began looking at them one at a time. Some she focused on, fascinated by every word. Some she skimmed through.

Helen returned to her grandmother's collection of books and pamphlets. Some looked almost new, the spines cracked just enough to indicate they had been studied, albeit briefly. Others were dog-eared from repeated reading. It was the dog-eared pages that she focused on, wanting to know what her grandmother was thinking.

The last tape Helen looked at before concentrating solely on her reading was one featuring evangelist Luis Palau. As tears rolled down her cheeks, she listened to him saying, "So the answer to all of this is simple. Just ask God to come into your hearts. For those of us now, living before the Rapture, we can join our Lord in Heaven before the Antichrist even comes to power. But even after the Rapture, the love of God and His mercy are still available. But you've got to take the first step. You've got to get down on your knees and ask God to come into your life. Admit you are a sinner and open your heart to Jesus. If you do that simple thing, that simple act of faith, you will have eternal life."

It was dark outside when Helen, sobbing almost uncontrollably, left her chair, went on her knees, and began to pray. Finally she understood. Finally she had come to where her grandmother once hoped she would be. Finally she understood what her grandmother had carried in her heart all those years.

"Dear God," Helen prayed. "Please forgive me for being so stubborn. Somehow I always knew Grandma was right when she told me that I needed you to wash away my sins. I read about your son. I spoke of him with my lips. But now I know that was not enough.

"Lord, I ask you now, please come into my heart and into my life. Forgive my sins as I..." And as she prayed, she felt the enveloping warmth that had comforted her. Now she realized that God whom she denied had always been with her. It was she who had refused to open her eyes, her mind, her heart to what was always there for her. Her grandmother had been but one of many vessels for His love. And while she missed her grandmother in a way that would never fully heal, she at last understood that it was God who would hold her, nurture her, love her unconditionally, if she would only reach out and embrace Him.

"....in Jesus' name, amen."

NINE

Day Four

They gathered together in wonderment and joy whenever they could find even one other who shared their understanding of the events of the past few days. They had heard about the Messiah, of course. Many of them called themselves Christians because their families had been at least occasional church goers. But faith had lost its meaning when they became adults. The songs were beautiful. The stories were moving. But they were just that, stories by a people with nothing better to do with their time than to tell of a man who was the Son of God through a pregnant virgin whose fiancé needed only a dream to believe such nonsense. It wouldn't play in Hollywood, but those were simpler times.

Franco Macalusso was something else. This was a man who made missiles disappear from the sky. This was a man whose deeds were recorded on videotape and shown on the evening news. This was truly the Messiah, not some myth written about by people who mostly never really knew him. He was the reason they returned to the churches.

He was the one to whom they gave praise and honor. He was the one who made them feel blessed to be living in such a time of peace, harmony, and hope.

The *Detroit Free Press* put it most succinctly with its headline, "Macalusso Saves The World." The *New York Times'* headline read, "Public Has No Doubt: Macalusso Is The Messiah." "Heaven Applauds The New Messiah," a *Jerusalem Post* story read.

There was a handful of people who were not Christians, were not particularly religious, who began reading the books and viewing the videotapes loved ones left when they disappeared. Like Edna Williams, a few others had deliberately left material for relatives or friends they knew would come to their homes to go through their possessions. Others simply had the material carefully placed on shelves or on tables next to a chair used for reading. It was found by chance by a well meaning landlord, neighbor, or police officer.

Sometimes the person finding the tape or books would take them home for study. At other times they might give them to someone they thought would be curious about such strange ideas, never really reading or viewing them themselves. And of course some dismissed it all without looking, having either no interest in such matters or feeling it was all a bit of pre-Macalusso superstitious nonsense.

The information this handful of people were discovering was both so joyous and amazing that some tried to share it with co-workers and others. To their great sadness, the full story of the Rapture was being fulfilled, including the hardening of the hearts of the non-believers in Jesus who accepted Franco Macalusso as the Messiah

A few of the new believers were reprimanded by their supervisors for creating dissension and trying to bring some deviant cult thinking into the workplace. Others found growing hostility within their families, fathers arguing with sons, mothers with daughters, husbands with wives, and children with each other. The only peace, other than the new joy they were experiencing by knowing the truth, came when they gathered in two's and three's in Jesus name. They would meet in coffee shops, living rooms, and even in those few churches where so many were raptured that those left behind, now believers in Macalusso's power, would allow anyone to use their no longer needed space.

What went unspoken was The List, a registry established by Len Parker taking advantage of internationally linked computer repositories already in use by law enforcement agencies. The List noted the "fanatics" who had come to the old ways since the coming of the new Messiah. It was not a crime to be sacrilegious, of course. The benevolent Messiah would never tolerate hostility towards those so weak as to be changed by a book whose 2,000 year old message was proven so wrong. Instead, their names and locations were noted so they could be re-educated if possible, and if not, at least prevented from spreading a poison throughout the world. "Look upon it as silencing the serpent in the new Eden," Parker had explained to the leaders of the Macalusso followers who would be responsible for coordinating The List in their respective countries.

Separately from The List was the quiet confiscation of the material left behind by the disappeared whenever it was discovered by the authorities. Such books and videos were of no value when the new Messiah was present to interpret the past and the present. He talked of "The One Who Came Before Me." He addressed religious leaders who had not disappeared, asking, "Did The One Who Came Before Me stop wars? Did The One Who Came Before Me bring peace? Did The One Who Came Before Me strike the missiles of destruction from the sky?

"Of course not. Only the Messiah can do what I have done. Only the Messiah can change your hearts which have been filled with such hate.

"I am the one foretold. The One Who Came Before Me was not worthy of the adoration of the ages. Only I have brought true and lasting peace. That is why, now that my time has come, there must be no other."

Yet those who gathered in two's and three's knew better. They had found faith in the one Macalusso was calling The One Who Came Before Me. They now knew that Macalusso was not the true Messiah.

The boldest among them felt the need to declare the truth to the world. They listened to talk show hosts soliciting call-ins about the events of the last few days, then phoned in order to bring the truth to the audience. They tried to explain the passages in the Bible foretelling this time, tried to get people to study the Bible and think for themselves.

A few researched the lives of the disappeared. They talked of how beloved they had been, how spirit filled, spirit led. They talked of the good works that had come so naturally to them that they were unaware how different they were from so many others. They tried to explain that the disappeared were twice blessed, both with their gentle goodness in this life and with their being raptured into the special place God held for His true believers.

For the most part, they were met with pity, anger, or hostility.

"I can't understand how your last caller can be so naive about the Messiah," said one woman calling in to the Sandy Beverly Hour originating on talk radio 1010.

"Look, Sandy, anyone with half a brain can see the wonderful things the Messiah has done.

"What did Jesus do? Maybe there's something I missed in all those Sunday School classes my parents dragged me to, but excuse me, didn't he die? On the cross? A couple of pieces of wood, three nails, and whatever? And the guy's history, just like anybody else.

"Now can you tell me how some guy who can't even bring himself down from the cross can be expected to challenge a man who can make the weapons of war vanish with a single word? Of course Franco Macalusso is the one we have been waiting for. I mean, like how can these jerks even begin to think otherwise?"

"I'm with you," said Sandy. "These fringe groups... these haters... have to be a little crazy, you know? That's why we have free speech, but sometimes I wonder if we let people go too far. Thanks for calling."

Sandy clicked off the line and checked the message her producer had punched up on her monitor screen for the name and location of her next caller. "I have Charlotte in Seattle. So what's on your mind, Seattle?"

"Sandy, I'm so excited. It is you, isn't it?"

"Yes, Seattle. Live and on the radio. So what do you have to say?"

"I just want to agree with your last caller, Sandy. It is okay if I call you Sandy, isn't it? I listen to you every day and I like to think of us as old friends."

"It's okay, Seattle. I think of you as a friend as well."

"You do? Gosh, I'm so nervous."

"Get to the point, Seattle," said Sandy, her voice growing slightly hard.

"Sorry, Sandy. Ummm... I just want to say that President Macalusso has brought peace to my family as well. We're.... what do you call it? Dysfunctional? Nobody's talked with anybody for twenty years. I tried to do my family tree a few years ago and nobody would tell me anything about anyone because everybody hated everyone else.

"Now...I don't know. The night the Messiah came, this cousin called my grandmother who called her brother, Ralph, who called a niece he hadn't spoken to in I don't know how long. Ever since she ran off with that Greek boy while she was studying in Paris or some such place. I mean, you should see our telephone bill with everybody connecting with everyone else. It's wonderful. The phone company's getting rich and we're making up for years of fighting no one can remember why anyone started."

"What a wonderful story, Seattle. And you know, you're not alone. We've been hearing stories like that from Frisco and Atlanta, from Detroit and the Big Apple. It's like President Macalusso freed us from the pettiness that had come to dominate all our lives. If the churches had been preaching the gospel according to Macalusso as they should have been, you can bet the nation never would have come to the brink of war like it did.

"And now we have James in Toronto. Tell me, James. What wonderful things has President Macalusso done in your life?"

"Sandy, don't you have a Bible in that studio of yours? This Macalusso guy is clearly the one called the anti...."

"Serious callers only," said Sandy, cutting him off in mid-sentence. "This is a time for celebration, not bad jokes.

"Norman in Detroit. What exciting changes has the Messiah brought to you?"

The caller from Toronto was not alone. Many new Christians, "the haters," were berated for their lack of belief in the one being called the true Messiah. A few were attacked, beaten, or even shot. Fire bombs were hurled into homes. Hate messages were scrawled on doors. Children were taunted for the stands of their parents, even if they professed to believe what their friends were saying about President Macalusso.

Bronson Pearl had not told Helen he was returning to the United States, his assignment in the Middle East finally over. He had slept on the plane coming in to America. He had shaved, brushed his teeth, made himself as presentable as possible. He would have liked to take a room at a hotel near the airport, get a shower, some more sleep, a decent meal. No, he would have liked to have gone home to his wife. But he longed for Helen too much to stop at some hotel, and until she agreed to his proposal of marriage, the home he longed to share with her was just a delightful fantasy he knew might never be fulfilled.

Hadn't she understood the significance of the last few days, he wondered? Hadn't she seen how fleeting life could be? One minute she was in his arms, and seemingly the next he was standing in Armageddon, broadcasting the end of the world to her anchor desk in New York. They should have been together at such a time. They should be together now that there was peace. They should have been...

Helen was in a staff meeting when Bronson walked in to the WNN broadcast complex. She and Mike, the floor director for her show that day, were going over the order of stories, timing, and other details.

Mike did not notice the correspondent as he slipped through the entrance and leaned against the wall. Helen, however, was transfixed. She knew he was alive, knew he had survived the violence. Yet seeing him in the flesh, knowing she could rush across the room to embrace him... It was all she could do to stay seated and pretend to be listening to whatever Mike was saying.

Bronson saluted Helen, a gesture they had both seen in an old movie they enjoyed.

Helen smiled, tears coming to her eyes. Then she mouthed the word "Yes."

Bronson looked at her quizzically. He shrugged his shoulders and raised his arms.

"Yes," she mouthed again.

"Helen?" said Mike. "Are you with me on this?"

"Yes," she said aloud for the first time, though she had barely heard anything he said.

"So you want to lead with the assassination of Abraham Lincoln? They caught John Wilkes Booth, but there's this whole conspiracy angle for Special Reports."

"Yes, Mike. That sounds perfect."

"You haven't listened to a word I've said," said Mike, bemused as he turned, looking to see what had so completely caught Helen's attention. Smiling, he said, "So go see him. Go to your office. Take a break. Elope. Whatever. Just be back here in half an hour so we can get this thing finished."

This time Helen heard most of the words. "Thanks, Mike," she said, rising from her chair and hurrying over to Bronson. Oblivious to the crew, she put her arms around him and said, "Yes. Yes, I'll marry you."

They had moved quietly into the WNN headquarters building. Young men, idealistic, well trained, chosen for their loyalty to the concept of the New World Order as defined by Franco Macalusso. Their uniforms were a hybrid of the European Union and the United Nations, the colors recognizable throughout the world as belonging to men and women whose authority could transcend that of duly elected governments.

The soldiers wore 9mm automatic side arms, not much different from the weapons issued to the police. If they had anything more, they kept them away from the building, away from sight. Those chosen for what Macalusso had declared to be the monitor command were polite, discrete, curious enough about what they were witnessing that it was obvious their skills were law enforcement, not the electronics of broadcasting. They were visibly excited about seeing such "names" as Helen Hannah and Bronson Pearl, but they remained quiet, deferential, and very much out of place.

Bronson had seen the type of soldier before. Macalusso had begun preparing such a force when he was still with the United Nations. They were with him as European Union security. And now that he had revealed himself to be the Messiah, they were even more prominent.

It was the latter that troubled Pearl, though he said nothing. If Franco Macalusso truly was the Messiah, why did he need such security? He had stopped the violence, somehow taken the missiles from the skies. Those who believed would follow him without question. Those who questioned would not challenge him.

So why the armed men in key communication centers?

It was a question without time to answer. It was a question he almost felt guilty about considering given what he had witnessed with his own eyes. Perhaps it was best ignored for the moment. After all, he had returned to the anchor desk, to the woman he loved, to the job that sustained them both when all about them was insanity. Now, as he held her hand below the set, hidden from view, he listened as she read the introduction to the news, then talked of his return from the Middle East.

"It's good to be back, Helen. Actually, it's good to be anywhere."

"You're right about that, Bronson. For those who just tuned in, we're waiting for our feed from Jerusalem where President Macalusso is scheduled to address the world. He has promised to shed some light on the absolutely incredible events of the last forty-eight hours."

"Clearly the world is waiting for such information. From the numbers I've been hearing, this will be the most watched telecast in history. People everywhere desperately want some answers."

As Bronson was speaking, Helen touched her ear piece, then looked up at the control booth and nodded. "We've just been told that the feed is ready from Jerusalem, Bronson." She turned to the camera and said, "We now switch to WNN in Jerusalem and follow-up coverage in London. This is Helen Hannah in New York."

The rally was held in what appeared to be a stadium. Spotlights positioned near the top regularly swept the crowd estimated to be at least 75,000 people. Another 100,000 men, women, and children were outside, watching the speech on banks of giant television monitors.

Helicopters hovered overhead, their sides painted with the logos of more than a dozen television networks from around the world. WNN alone had six cameras in the stadium, two more outside, and a gyroscopically stabilized unit in one of the helicopters. Thirty reporters roamed among the mobs, soliciting comments from those who would be listening to the speech. Similar outdoor viewing/listening posts had been established in other parts of the world so that the speech could be witnessed live in communities of all sizes. At least two billion people were expected to hear or see the speech as it was given, either in public meeting areas or on television and radio. At least another billion or more would receive a delayed version in one form or another.

Franco Macalusso walked calmly down a long aisle in the center of the stadium, a follow spot focused on him as he made his way to the podium. On catwalks overhead, snipers had been positioned with high powered rifles equipped with spotting scopes. Reporters who had questioned the need for such weaponry were told that they could not mention it on the air, photograph it, or write about it. They also were not to discuss other security measures taken throughout the area. As a result, the television image made Macalusso seem to be walking unprotected and unconcerned as the audience rose to its feet, cheering.

"Franco! Franco! Franco!" came one cry from the crowd.

"Praise the holy one!" shouted others.

"He has come for us!" "At last, the true savior." "Praise his name!" "Franco! Franco! Franco!"

There were protests in some of the regional broadcast areas. A group calling itself the Friends of Jesus stood silently near where the London monitors had been set up. They had formed from the members of several small study groups which had come together after reading and viewing the material left behind by the disappeared. Their clothing was stitched with biblical references to the stories about Jesus, the end times, and the Antichrist. They were ignored by some, taunted by others, spat upon, called "crazy" and worse.

A group calling itself Christians Questioning, another of the post-Messiah "haters" groups, passed out pamphlets in Los Angeles, the writing discussing the comments of Macalusso versus what they read in Scripture. They were counter picketed by a group with the misnomer Christians For Macalusso. Formerly non-believers, though raised in one of the Christian faiths by believer parents who had disappeared, they were ardent converts, evangelically spreading the new word.

Other protests occurred in New Delhi, Manila, Mexico City, Vancouver, and elsewhere. Sometimes the people were ignored. Sometimes there was violence. There were a few arrests, local police usually siding with the people angered by the protesters. And in a handful of areas, the protesters, the "haters," were jailed in "protective custody" to prevent them from being seriously injured or killed by unusually angry crowds.

As though aware of the protesters and their reasoning, the official feed camera closed in on an object Macalusso was carrying on his walk to the podium set up in one end of the massive gathering place in Jerusalem. It was a large, leather bound Bible that had obviously been frequently used. As he reached the top, he raised the Bible high in his right hand.

"Ladies and Gentlemen, I hold in my hand what can only be considered the most important, yet misunderstood book in the history of the world. It is in this book that my coming has been foretold. It is in this book that your generation is alerted to my presence. It is in this book that you have also read of the Great Deceiver, The One Who Came Before Me.

"The prophet Zechariah spoke of my coming today when he said, 'And his feet shall stand in that day upon the Mount of Olives, which is before Jerusalem on the east". A long time ago, The Man Who Came Before Me spoke in my name and deceived many. His deception continued for almost two thousand years, and now I have removed those who believed his life. They were the followers of the Deceiver, people who chose hatred and intolerance over peace and unity."

He paused, watching the audience, gauging its reaction. They had never grown fully quiet, his amplified voice bouncing off a wall of sound. Yet now they grew louder, cheering the words he had just spoken.

"I have removed the tares from the wheat."

Some of those present had tears in their eyes. Several men and women had their heads bowed, their eyes tightly closed in prayer, one open hand raised towards the sky. "Thank you, Franco," they said. "Oh, Franco, thank you."

One man, listening to the opening words, grew angry. "My sister disappeared," he shouted at Franco, though no one more than a few feet away could hear him, so great was the din of voices. "She was a beautiful woman. She was a widow who raised five children in the church. She knew the Lord, loved the Lord, as I did not. Those children, my nieces and nephews, were successful before they, too, disappeared, because she turned them over to Jesus, someone I did not know until I read what her family left behind. You have worked tricks for our minds. He changed hearts, raised up the meek..." His voice choked with anger both for the loss with which he was still trying to cope in his new found faith, and for the blasphemy so smoothly rolling off the tongue of this pretender. "How dare you say my sister was deceived?"

There were other angry cries, though the television audience never heard them. Some of the people were ignored. Some were seen as crazy, those around them moving away for fear whatever caused them to act so foolishly might be contagious. And some were heard by the roving security force. They would be grabbed, forced to their knees, and with the pretense of searching them for weapons, injected with a drug that assured their silence while still letting them stay on their feet as they were escorted away.

In the WNN studio, Helen had also become angry. "Bronson, it's a lie. This man's lying. I read what Grandma left for me. I watched..."

"Shhhh," said Bronson. "I want to hear this. I met the man, spent hours with him. He's fascinating."

"He's a vehicle for Satan's lies."

"Helen, just watch. Please. I want to hear what he has to say."

"He says lies, Bronson. Don't you understand. This is the one Grandma talked about with us that day we went to visit her church together. This is..."

"Helen, please, after he's off the air."

"I have come in peace, and I have brought peace to the world,"

Macalusso continued.

"Franco! Franco! Franco!"

"I have saved you all from certain destruction."

"Praise his precious name. Franco! Franco!"

Then, gesturing to the Bible, he continued, "This book has told you that by my fruits you would know me. Now that you have seen the good works that I have done, you can rest assured that your salvation is at hand. Salvation is knocking at your door."

Helen glanced around the newsroom. Everyone was riveted to the set. Joanie Harris was crying, laughing, experiencing a personal ecstasy unfamiliar to her normally wild living character. Mike was fixated on the screen, fascinated by every word. Even Bronson was staring, though Helen could not read the slightly bemused expression on his face. Clearly he was enjoying the show, though she started to relax only when he whispered, "This reminds me of Hitler in the 1930s. Did you ever see those clips? It was like something Cecil B. DeMille would have created for one of his Bible epics only it was real. This guy's got the same gift of oratory. Fascinating."

Then she felt a tightness in her chest as he added, "Thank God this one's for real. Hitler was a dangerous fraud. I've seen the power of this man with my own eyes."

"I am here to tell you that today mankind is ready to take its next great step of evolution. I will show you wonderful powers that lie within you now, waiting to be unleashed. This is not what one American of my acquaintance calls 'pie in the sky by and by.' These are powers that have been your birthright from the very beginning. But first, those who were not ready, those whose minds were so closed that they could not possibly hear the truth; those whose hatred of the truth of human potential were holding us all back, they have been removed. Only the fittest can survive, and that is why you are hearing me today."

The cheering was deafening. The security personnel warily watched the crowd. They had been warned that followers of the Deceiver, The One Who Came Before Me, might cause trouble, but so far there was no one who posed a danger.

"What has held you back until now were those who refused to believe in the power of the human mind. Those who believed that our true power came from outside of ourselves. I tell you today, the power is within you now. It always has been. And now, finally, it is time for you to see just what you are capable of. I will be your guide. But always remember, I am not the power. The power is within you."

Despite her new understanding, Helen realized that she, like the majority of the people left in the world, was riveted to the television monitor. There was something more than charisma that gave power to President Macalusso's words. It was as though there was a force within him that was so seductive it could tug at the very soul of the weak, the spiritless, the questioning.

She glanced at Bronson Pearl and realized that his facial expression was no longer dispassionate. Like the rest of the people watching inside WNN, he was mesmerized by the screen. She needed to break the spell, needed to speak with Bronson alone.

Helen squeezed Bronson's hand. He glanced quizzically at her, just as she remembered the security guards who had become a part of the WNN routine of the last few days. Then she glanced at her lapel, realizing she was still wearing a wireless microphone. Anyone could listen to her comments even though they were no longer being broadcast.

Reaching across the desk, Helen took a pen and paper and

wrote, "Things are not as they seem. I need you to leave here with me right NOW!"

Bronson looked at the note, puzzled. This was the most important speech by perhaps the most important person in history. Certainly there would be no bigger experience for them as journalists in their lifetime. Having to watch a tape or read a transcript later just wasn't the same.

He looked at Helen, shaking his head no. Then he pointed to the monitors and held up his hand as though to say, "Wait. Not now."

Helen jerked back the paper and angrily wrote "PLEASE!!"

Bronson looked at her more closely. Helen was an experienced professional with the same aggressiveness he had. She should have been just as excited by what was taking place. If she was this insistent, there must be something more important. And if there wasn't.... Well, it just better be important.

Bronson rose to his feet and quietly started across the room. As much as he was taken by what was happening, a part of him was a professional cynic. He knew President Macalusso was special. He had witnessed first hand what occurred with the missiles and machinery of war. Yet he had also witnessed the undercurrent of hate that remained, the anger against Christians, the use of security personnel. Something was wrong, and if Helen was worried, he should also take precautions.

"I'll watch the rest of the show in my dressing room," Bronson whispered to the floor director who was surprised to see him leaving.

Helen left a few moments later. "Bathroom," she said, smiling resignedly.

"If this speech runs long, there will be a water shortage from all the flushing when it's over," laughed the floor director, returning to the set.

Overhead in the control room, Len Parker was the only person not watching a monitor. He knew what the speech would be, what the reaction should be like. He was more concerned with those who might cause trouble.

Quietly, Parker tapped the shoulder of a uniformed soldier sitting at a control desk, watching President Macalusso. He was fascinated, and it took him a moment to realize Parker wanted him. "Rewind surveillance camera three's tape a couple of minutes, then run it on Monitor 6," whispered Parker, pointing to the screen only he and the soldier could see.

The youth did as he was asked. Parker watched until the paper was passed to Bronson the first time. "Stop! Now give me a close-up on the paper."

The paper began to fill the screen.

"Now enhance it so I can read what it says."

Bronson Pearl walked towards his dressing room. No one was in the halls. In the distance he could see the studio security staring at the large screen television in the network's lobby. Everyone was watching Macalusso's speech.

Bronson also had a monitor in his office. He positioned it so anyone glancing in would think he was resting on his couch, watching the broadcast. Given his level of exhaustion the last few days, no one would question. Then he turned on the set, adjusted the volume, opened the door a crack, saw no one, and left.

Helen had gone in the other direction, not bothering to stop by her office or anywhere else. There was no one wandering the building, probably no one on the streets. Everyone was gathered where they could see and hear this most important address to the world. She reached the side entrance, opened the door, and walked down the street.

It took less than five minutes for her to reach Bronson. The way the buildings and parking areas were situated, only one section of the street was away from the possibility of prying eyes and ears from the network. There were no windows on that side of the building, no coffee shops or bars. They had gone there before when they sought privacy. Bronson had proposed marriage there the first dozen times he had tried. Eventually it had become a joke between them, though he was certain that was where she would go.

Helen embraced Bronson with all the emotion of the past several days. She clung to him with the fierceness of a mother tiger embracing a wounded cub. Then, gradually she began to relax, her body shaking from the release of tension. Finally she stepped back from him, her hands on his shoulder, her head bowed. She breathed in deeply, then exhaled slowly. "Lord, give me the strength..." she whispered.

"What's this all about, Helen? I don't think I've ever seen you this upset."

As Helen started to speak, she noticed a movement in the distance. One man was in a suit, the other in uniform. She couldn't quite make out their faces, yet knew they were from WNN. No one else was around. No one else was of concern.

Helen took Bronson's arm and hurried him around the building to where she had parked her car. "Just get in. It looks like you're not the only one who wants to know what I've discovered."

Helen drove slowly, not wishing to attract attention. So long as she blended with the other cars, she was fairly certain they were safe. Eventually she drove onto the freeway, getting off at the first exit, getting on again, then doubling back, all without going above the legal limit. Finally she returned to the city, going to a parking garage near her grandmother's apartment. Satisfied she had lost whatever surveillance had been used, she used her key to let herself into her grandmother's apartment building.

"I know this is about President Macalusso, Helen. You haven't been the same since the day they tried to start the war.

"I know you saw it on television, but you really had to be in the midst of it. The missiles are launched, the battle is in earnest, and suddenly this helicopter starts to land at the Mount of Olives. Just as the door opens and Macalusso starts to step to the ground.... BAM!.... they disappeared as easily as a playing card in a magician's hand. People were vanishing everywhere. The missiles could no longer be seen and heard. Some planes just dropped from the sky. Others returned to their bases."

He paused, recognizing that Helen was not sharing his enthusiasm, yet he was too excited to stop talking and ask why. "And the timing! If he'd have arrived a minute and a half later, this world would have been one giant mushroom cloud. From where I was standing, it was pretty obvious those idiots were going to blow up the entire planet. Every leader was at fault. Every one of them. They all gave their codes to launch, and this guy stops them all in their tracks. He raises his hands, says a few words, and it's over.

"No impostor or charlatan could pull that off. This guy is something beyond anything I've ever seen.. If this guy isn't who he says he is... then who is he?"

"I'd rather you saw it for yourself, Bronson. Grandma knew I wouldn't understand before she was raptured. She left this to help me. Now it's your turn. Just watch the tape and then we'll talk, though I have a feeling your questions will have been answered."

Helen walked over to the VCR, inserted the tape, and turned on the television. Then she used the remote control to find the place she wanted him to view. It began with Rexella and Jack Van Impe in their studio.

"So, Jack, millions of people will suddenly vanish off the face of the earth," said Rexella. "The world will be in peril as never before and then suddenly this great leader, unlike anyone the world has ever seen, will rise and seem to bring great peace to the world."

"Ah, Rexella. And the Bible spells it out in perfect detail. He's going to quarterback a seven year peace treaty, as Daniel 9:27 shows us. Then he's going to seem to bring peace to the whole world as First Thessalonians 5:3 reveals. He is going to be the most compelling political leader that this world has ever seen. But he's much more than that. He's nothing less than a great deceiver as Second John 2:7 shows. He's the one the Bible calls the Antichrist in First John 2:16. And he has only one goal, to deceive the world into believing..."

Helen and Bronson watched, oblivious to the fact that they had been followed. Miniature monitoring devices had been placed on all the cars driven by key WNN personnel. They were meant for tracking, though the reason given to the mechanics in the shop where the work was handled was that the devices would enable the network to rescue anyone in trouble on their travels. Instead it assured long distance surveillance that would allow agents following the car to stay out of sight yet never lose their quarry. As they sat watching the apartment building, one of the men began working with a small electronic hand unit kept in a special holder beneath the dashboard. The other turned on a small television monitor mounted on the floor to the right of the driver.

The tape finally finished. Bronson stared at the set as Helen turned it off. "Well?" she asked.

"It's fascinating, all right. Perfect for a WNN special report one day. How many of those people are still around?"

"Bronson, what are you talking about? Some day? Don't you see that this is about what we're experiencing now? Don't you see that

Macalusso is going to tighten his hold on the network, on communication in general, and soon a report won't be possible. Do you think a man who is the Antichrist is going to let us reveal his secret to the whole world? But that's what we've got to do, Bronson. We've got to tell..."

"Helen, back up a bit. I know you're grieving over the loss of your grandmother. And I grant you that this stuff is interesting. It does give a reason for what happened, but so does Macalusso and I don't see where one statement is any better than any other. Certainly an old cynic like you isn't taking this literally."

Helen glared at him. "I'm not grieving over the loss of Grandma!" she said. "Not the way you're thinking. I know she's not dead, at least not as we normally think of death. How many of the disappeared are there? Millions at least. We all know that. And there has been not one report of a corpse, of some mysterious burial ground, of mammoth trucks carting off bodies to be burned or destroyed by acid or...."

"Bronson, I miss that woman. I miss that woman more than I missed my own parents because I knew her longer and came to understand how very different, how very selfless her love was.

"You met her. You knew her. You know she's not dead somewhere just as I do. So the truth is that either she was raptured in the way you just heard about on the tape or Macalusso is telling the truth. That would make my grandmother closed minded, evil, a follower of something false, and a menace to society. Franco Macalusso's no hero. He's the Antichrist and we need to expose him."

"Aw, for God's sake, Helen, you're a journalist. We're talking about having been witnesses to the greatest event in the history of the planet and you're talking to me about the bogey-man."

"What does it take to convince you, Bronson? Can't you see

it? You've heard Macalusso. You've heard what he said about the disappeared. Either he's telling the truth and everything you've ever said
about Grandma is false, or he's the Antichrist. There is no other explanation, not with the dramatic events of the last few days. It's all right
there on that tape and here in the Bible. You've got to see that."

"I'll tell you what I see, Helen. I see someone who needs to
step back for just a minute. We all want answers. We all want to believe our lives have been what we've thought they've been. But you
and I are in a business that does not allow our desire for one answer to
cloud our journalistic judgment when the truth is likely to be very different.

"It's time for a reality check. We've been through a lot. We've
been separated at a time when we thought we would never see each
other again. Your grandmother is one of the disappeared. You made a
commitment to marry me despite all the fears inside you. And just a
couple of days ago, we all thought we were covering the story of how
the planet was going to be turned into one giant nuclear desert. We
were doing our jobs because that's how we stay in control of our sanity,
but all of us knew that if the tapes weren't destroyed, and if they could
survive long enough after our deaths, they would serve as history les-
sons for whatever life form took our place.

"Our fears weren't warranted, not as we thought. And this
thing with your grandmother....Helen, I'm sorry. I loved the woman,
too. I don't know why she is part of the disappeared, but Macalusso
might be able to tell us later. I've interviewed him a couple of times
already. I'm sure I'll be doing it again. I can ask him one on one. Certainly he knows the stories of everyone he removed or he would not
have done so. Now you've got to get a grip on yourself so we can go
back to the studio and..."

"I'm not going back," said Helen, firmly.

"What are you talking about?"

"I'm not going back. If you're still blind to what's going on...well, that's between you and God. But I know the truth about Macalusso. I know the truth about my grandmother. And I'm not going to destroy her memory or promote the greatest evil the planet has ever faced by joining you in telling the world what a great guy he is."

"Of all the people I know, I would have thought you'd be the last to get caught up in the ideas of some.... of some.... religious cult."

"What you can't seem to understand, Bronson Pearl, is that I am using every bit of objectivity, cynicism, observation, and all those other traits that I've learned as a journalist. I'm emotional about Grandma. I'm emotional about almost losing you. I'm practically a basket case that I said yes to your marriage proposal and find myself actually liking the idea. But I am coldly objective about what is taking place right now.

"You're the one with the steel trap mind that closed before reality could set in. This is for real, Bronson Pearl. What's it going to take for you to believe that."

"When Franco Macalusso dons his red suit, reveals his horns and tail and makes his speech holding a pitchfork, then..."

Helen glared at him. The joke was the wrong one at the wrong time, and Bronson realized his mistake.

"Look, Helen, you've got to agree that for both of us, seeing has always been believing. We've both fought for assignments that would get us into the forefront of action taking place somewhere in the world. We wouldn't even rely on the video feed to the network. We didn't want to see it filtered through a videographer's eye which was already having a camera lens act as 'editor.' But I'm not certain you're still doing that. I think you've got a belief system and want to only see what supports it."

"Maybe, though I think it's closer to the truth to say that you're refusing to see anything that doesn't support what you want to believe. Maybe you're not ready to fall on your knees and give your heart to God, to embrace the teachings of His Son, and frankly I'm not asking you to do that. All I'm asking you to do is to look at this stuff truly objectively. Don't just remember the missiles disappearing from the sky. Think about the security forces that are quietly moving into our lives. Think about the life my grandmother lived and the way she would have had to live to be the type of person Macalusso said she was. Think about me and the fact that if I didn't really believe there was something to it, I wouldn't be asking you to take the time to really look into it."

Helen paused, emotionally drained, her voice filled with disappointment. "Of all the people I know, I'd have thought you'd be the last one to dismiss something this big without even looking into it."

"I'm not saying there's nothing to it," Bronson began, aware of Helen's looking askance at him for such a statement. "My father spent every day of his life believing it. It made him a happier man. Maybe it even made him a better man. But at the end of the day, he still ended up dead, just like all of us will."

"His earthly body may have died, Bronson, but his soul is still very much alive."

Bronson stared at Helen for a moment as she stood in front of him. Then he took her hand and brought it to the side of his face, holding it against his flesh, feeling her comforting touch. "I wish I could believe that, Helen. Honest to God I do."

He stayed there for a moment, Helen using her free hand to stroke his neck and back. This was a difficult time for them both, and to her amazement, as deep as their differences had so unexpectedly become, she loved him all the more. He was trying, talking with her, showing her the respect she had always wanted from a man, even though she knew he felt her reaction was emotional, not logical. Then he rose and started walking around the room, talking as much to sort out his thoughts as to try and convince her.

"Look, I've met President Macalusso. I've seen what he's done with my own eyes. I followed his career at the United Nations. I've done backgrounders on his business interests. I've done voiceovers for the documentary on his life and career. I've interviewed him when he became President of the European Union. And I was there in Israel, there in Armageddon." Bronson paused, realizing the word he had just used and its import.

"Franco Macalusso is the furthest thing from evil that I have ever seen.

"Think about what he's done. He rid the world of hatred."

"Except for those people who disagree with him, who love Jesus, embracing Him as their Lord and Savior," said Helen.

"He saved us all from what was certainly to be our imminent destruction. And now all he wants to do is unite the world in peace.

"I know you want me to look at the Bible. Helen, I've looked at it. I've spent too many nights alone and bored in strange hotel rooms with nothing to do but read the one the Gideons put in every room. I've read it cover to cover, and once I even bought a commentary so I could better understand the history surrounding the events it discusses.

"Yes, I have an interest in religion, too. But I'm still a journalist. We get Jesus filtered through the ages. He was dead before the gospels were written. He was dead before Paul wrote his letters. I wasn't at the wedding feast when He did as His mother asked and turned water into wine, and neither were the reporters who later told the story.

"But I was there for the arrival of Macalusso. I saw him raise his arms and make missiles vanish from the skies, fighter jets and bombers return to their bases, weapons cease functioning, and millions of men and women stop in the midst of battles. I saw him, Helen. I was a witness. This man is who he says he is, Helen."

"Maybe it's time for you to step back and look at this as an objective, professional journalist. We have a guy apparently doing some fantastic things and making even more fantastic claims about himself. He's impressive. He's unlike anyone we've ever encountered in this century. But we also have some very strong evidence to show that when he says he's the Messiah, he just might be an impostor. Let me get some paper, a Bible, and a few of Grandma's reference books. We can sit down at the table and start checking this out."

For a moment Bronson started to object. Then he realized that, at the very least, Helen needed to use the facts to disprove her own theories. At the most, she needed to show him the error in his own thinking. Either way, they would be stronger for working together. "Okay," he said. "Let's take it from the real beginning. The Bible says this Antichrist character will come out of the Roman Empire, right?"

They sat in the car, watching and listening. The tiny camera, mike, and transmitter had been placed in an overhead light fixture in Edna Williams' home. It was similar to several hundred other such devices, each placed in the homes of those disappeared whose family members included someone prominent in government or the media. The devices had a rechargeable battery and were also wired into the electrical system to extend their lives. They were kept off, being triggered by remote control devices carried in the cars of trusted members of Macalusso's personal security force as necessary. Each of the cars was equipped with a small television monitor and recording unit to assure the collection of evidence.

Helen Hannah had been monitored on each of her visits to her grandmother's home. Nothing was said to her after the fact. Nothing would be said for the immediate future. She saw it as her safe haven from observation and that was the way the security personnel wanted it.

Now she had brought Bronson Pearl there, a complication, though a minor one. No individuals were as important as the Messiah in the minds of the public. As trusted as Bronson might be, the right story about him would assure popular opinion went against him should he need to be arrested or killed.

The image on the monitor was fuzzy, like the picture on one of the early black and white television sets trying to receive signals in a fringe area. The people were identifiable and their voices were coming through very well. But computer enhancement would have to be used before any trial.

Agent Domi checked the recording meter as Helen was heard on the small speaker saying, "That's right. The Antichrist will come from the Roman Empire, and according to this encyclopedia, the European Union is geographically equal to what was known as the Roman Empire of biblical times."

Agent Domi smiled and said, "The sound's perfect, and that's not a bad picture for a camera half the size of a frozen pea. The power pack's the biggest thing we had to worry about."

"I just hope they don't spot it," said Agent Probert.

"Not a chance. The tech guys have had so much experience with these things, there hasn't been one installation anywhere in the world where anyone's caught it. We just can't tip our hand too early. That's why so many followers of the Deceiver will be a long time before they're brought to justice. We need to see who's influencing others and who will face the Messiah's wrath alone."

"You'd think he'd know what's in their hearts."

"I'm sure he does. But we're a people of laws. He's got to

handle matters in ways that are familiar to us. Otherwise people might get upset."

"With the Messiah?"

"It could happen. This is all so new to them. We understood what was happening when he first started recruiting us. And look how long it took for us to be convinced. These people are just beginning to see."

"Except for those who follow the Deceiver."

"And that's why we're here."

It was midnight before Bronson was becoming convinced that there was more to what Helen had been saying than emotion, yet he was still concerned that she was over reacting. They had emptied the refrigerator of food, gone through two pots of coffee, and were becoming exhausted. However, neither felt they should stop. They had another Van Impe video playing on the VCR, and all around them were books filled with page markers. Bronson was using a Bible, scanning each page with his finger until he found the passages he was seeking. In front of him was a piece of paper divided into two columns. On the left was a column marked "Prophecy." On the right was a column marked "Fulfilled."

The Rapture was first. There was no question that it had happened, no question that it had been foretold. Bronson had admitted as much to Helen when he apologized. She was right. Edna Williams did not fit the Macalusso profile of the disappeared. Nor did a few of the others each or both of them knew. The truth had to be 180 degrees apart from what he claimed.

Then there were the heart attacks. Neither had been assigned to that story, the team coverage headed by the WNN medical specialist. But they both knew about them.

The incidents began right after the Rapture. At first the victims were thought to only be those who were elderly, frail, and experienced the shock of seeing friends and/or loved ones suddenly vanish. Then they realized that such deaths were far in excess of anything statistically normal, even in areas experiencing a natural disaster such as a flood or hurricane. The sheer number of heart attack deaths had to be the fulfilment of prophecy. Nothing else made sense.

Most of the notes Bronson had made were cryptic — about Israel, a Great Leader, Peace, Miracles, and a Treaty. Each represented a prophetic promise, and each had been fulfilled except for the signing of a peace treaty between Israel and the rest of the world. Such a treaty, with a seven year life, was the only prediction that had yet to be realized.

Bronson put down the Bible, picked up the paper and studied it. He looked from the left column to the right, left to right, again and again. Each time the conclusion was inescapable. Each time he did not want to have to deal with what he was seeing. Finally he stood up, put his arms on Helen's shoulders, kissed her head, then began pacing the room.

"I'm sorry, Helen, I just can't accept this. I see why you keep talking the way you do. I understand where you're coming from. This stuff is interesting. No, it's outright compelling.

"But this is more than 2,000 years after much of this stuff was written. There have had to have been other times when similar events occurred, and maybe there were...

"I don't know how to say it. I'm a journalist, a professional reporter. I'm supposed to be the most trusted man in America. I even have theme music. And I just can't quite believe that we should be worrying about the bad dreams of some ancient shepherd. I just can't...

"Look, Helen, I'm heading back to the studio. I'll cover for you as best as I can to give you some time to think about this, to come to your senses. I see what you're trying to show me, but every bone in my body says you are going right off the deep end and I can't buy into your fantasy no matter how much I love you."

He headed for the door, then paused, looked at her, and said, "You tell your God that if He is the real God, and if He has something to say to me, He knows where I live. Maybe you have to be touched in some special way, and if that's what has to happen to me, then fine, so be it. For now, with all that I've seen over the last few days, I can only say that a God in the world is worth two in a book."

TEN

Day Five

There had been intense media pressure concerning the actions of those called the haters, the people who insisted upon following the man the declared Messiah was calling The One Who Came Before Me. The incidents of the previous few days emboldened a number of tabloid-style television personalities to try and start their own religious shows to take advantage of suddenly available time blocks. Christian broadcasting had ended with the loss of their ministerial staffs and supporters. Rather than scrambling to fill the time slots with old movies and innocuous documentaries, Macalusso centered programs were tried. Most were local efforts, but the most popular evening time slot was grabbed by Kenny Casswell, also the host of the widely syndicated "Kenny C's People." He had been notorious for such specials as "I'm dating my daughter's boyfriend" and "Three marriages, no divorces" which had been condemned by the televangelist he replaced when the popular minister joined the disappeared. He had both the "gift of gab" and the hypocrisy to claim his new show represented the previously little known "spiritual side" of Kenny C. He also made a point to put down those who had disappeared since they were deprived of the chance to work with the real Messiah.

"I can't speak for the good Lord above," said Kenny Casswell during the opening commentary on the "Franco Hour Of Power With Kenny C" show. "God is the ultimate judge, and what he says goes. I just know that there must have been a lot of sin filled, hate filled, lust filled, hypocrites to have so many removed before the coming of the Messiah. I just wish my ex-wife could have been one of those trouble-makers the Messiah removed. Too bad she never was involved with our beloved Macalusso. He would have shown her a thing or two when he announced who he really was. But I guess I'll just have to live with the idea that the Messiah doesn't have the problems with her that I do.

"And now, before I bring out the lovely Angel McMillan who sings the praises of Macalusso as sweetly as her name implies, I want to say, thank you glorious Messiah. Thank you for this chance for me to talk about you in prime time. And thank you for Angel McMillan whose album of your favorite songs will soon be released. It is called Music For The Messiah and is available in record stores everywhere."

Local newscasts began featuring stories of church defacements in their "happy news" sections. Attacks against those rare individuals who dared speak the name of their newly discovered Jesus with trembling and awe were beginning to be considered positive stories.

Increasingly the followers of Jesus were being called "haters" by the believers in the power of Macalusso. They were seen as an evil force, perhaps subversive, and certainly in need of being stopped.

Franco Macalusso's addresses spoke of tolerance, love, and harmony. However, he also made clear that anyone who was against such universal needs was also against humanity and must be stopped. The counter measures were to be peaceful, he stressed, and made with the utmost caring about the misguided individuals who were their targets. But the truth was that much of the news blocked out for its negative impact showed men and women using force to enter the meeting places of the haters. Uniforms had been given to the Women Who Watch and other loyal groups who supplemented local police and military when isolating the haters. They needed to be kept in hospitals, minimum security prisons, and specially created camps until they could be convinced of the error of their ways. To the Macalusso lovers, they were heroes of the New World Order. To those named the haters, who were called "the Messiah's Marauders," derided for daring to challenge those who had discovered the truth about Jesus, the name so powerful the new "Messiah" dared not utter it.

Men and women took cans of spray paint and wrote "Death To The Haters" and other hostile slogans on the doors and walls of churches and store front meeting halls.. They went to the homes of people they knew or suspected of being active Christians, marking their windows with the word "haters."

Some looked upon the Christians with pity, knowing that there would come a time in the near future when they would face the wrath of the Messiah. Already there were arrests, mass jailings, and sentences that ranged from forced re-education to life in prison. Others were filled with hatred, smashing windows, smashing cars, taunting the haters. Fire bombs were thrown into homes and apartments. Beatings were increasingly common. In one community, a group of Messiah Zealots calling themselves The Army Of Macalusso Consciousness, surrounded a cluster of homes where the residents had been praising Jesus from a time shortly after the resurrection. The residents, who were herded onto a school playground at gun point, called themselves the Descendants Of Peter, reminding those with whom they spoke that Peter needed the Resurrection to become a full believer. They had not known Jesus before the Rapture, indeed had avoided places where they might hear the Word. Instead they had stumbled upon the same books and videos that were creating a resistance movement, read them, and believed for the first time in their lives.

Since they had seen the Rapture, it became for them what the Resurrection must have been for Jesus' friends. With knowledge of the disappeared fresh in their experience and the left behind writings to guide them, they knew first hand the unerring truth of Bible prophecy. They went from religious ignorance to being men and women of totally committed faith. And when some were shot for their proselytizing, they died rejoicing in what was happening, having first refused to renounce the Lord.

Billboards independently made by extremist followers of the Messiah began to appear with warnings saying, "Haters Repent. Macalusso brings joy. All else brings death."

Bronson Pearl was troubled by the growing violence. The world was more peaceful than it had ever been. Old enmities seemed to have fallen away. There was peace in areas of the world where previously a night without gun shots, sirens, search lights, and screams would have seemed a miracle. People no longer lived in fear. Yet the antagonism towards the new Christians was growing in ways that did not seem to fit with the person of the Messiah. Even if they were following a false prophet in their sudden belief in Jesus as the true Son of the Living God, they were gentle people. They prayed for those who declared them to be enemies. They had compassion for those who professed allegiance to the new Messiah. They threatened no one except through unconditional love.

Peter and Paul Lalonde

Equally troubling was something Bronson had begun to notice in the speeches and writings coming from the Messiah. He did not know why he had missed it at first. Normally he was careful when interviewing to listen to not only what someone was saying but exactly how they were saying it.

Perhaps it was his turmoil over the fight he had with Helen that made him think about all of the events since Armageddon. Perhaps his carefully honed skills as a journalist were kicking in after too many days of over work leaving him numb with exhaustion. Whatever the case, he realized that he had never heard Franco Macalusso utter the name of Jesus. Macalusso had made reference to Jesus, of course. He had called Him the Great Deceiver. He had called Him "The One Who Came Before Me." Yet he had never actually said Jesus' name.

Certainly this refusal to name Jesus might have had something to do with his utter contempt for a false messiah. Yet there was something more troubling. A true Messiah could only be sent by God. He would be God's emissary on earth, the person who would usher in the Kingdom of God that Jesus discussed 37 times in the synoptic gospels according to one of Edna Williams' study guides.

More important, the Bible said that each time the name of Jesus is spoken, the name has a power to it that neither Satan nor the Antichrist can match. If Franco Macalusso was, indeed, the Antichrist as Helen believed, that would account for his fear to utter the name of his enemy.

Another problem came from the limited references to a faith in God. Certainly Jesus confronted all manner of horrors and never forgot where praise was due. This man was not like that. He spoke of himself. He spoke of the power within each person. Yet he never reminded the world to love God before all else as God had caused to be written again and again. And though it was possible that the Bible was wrong on this

217

matter, he doubted it. After all, the admonition was almost as old as time, etched in stone during the Exodus, and referred to again and again for thousands of years. For the Messiah to come and ignore this... He found it extremely troubling.

There was also the matter of the intense use of secular instruments by Macalusso. Why would the real Messiah worry about WNN's daily operations, its programming, and its ability to saturate much of the world with its signal. Why would the real Messiah have such micromanaging desires with them and who knew how many other broadcast facilities world wide.

Maybe there was something to what Helen had been trying to show him. Maybe....

"Good morning, Bronson. Mr. Parker wants to see you right away," said Mike, the floor director.

And that was the other thing. Len Parker had gone from being an observer to being someone with power and authority far greater than seemed appropriate. He was in security, a body guard or soldier or whatever it was such people did. Now he was acting as censor when the narrowing of the news was totally inappropriate for a broadcast facility such as WNN. It was all very curious.

As Bronson started to walk towards Parker's office, a young woman dressed in the same uniform as the other security officers, though without a weapons belt, brought a stack of papers to him. "Here's today's copy and some suggested banter notes, Mr. Pearl."

"Thanks, Kerry. But why the new look?"

"It was Mr. Parker's idea. He wants the support staff to show their faith in the Messiah. I feel a little silly this way, but if it's a way of proving my loyalty, that's okay with me."

Bronson shrugged, flipping through the notes as he went through the door leading to the steps going up to the control room.

"Hey, Bronson, Mr. Parker wants to talk to you ASAP," said one of the engineers.

Bronson ignored the comment, setting the notes to one side, then taking his pen and checking a line here, crossing out a line there, and generally starting his usual pre-air time editing process. Before he finished the first page, another technician entered the room, saying, "Bronson, have you seen...."

"Parker? Not yet, but I'm getting the message. I guess it's important." He pocketed his pen, picked up the papers, and walked down the hall to Len Parker's office. He opened it without knocking.

Parker was sitting behind a large desk on which several pieces of specialized equipment had been placed. There was a small television/VCR combination, three different sizes of tape recorders, a computer terminal, and several electronic devices Bronson did not recognize. There was also a small stack of folders taken from the Personnel office. Parker was reading Helen Hannah's file as Bronson entered the room. He looked up, scowling.

"Trouble in Paradise, Len?" Bronson asked, facetiously. He had seen Len Parker's type in many places of the world. He was the type of man who gained his self-respect by attaching himself to someone he thought was a rising leader in business, industry, or government. His future, his self-esteem, all were tied to the success or failure of the person with whom he was aligned.

Such men could be ruthless, though if their leader was toppled, they would frequently claim to have just been following orders. Bronson found them all pathetic little cowards, grown up versions of schoolyard bullies. He was always surprised and a little saddened when others yielded to their desires. Even at the network, he was one of the few employees who did not tremble at demands for his appearance such as the summons he had just received.

"Where's Miss Hannah, Mr. Pearl?" asked Parker, coldly.

"How should I know? Have you tried her apartment?"

Parker rose from his desk, his body tensed like a panther about to strike. He let his suit jacket fall back to reveal that he was carrying a sidearm. Then he moved to the door, closed it, and angrily said, "Cut the bull, Pearl. Where is she?"

"I told you, I don't know," said Bronson, just as firmly. "Now what's going on here."

Parker did not reply. Instead he returned to his desk and switched on a small amplifying unit attached to a micro cassette tape recorder. Then he pressed the play button, surprising Bronson with the sound of his own voice. "I'm not saying there's nothing to it. My father spent every day of his life believing it. It made him a happier man. Maybe it even made him a better man. But at the end of the day, he still ended up dead, just like all of us will."

Helen's voice came next. "His earthly body may have died, Bronson, but his soul is still very much alive."

And then there was Bronson again. "I wish I could believe that, Helen. Honest to God I do."

Parker stopped the tape and stared coldly at Bronson. The journalist had been in dangerous situations before. He had traveled behind the lines of government forces in order to do interviews with guerrilla forces in several different South American, African, and Eastern European countries. He had to travel in disguise to avoid arrest or worse. And always he had understood the risks, the potential value of what he was doing.

This time Bronson realized he was out of control. He was the target of surveillance by a man who should have had no reason to do such a thing. Even worse, Helen was involved and he had no idea how. He hoped he would not show his fear because it would only be with a show of fear that a man like Len Parker could be truly strengthened.

"So just what do you believe, Mr. Pearl?" asked Parker.

"You've got the tape. For all I know you've got pictures of my every move. You figure it out."

"Does that mean you don't know? That you haven't made a decision about the Deceiver and the Messiah?"

"Look, I walked out on the woman I love. If you have a tape, you know that. That should tell you what I believe."

"Not good enough, Mr. Pearl. A lover's quarrel perhaps, not necessarily a theological difference. We need to know that you support our Messiah."

"I'm sure not here because I support you."

Len Parker refused to rise to the bait. He sensed that Bronson was trying to change the subject, to avoid answering the critical question. Did he not know that what he failed to reveal in a friendly manner could be learned through less pleasant means? Did he not know that if he chose to bother himself with someone so meaningless as this journalist, the Messiah could read his heart?

"Helen Hannah's missing, Mr. Pearl. Her car is parked near the apartment of Edna Williams, but she's no longer inside. We just hope she's not going to do anything stupid." He paused, looking coldly at Bronson, then added, "And put herself in danger."

The threat against Helen was the wrong way to handle Bronson. Like all successful journalists, he was an extremely aggressive man. Like all men in love, he had become extremely protective. The idea that Len Parker would talk of hurting Helen...

"By danger, I assume you mean from yourself, right?"

Parker shrugged, enjoying what he still thought was his upper hand. "It's my job to protect the interests of the Messiah and the peace and unity he has brought to this world."

"What exactly is that supposed to mean?"

"Anger and hatred are the enemies now. And I'll do whatever I have to in order to eliminate every source of those emotions remaining. Obviously when someone so prominent as Miss Hannah is running around like a half-cocked loaded gun, she has to be stopped for her own good and that of society."

"From what I've seen, the only anger and hatred has been brought by zealots like you. It's the extremists who are defacing the churches and attacking the Christians. Now you're talking about eliminating someone who disagrees with what so many of us have been thinking about the events of the past week.

"I've heard that word before, Parker. Sometimes they call it ethnic cleansing. Sometimes they call it re-education. Eliminating is more to the point, isn't it? You're going to kill Helen and anyone who shares her beliefs, aren't you?"

Parker realized he may have gone too far. He calmed himself and said, "Look, Mr. Pearl. Don't act like I'm the enemy or misinterpret my words. I'm a military man, an intelligence analyst, someone who's been around facts and figures. I've never so much as given a speech while you make your living with words.

"Perhaps the word 'eliminate' has the wrong connotation. I'm not your enemy and I'm not Miss Hannah's enemy. I'm just trying to serve the Messiah and help him bring peace and unity to the world. Who could possibly have a problem with that?"

"Said the spider to the fly..." mumbled Bronson, turning and leaving the office. For the first time he realized that Helen might have a point. But where was she? Where was Helen?

Agent Domi was startled by the ringing telephone. The apartment was empty, the woman who once lived there among the disappeared. The telephone seemed like a voice rising from the grave. It was spooky and he was uncomfortable.

Three rings. Four rings. "Peace in the name of the Lord. This is Edna Williams," said a voice on the answering machine. "Please leave your name, telephone number, and a brief message. And rejoice in this day that the Lord has made."

"Helen? Are you there? Please pick up the phone, Helen. I've looked everywhere else. You must be there. Helen? Helen?"

Agent Domi recognized the voice of Bronson Pearl. So it was true, he really didn't know where she was.

He was not too surprised, given the argument they had the other night. But it was useful information to give to Len Parker. He made a note in a pocket notebook, then returned to the strongbox from which he removed the Jack Van Impe tape. He glanced at it, then casually tossed it aside as he continued his search for whatever else he might find.

Bronson Pearl was not certain when he thought of the plan. There was that time in South America where a revolution was won by a weak, little supported force that captured the state run radio station and was able to broadcast news reports that convinced the people that their popular leader had been defeated. By the time the truth began to leak out, the self-proclaimed Commandante For Life, whose followers numbered a few hundred at best, was firmly in control of the nation.

Bronson also understood that the financial stake Macalusso had taken in WNN might have little to do with business. Perhaps he wanted to use the broadcast facilities to control the knowledge and actions of the people. Whatever the case, WNN was critical to some portion of his plans, something a true Messiah would not need. After all, Jesus spent his time walking the streets of Jerusalem and other cities.

He talked quietly to the people, teaching, healing, and speaking of the Kingdom of God. The only time he became extremely angry was when he drove the money changers from the Temple. He touched the world usually one or two people at a time. Yet His influence remained almost 2,000 years after His death, and that influence affected all corners of the globe.

What Macalusso had done dwarfed anything at the hand of Jesus before the Resurrection. If he needed the largest news and broadcast organization in the world for any purpose, if he needed to dominate a broadcaster whose faith was deeper than any secular loyalty, something was very wrong. Perhaps it was time to challenge the man in whom he had once believed was undoubtedly Heaven sent.

Len Parker sensed that he had to move quickly. His faith in the Messiah was such that he could not imagine anyone worth living not sharing his commitment. Unfortunately there were extremist fools and it was his job to handle them, the reason he was talking with Mike in the control room. "I understand that you're the guy who can help me, Mike," said Parker. "I have a bit of a concern."

"What's up, Chief?"

"I'm a little worried that someone might say something damaging on the air. Something that might slow down the move toward a permanent world peace, and that's something I'm sure we all want to avoid."

"I'm surprised you're worried about something like that. You've watched our feeds from all over the world. Everyone is happy now. We have peace in the world. I mean, real peace. Not the nervous tension and secret sniping of the Cold War. I don't think any comment from some Hater is going to change that."

"Probably not, but with all the Messiah has done for us, I don't want to risk embarrassing him or causing him pain. I'm checking with you because I want to make sure we don't run into any unnecessary obstacles along the way, that's all. Are we protected with our broadcasts?"

"A little, though probably not what you have in mind. I think you'll probably want to go to a 12-second delay system rather than the 5 second run that's standard."

"What does that mean?"

"It just means you'll have 12 seconds to review every transmission before it gets sent out to the world. If someone says something you think might be harmful, you simply pre-empt the transmission with something else and claim technical difficulties. We do it on live call-in shows all the time."

"Okay, set it up and make certain I can do it from my office as well as from the control room. And don't mention this to anyone, okay? We don't want to alarm anyone or make them think we're worried about the haters. We've got the security to handle any violence, but we'd like to get all our defenses in order."

"Consider it done, Mr. Parker."

Although Len Parker was suspicious of Bronson Pearl, he was sure enough of his powers to intimidate, sure enough of how he was viewed as a representative of the Messiah, that he continued to use Bronson as an anchor. The situation appealed to the journalist for he felt that so long as his face and voice were familiar, he might influence the outcome of whatever was happening. He was also certain that, wherever Helen was, she would keep track of events through WNN.

The evening newscast was his first since Helen's departure, and he and Mike agreed to say nothing about what was happening. The opening began as usual, the announcer saying, "Across America and around the world, you're watching WNN with Bronson Pearl and Helen Hannah."

Bronson looked into the camera, smiled and said, "Good evening. I'm Bronson Pearl. Helen Hannah is on special assignment.

"As the situation in Europe and the Middle East continues to look better than ever, many are hoping that events will take another quantum leap sometime soon. President Macalusso has been meeting with world leaders in Bonn Germany for the past nine hours and an announcement is expected any time now. Of course, we'll bring you that live when it happens. Right now, with more on this situation in Bonn, is WNN German correspondent Samantha Metcalfe."

The screen switched to an image of Bonn, Germany, where the reporter was standing in front of a nondescript government building. "It has now been confirmed that foreign ministers from the European Union, as well as leading religious dignitaries from around the world have been meeting all night in this German government building. The attendees began arriving late last evening, an apparently unexpected meeting resulting from the demand of the man we had all believed to be little more than a businessman/politician who rose to the Presidency of the European Union. Instead, it is now agreed by virtually the entire planet that he is more than that."

"Roll footage of the religious leaders," whispered Max into his headset linked to the control room. In moments the screen was filled with what appeared to be a press conference being held by two men, one a man once declared to be an Islamic extremist, the other a Jewish Rabbi. The Islamic leader spoke first.

"We have all seen some remarkable events over the past several days, and clearly no one can deny the fact that our entire world has undergone an extraordinary change. Even with the planet being saved from the brink of almost certain destruction, and with the haters of peace and unity having been removed, the most incredible sign we have seen has been the realization by the entire world that President Franco Macalusso is indeed the Messiah he claims to be.

"There is no question in my mind that we are now once again living in Biblical times. He is the Messiah of Israel, the Messiah of the entire world is alive today. He is walking among us, living as one of us, bringing us the fulfilment of Biblical prophecy."

"But what evidence is there to support this view?" asked the reporter, almost apologetically. He, too, had witnessed the events of the past few days. He, too, was now a believer. Still, there was a formality he had to follow for the broadcast.

"As my brother has said, that will be revealed within a few days," said the Rabbi. "For now, the first issue that has had to be re-solved is that of peace. That is how we knew that we would recognize the true Messiah. He would bring peace. Did the one called Jesus bring peace? No. Only the true Messiah can do that."

As the Islamic leader began to speak again, there was a quick cut back to Bronson sitting at the news desk. "I have just received word that we're ready to go live to the embassy in Bonn. Apparently an agreement has been reached. Samantha?"

"This is an exciting moment for the world, Bronson. You can see for yourself what just happened a moment ago. The leader of the Arab world and the leader of Israel, one man a follower of Islam, the other a Jew, have just shaken hands indicating the final peace agree-ment has been reached. We have been told that an official spokesper-son will explain what has happened, and then there will be an address by President Macalusso and the other world leaders in a few minutes."

There was a hush among the dozens of reporters, security per-sonnel, and government aides as Heinrich Dieter stepped to the micro-phone. "I am pleased to announce that the Messiah has achieved something today that no man has ever been able to do before. He has brokered a full and comprehensive peace agreement between two brothers who have been separated for more than 6,000 years. This seven year, far reaching agreement goes well beyond a simple peace between Arabs and Jews. It involves all the major leaders of the world, establishing a newly agreed upon constitution for Planet Earth."

"Mr. Dieter!" shouted one reporter. "What does that mean? Have government leaders been secretly meeting?"

"I'm afraid I can't tell you anything more than I've just explained. I was caught by surprise myself. President Macalusso will be talking with you shortly, and at that time he will be able to answer your questions. We also have more than two dozen heads of state, each of whom has agreed to speak if requested."

In the studio, Bronson Pearl was as startled as others watching the news. Normally when a major event is about to take place, reporters are briefed in advance so they can prepare their commentary and analysis. This time the news was so unexpected, it took him a moment to recover.

"You have heard the announcement. There is a seven year peace treaty between people who have been at war for six thousand years. Of course, there have been treaties of one sort or another in the past, but they have always been more honored in the breach. This is different because this time it was brokered by President Macalusso whose powers were so clearly demonstrated just a few days ago.

"We're going to break for a message, and when we return, we'll talk to our chief political correspondent in Washington to get his take on this startling event. We'll also carry President Macalusso's address live whenever he chooses to make it."

Bronson smiled into the camera until the red light went off, indicating the network had gone to commercial. He remembered what

Helen had showed him, remembered the story of the seven year treaty. Increasingly he thought Helen might be right. He still did not understand all the miracles he had witnessed, but he was beginning to believe that Franco Macalusso, though the most unusual man of this century, was perhaps less powerful than his past achievements made everyone believe.

Helen Hannah had thought she was being cautious when she left her grandmother's house. She had no idea the extent of surveillance taking place, not only in relation to herself but also to so many others around the world. She did know that her actions were not going to be popular ones. She also realized that her car was familiar to the staff of WNN, her license plate recorded by security, her parking sticker highly visible in the lower left hand corner of her windshield. During the days preceding the Rapture, the car's markings enabled her to travel freely anywhere, from the Employees Only lot of WNN to the center of breaking news events from which most civilians were excluded. Since she made her decision to leave, the markings had become too easy a way to spot her.

Helen walked the first several blocks to the area known as Midtown. There were clean, safe, inexpensive hotels used by business travelers on tight expense accounts. They were not the type of places that Helen Hannah or any other media celebrity would be expected to use. As a result, no one looked at her with even a hint of recognition. They might have been familiar with her, certainly the television set in the lobby bar was set to WNN she noticed in passing, but because they didn't expect to see her, they didn't see her.

Helen had watched the newscast Bronson was anchoring, smiling sadly at the news he was reporting. Surely he understood now. And if he didn't, the announcement of a seven year treaty had to shock him towards reality.

She missed Bronson, wanted to see him, talk with him, hold him. She so desperately needed him to understand the truth, to grasp what she had been saying. "God, please, show me what to do," she prayed.

When Helen was finished, she took the Gideon Bible from the hotel drawer and left the room. She took the elevator down to the lobby and walked out the door, moving briskly towards her grandmother's neighborhood. Darkness had settled over the city and it seemed safe to return for her car. She was certain any surveillance had been ended. She had no idea about the tracking device that assured some of Macalusso's men would again pick up the pursuit.

Helen drove through the streets of the city, slowing at the WNN parking garage, then driving twice around the building before actually pulling in. Her pass made the gate rise, and she knew that at night there was only an aged security guard in the front booth. He had worked for WNN from the beginning. He was not one of the new people, the hand picked men and women whom Macalusso had added to the building's security force.

Helen turned off her lights and drove slowly to where Bronson Pearl's four-wheel-drive vehicle was parked. They had long ago given each other keys to their respective vehicles since they worked together so frequently. She used hers to open the door,
then placed a large brown envelope on the passenger seat. She closed and re-locked the door, then hurried back to her own car, starting the engine and again driving without lights down the exit ramp.

What Helen did not realize was that the tracking sensor had activated a small alarm in Len Parker's office. He called Agents Probert and Domi who had handled the original surveillance. They ran to their car and were in pursuit as soon as Helen again put her card in the release slot to open the exit lane gate.

This time there was no effort to hide the fact that Helen was being followed. Len Parker was certain she was one of the haters, a follower of the Deceiver who was unrepentant, could not be threatened, and would have to be eliminated. Ironically, Bronson Pearl had prepared the viewing audience for her death by mentioning that she was on special assignment. It would be easy to create a story where she becomes the news herself, her death declared a great tragedy at the height of a brilliant career.

Helen looked in the rear view mirror and realized she was being followed. The dark vehicle, its headlights on bright to keep her from seeing clearly, was closing in. She stepped on the gas and began racing around the city's streets.

"Don't let her get away," said Agent Domi to his partner. Probert, the more experienced driver, was behind the wheel.

Helen had spent enough time as a general assignment reporter in the city to understand the rhythm of the streets at all hours of the day or night. She knew where pedestrians were likely to be walking across the street regardless of the traffic signals. And she knew which streets were busy only in the day time, the buildings used for warehouses, manufacturing, photography studios, and the like. No one lived on those streets, and there was seldom reason for pedestrians to walk there after dark. Restaurants, apartments, bars, theaters, hotels, and other locations were far enough away that she knew she could safely accelerate before again having to blend with the night time traffic.

Helen also knew the myriad alleys that honeycombed the backs of buildings. By daylight many were blocked by delivery trucks. By night, except for the occasional lover or burglar, there were seldom any vehicles parked there. The only pedestrians were derelicts seeking safe shelter after dark, and they stayed to the side, sleeping on cardboard stretched over steam grates.

Under normal circumstances, Helen would have easily outmaneuvered her pursuers. She knew which one way streets she could take going the wrong way with little risk of striking cars. She knew where she could make good time cutting through an alley and where an alley formed a T requiring a slow, careful turn right or left. But the signal being sent from the homing device attached to her car enabled them to maintain the pursuit.

Frustrated and frightened, Helen turned into the first alley she approached, never thinking about where it went. She opened the door, rolled out low, slammed the door to extinguish the inside light, then got to her feet and began running.

On one side was a fire escape. It was designed so that the ladder rose up, ten feet above the ground, usable only by someone coming down from an upper floor. The only way to climb was to find a large trash can or other object from which she could jump and grab hold of the rungs.

Hearing the pursuers' car, she realized there was no time for anything but running. What she did not see was that she had chosen a dead-end alley. High walls, thick weeds, and mounds of trash greeted her before she had run a few yards more. At the same time she heard the other vehicle stop, the doors open, and the voices of her pursuers.

"She must have gone up to the roof," said Agent Domi, analyzing the situation as he could see it. Helen realized that she was lucky she had parked the car at the mouth of the alley. Otherwise they would have known she was trapped. "I'll go up from here. You swing around to the other side and make sure she doesn't come down over there."

Helen had flattened herself on the ground, covering her body with trash to try and blend in with her surroundings. In the daylight she would have been obvious. In the harsh light from the occasional street lamp illuminating the alley, she was perfectly camouflaged. Now, with the men apparently going in two wrong directions, she felt safe breaking cover. Slowly she stood up, moving stealthily towards her car. As she started to reach for the door, a hand touched her shoulder and another grabbed her wrist.

Before Helen could cry out, her assailant pushed firmly against her shoulder from behind while pulling her wrist backwards. She was forced to the ground, knowing her shoulder would be dislocated if she tried to resist.

Two other hands grabbed Helen's free arm, bringing her left wrist back to where her right wrist had been pinioned. Then handcuffs were clamped on her wrists and both assailants released their hold. "If you yell, we'll Mace you," one of the assailants warned. "No one can hear you, but we don't want to draw a crowd. You're coming with us, and any further resistance is just going to get you hurt."

Bronson Pearl was angry, frustrated, and confused. The more he thought about what he had seen and heard, the more confused he became.

First there was the Rapture. The event had to be the Rapture, at least as Helen explained it and as the Bible confirmed. Too many good people had disappeared. Too many of those left behind put the lie to Macalusso's explanation for what had happened.

But there was also the incident with the missiles and the armies of the world. There was instant peace in the midst of what appeared to be total war. Surely this was the warrior king so many people believed would be the Messiah. Jesus was the good shepherd, killed for the sins of the world, yet the army of the Caesars continued its violence for many years after His death on the cross. And yet Macalusso could not speak the name of Jesus, and hadn't the Bible discussed the power of that name over all the evil of the world?

"Besides," thought Bronson, angrily. "I just can't believe that the prophets of the Old Testament could see into the future. I can't believe that whoever wrote the book of Revelation knew what our lives would be like today."

He opened the car door and noticed the envelope containing a Gideon Bible and a single white cassette tape, the type used by commercial production facilities. He knew that Helen must have placed the envelope there.There was no writing on the cassette tape, no label. He placed it in his cassette player, started the car, and began listening as he drove.

First there was the announcer telling him, "You're listening to Point of View on the USA Radio Network." This was followed by the voice of Marlin Maddoux, someone with whom Bronson was unfamiliar.

"Welcome back to Point of View. I'm Marlin Maddoux. Today we're talking about one of the questions that every Christian has been asked at one time or another. If God really exists, then why doesn't he simply show himself to the world?

"I mean, He's God. He can do anything He wants. Right?

"Well, today we're going to answer that very question by talking about one of the most important elements of the Christian experience, Faith."

"And faith is what lets us know in our hearts that even long after our loved ones may have departed, their spirit still lives forever in the presence of the Lord. As the Bible says, absent from the body, present with the Lord."

Bronson, listening intently, touched the rewind button, replaying, "...that even long after our loved ones may have departed, their spirit still lives forever in the presence of the Lord."

Suddenly he stopped, turned his truck around on the dark road, and began accelerating rapidly.

It was almost one o'clock in the morning when Bronson reached the cemetery. The big iron gates were locked, but there was still access through breaks in the fence large enough for one person to squeeze through. He took a small penlight from the glove compartment and began walking the all too familiar grounds, finally stopping by a head-stone that read: JAMES STEVEN PEARL 1929-1991. Below that was a scripture reference, 1 Thessalonians 4:16-17.

Bronson approached the headstone like a shy little boy inter-rupting his father's quiet time of reading the newspaper after work. He dropped to one knee, brushed some dirt from the stone, and sadly said, "Hi, Dad."

Suddenly Bronson felt awkward, as he had when he was a teenager too cool to ask his father the questions for which only the older man had answers. For a while he had been openly disdainful of his father. James Pearl was a newsman and one whose respect he came to crave, so much did he respect the man. But James was also a man who left school in eighth grade to support a widowed mother and several younger siblings. He never went to high school, never set foot in a classroom other than his church's Bible study groups, and that didn't seem to count. Yet he was a voracious reader, more aware of politics, religion, and the affairs of the world than Bronson had become as an international correspondent. And he utilized this background to become a success in a field dominated by men who sometimes held multiple degrees.

James also read the Bible. Each day he would work through portions of the Old and New Testaments, at first just seeking to com-plete the book which he did once a year. Later he went to the library and found commentaries, histories, and interpretations of the text. He became somewhat of a lay theologian, a simple man of deep faith and understanding. He never became angry with his son's failure to use his superior education to try and learn even more about the Lord than James had done. Yet Bronson knew that his own questioning heart was far more of a disappointment to the older man than his entry into broadcast journalism instead of the print world.

The two men just began to know each other as friends in Bronson's adulthood when James Pearl developed the prostate cancer that eventually took his life. As with everything else, the elder Pearl had been stoic about the pain until he found himself passing out at the wheel of his car. He only crashed once, and fortunately only a mail box was injured in that experience, but that was enough to truly scare him. He went to see the doctor who told him that the only way something could have been done would be if he had come earlier. They could try aggressive chemotherapy, radiation treatment, radical surgery, and all manner of medicine. But the fact was that the cancer had entered his lymphatic system. His body was riddled with it. It was only a matter of weeks or months no matter what was done in the name of treatment.

And so James decided to do nothing but enjoy life, which he did for almost six months longer than anyone thought would be possible. It was only during the last week that he was too weak to be out of a wheelchair, and when he went into a coma his last day of life, he did so at home, surrounded by loved ones, assisted by a home hospice worker, at peace.

The death had been emotionally shattering, though Bronson subverted and thus prolonged the grief as he worked to meet the demands of his own life and career. Still he mourned. Not for the past. They had shared too little in days gone by. Instead his grief was for the present and future they would never have together.

This time Bronson did need to talk about the Bible, about faith. As he sat staring at the grave barely illuminated by a quarter moon on a cloud filled night, he said, "What was it, Dad? What made you decide with all your heart to believe this stuff? I mean you never saw in your whole lifetime what I've seen in the past week.

"This Macalusso guy is...well, he's the real thing, Dad. He must be. I saw him. I saw him do stuff that no one could possibly do. He's done something that not even Jesus could do. He brought peace to the whole world. And yet...

"Dad, just about the whole world believes everything this guy says, and my mind tells me they're right to do so. But my heart...

"I don't really believe, Dad. I don't know if its the discernment you always talked about or if I'm just a cynical fool. All I know is that something's holding me back. I can't explain it, but it's something that keeps tugging at me.

"Helen's part of it. She's convinced he's evil. She calls him the Antichrist and keeps showing me all sorts of books and tapes and Bible passages that justify her position. And she may be right. But there's something else. Something..."

Tears began to stream down Bronson's face. He realized that this was the first open, honest, heart felt conversation he had ever held with his father, and his father was dead.

"Oh God, Dad! I wish you were here with me now. I know you'd know what to say. You always did. I just didn't know when to listen."

Bronson touched the tombstone, the cold slab of marble offering no comfort. Yet as he touched the smooth material, the moonlight momentarily broke through the clouds, once again illuminating the grave. JAMES STEVEN PEARL 1929-1991. 1 Thessalonians 4:16-17.

It was the Bible verse that caught his attention. He had read it when his father's Will requested the verse be part of the memorial, but he had long forgotten the particular passage. Sensing that somehow it was important, that his father was trying to give him understanding long after death, he hurriedly returned to his car and opened the Bible. "For the Lord himself shall descend from heaven with a shout, with the voice of the archangel, and with the trumpet of God: and the dead in Christ shall rise first. Then we which are alive and remain shall be caught up together with them in the clouds, to meet the Lord in the air: and so shall we ever be with the Lord."

Bronson sat for a moment, rereading the verse, thinking. Helen Hannah's grandmother had been one of the disappeared. Between her leaving and the material she left behind, Helen had all the proof she needed about God, Jesus, and Macalusso.

Bronson was different. He understood Helen's emotions, yet he also accepted the potential validity of Macalusso's statements. After all, who but God truly knew what was in each of our hearts?

The real question was about the dead, those who offered no threat to Macalusso, no reason to be removed.

There was a portable shovel and some other emergency equipment in a box in the back of his truck. Never knowing where he might be caught on assignment, he carried the shovel, some flares, one of those emergency CB Radios that plugged into the cigarette lighter socket, a flashlight, jumper cables, and a bag of kitty litter to give traction on ice. Helen used to tease him about trying to make up for never having been a Boy Scout as a kid, but now he was relieved he had the tools. He took the shovel and carefully went back into the cemetery, walking to the grave.

The work was difficult. The shovel, a two piece unit that broke down for easy carrying, was sturdy but not designed for heavy use. It was a camping tool, and no one expected to have to dig several feet of dirt when sleeping in the open. He had to bend awkwardly each time he forced the blade into the ground, then carefully bend his knees before lifting so his back would remain straight. Otherwise he would strain himself and be unable to continue.

The earth was soft, the one blessing in what he was doing. Yet as he dug he felt as though he was someone in a bad horror movie. Old movie images of Dr. Victor Frankenstein sending his assistant Igor out to find a corpse kept flashing through his head. He was sickened by his actions, yet he knew he had to continue.

"Lord, if this is sinful, please understand," he prayed. "I have to know. I have to see for myself."

He kept working, this time with thoughts of Thomas filled with doubts. Thomas had come to believe when Jesus offered to let him touch the wounds in his hands, legs, and side.

I am no worse than Thomas, he told himself. And the story I may have to tell is as important as the one the disciples came to spread throughout the land.

And so he continued, hoping he would finish before daylight. He left his suit jacket draped over the headstone, but his shoes and pants were mud covered. His shirt was covered with sweat and darkened from the mud that clung to the wet cloth. His arms ached from the unfamiliar exercise, and as he neared the end of his effort, he worried that his actions were making a mockery of his father's unquestioning faith.

It was well over an hour after he started that Bronson's shovel at last touched the lid of the casket. It took another half hour to clear enough dirt away.

"Dad, I don't know if I want you to be in there or not. I love you, and the idea of seeing your rotted flesh fills me with dread. Yet if Helen is right, I have nothing to fear. I have only to rejoice. I have..."

Bronson was scared. He was saying words, he realized, just to avoid the action he had to take. "Lord, give me strength," he said, forcing open the coffin.

The first thing he saw was the suit. "My Sunday best," his father had called it, as proud of the polyester, off the rack, Sears special as Bronson had been of his far more expensive first Brooks Brothers original. His dad wore that polyester suit every time he went to church, and he wanted to be buried in it.

The last time Bronson had seen the suit, it covered his father's remains. Now it lay neatly folded at the bottom of the empty coffin, looking as though it was waiting to be hung and put back on the rack.

A wedding ring, Timex watch, and a thin gold chain with a small cross on it were on top of the clothes. In addition, there was an open Bible, face down on the other possessions. Bronson picked up the Bible, propped his flashlight against the dirt, and let the light fall on the page. The book had been turned to 1 Corinthians 15, several sentences highlighted with the yellow marker his father always carried for noting whatever he felt was important when he read. "For the trumpet shall sound, and the dead shall be raised. Death is swallowed up in victory. O death, where is they sting? O grave, where is thy victory?"

And then he knew. Not in his mind. In his heart. Bronson Pearl, for the first time in his life, was more than a believer. He understood the truth, the joy in the lives of the people the Antichrist called the haters. He laughed through his tears as he thought about having missed the great shuttle bus to victory, the one caught by those who had been raptured.

Now he believed. Lord be praised, how he believed. His father was not lost. Helen's grandmother was not lost. One had died. One had been raptured. All were together. And though he had been left behind, though he knew there would be a time of trial where he would have to deal with Macalusso, victory would ultimately be that of the Lord. Of that he was certain, and it was a faith he would profess to his death if that was what was necessary.

ELEVEN

Day Six

With the passage of time, the public's reaction to Franco Macalusso began to change. The rejoicing continued, of course. And families were still trying to come to grips with the loss of those who had disappeared, and with the shock of discovering that there were still some haters in their midst. But the horror of near chaos and total destruction was no longer a possibility. Peace was in the land. Factories, schools, and businesses of all sorts remained viable. As a result, most people were gradually returning to the familiar, catching the news at the end of the day or through the morning newspaper.

In the WNN studios, Len Parker realized the problem as he watched the latest speech from Macalusso. It had been taped for later broadcast, allowing him to arrange for the fine tuning of the recorded images.

"Hold it," said Parker, watching the tape in the editing room.

"Freeze that picture."

The image was stopped and it was as bad as he had thought. Part of Macalusso's appeal came from the excitement people witnessed him generating. They delighted in his walking through throngs of people to get to a podium. They were intrigued by the sheer numbers cramming remote viewing areas, often showing up just to be a part of the throng themselves.

Now there was less appeal. The people knew what had happened, understood the Messiah was in their midst, yet figured that since they must have led good lives by his standard, they should continue as they had before. After all, from what Macalusso said, they would not have been left behind if they had fallen short of pleasing him.

The latest speech was proof of that fact. There was a crowd befitting a minor celebrity, perhaps, but not one worthy of the Messiah. "Change that crowd. You've got some earlier footage. Edit in more people."

"No problem," said the editor. "The computer can even make him look like he's walking on water."

Parker glared. "Are you one of the haters?" he asked, angrily.

"A joke, Mr. Parker. Can't you take a joke? Lighten up. The Messiah's come and all's right with the world. I'll add the crowd."

Suddenly the sound of a woman's voice startled Parker. He turned quickly as he heard Helen Hannah say, "So even God needs your electronic enhancement?"

Helen walked into the room, her handcuffed wrists locked behind her back. Agent Domi was holding her arm, though she made no move to resist. Watching Parker's actions only reinforced the truth of the Bible's predictions. The Antichrist was powerful, the most powerful force of evil the world had ever encountered, yet he was nothing when compared with Jesus. "You don't think he can convince the world who he is without your editing out the people's right to decide for themselves."

"Well, Miss Hannah. I see your version of God didn't do much to help you. Or is a miracle going to break the chain of those handcuffs?" Then, turning to Domi, he ordered, "Take her to my office. I'll be right there."

It was the first mistake, though neither Parker nor the men most closely associated with him realized it at the time. Helen Hannah was beloved by the WNN staff. She was a respected journalist, but she was also a troubled woman with a difficult past. She could empathize with people from all walks of life because, to some degree, she had experienced pain that paralleled or matched their own. She was also a delightful character whose romance with Bronson Pearl was the subject of gossip and frequent amusement.

There was nothing Helen Hannah could have done to warrant her being held as she was. She had committed no crimes, and if her religious beliefs prevented her from believing in Macalusso, well, she would probably come around. She was a sensible woman, after all. And this was the Messiah, the loving lord of all sent by God.

So why was she handcuffed? Why did she hold Parker in such disdain? Why...?

Inside Parker's office, neither of the men made any effort to remove the handcuffs from Helen's wrists. They wanted them as a constant reminder of who she was and how much her life was in their hands.

"You've got no idea what you're up against, Miss Hannah."

"I have a better idea than you think, and I'm not afraid of you."

"Well, you should be! Don't mistake our talk of peace and unity for weakness.

"People want peace at any price, and so we will give it to them. They want to believe that they are more than just flesh and blood, and we'll tell them they are."

"I think the serpent did the same thing in the Garden of Eden," said Helen.

"Child's play, Miss Hannah. What we have done is beyond anything written until now. And all anyone has to do is worship the Messiah."

"You mean Franco Macalusso, don't you? And if they don't worship this man?"

"Then they die. The choices were gone the day of his coming.

"You have never seen the wrathful side of Franco Macalusso. Do you really understand who he is and what he's capable of? You worship him or you die what might be a death more horrible than you can ever begin to imagine. The choice is a no-brainer, Miss Hannah. It's too bad you don't see that."

Then turning to Agent Domi, he said, "Take her away."

It was night when Franco Macalusso made his next address, the timing of which deliberately coincide with the largest possible number of people in the world being awake. It would be rebroadcast, of course, but the greatest impact would be on those who heard it live.

The crowd in the stadium where the address was given was large. More than 100,000 people, almost half of them standing shoulder to shoulder, were listening to the speech where it was being made. Yet unlike the first address, the number of people watching large screen, closed circuit broadcasts had diminished. The WNN cameras seeking local color around the globe had their broadcast images enhanced before airing. A thousand people were transformed into ten thousand, and a hundred people were made to look like a sea of eager faces. It was the magic of television, and it was effective.

"Today is your day!" stated Macalusso. "I am about to show you wonders beyond anything you have ever imagined. I am here to lead you into a whole new world of human possibility.

"In this new world you will discover the powers of divinity that I have buried deep within your soul. But you must go together, as a single creation. And even though I have removed the tares from the wheat, there are still others who have chosen not to join in this great moment. They have become cancer cells in our collective body, and until they have been removed, you cannot take the giant leap into godhood. They are standing in your way. I am telling you right now, my children. You are all gods. The power lies within you. It always has."

The crowds listened, spellbound. This was a message in which they could believe. This was a message that asked little of them but promised much. They had long known there had to be more to life than the challenges of the Bible. Now they knew the answer. They, too, were gods. They had only to rid the world of the haters and their rightful inheritance would be given. They would have powers and abilities beyond their wildest imaginations.

As the speech ended, the people who had been in attendance moved into the streets. The few who wanted to return home to their families were stopped by members of what were becoming mobs. "Are you a hater?" they were asked. "Do you accept President Macalusso as your lord and savior?" "Are you willing to destroy those who stand in the way of our blessed destiny?"

Occasionally someone would mumble something about a babysitter, a sick spouse, a child in need. Such explanations would be greeted with derision, and if the person did not change his or her mind, violence invariably ensued. Some were beaten to death. One man in a suit had his arms pinned with his belt, his necktie removed and used as a garrote, his corpse lifted onto a telephone pole as an example to others.

WNN had reporters in the field trying to make sense of what was taking place. Janet Shutt was working just outside County Stadium, trying to get a sense of the mob. Tens of thousands of people had gathered to watch the Messiah's speech on massive screens positioned around the stadium. They were excited as they left, singing, praying, praising Macalusso, but also having an undercurrent of anger.

"I don't see how these haters think they can put themselves and their paranoid ideas ahead of the whole world," said one man Shutt stopped for an interview. "Look at the promise that has been made. We can gain the godhood within us if we but rid the land of this handful of.... Well, I'd rather not use such words on television but we all know what the haters are like.

"I mean, let's face it. These are the same narrow minded religious zealots whose ideas have stood in the way of peace for far too long. Now the Messiah himself is finally here as everyone with half an eye to see has witnessed, and these haters even put themselves before him."

"I can hardly wait for the fulfilment of the promise," said a woman who had stopped to listen to the interview. The camera shifted to her as she continued, "The Messiah says that we're all gods. He says that we have unbelievable powers within us all. Since that's true, we've got to do whatever it takes to get rid of the haters who are standing in our way."

The mob scenes were just the cover Macalusso had desired. The real action taking place was one coordinated by his military forces throughout the world. This was the night that the Antichrist was going to solidify his power by terrorizing, or even eliminating if necessary, the new Christians who refused to bow their heads and bend their knees in his presence. It would be a night much like Crystal Night when Adolph Hitler had his storm troopers destroy the homes and store windows of the Jews, after first assuring a total news blackout except as information came from his loyal officers.

This time WNN was given exclusive right to film, Len Parker hand picking the reporters who would handle the coverage. "The Messiah wants this to be a pool effort," he explained. "The footage shot by WNN will be made available to all other television networks without charge. We just can not risk the reporters' lives if the haters become violent and try to retaliate."

Bronson Pearl's body ached. He had been awake for 30 hours and knew his reflexes were slow, his thoughts not as clear as he would like them. What mattered was getting away from New York, from the

APOCALYPSE

WNN headquarters, from Len Parker.

As thorough as the Macalusso organization might be, they had only been in power less than a week. They did not understand the full nature of the regional bureaus, their attitude towards the top on-air people, and their excitement when working with the most respected professionals.

Bronson drove to Boston, to the WNN bureau where he told them he had been assigned to handle some field work. There was too much taking place with the forthcoming speech by the Messiah when Bronson arrived, and then with the need to record the aftermath when it was over for anyone to question his presence. He said he would be observing what happened, then would need a camera crew to take him to where he could make a satellite link. He needed to go live with a commentary, something they had seen him do from the Middle East.

As the violence took place, Bronson sat in the satellite uplink truck, watching the monitor, awaiting the time when he could be fed to every station in the world tuned to WNN. As he waited, he looked in horror at scenes that would have been outrageous if seen on a television action/adventure show. The fact that these were real events happening to real people made matters all the worse.

From Toronto, the first scene was illuminated by a single light mounted on a hand held ENG camera. There was no voice over, only the "cinema verite'" style of taping that let the viewer witness the event as though in the midst of it all.

Several soldiers wearing bulletproof clothing and carrying high powered hand guns, electronic prods meant to cause disabling muscle convulsants, and potent chemical sprays, used a battering ram to break down the door. It was a device normally used when entering locked homes used by drug dealers. It allowed rapid entry before the evidence could be destroyed.

The door smashed easily and the camera stayed with the soldiers as they rushed from room to room, pausing just long enough for them to check to make certain there was no one waiting in ambush with a weapon. Finally they reached the first bedroom, the camera pausing briefly on a sign reading, "Shhh. Child of God, beloved of Jesus, sleeping here." Then he followed the soldiers into the room.

The men grabbed a small child from his bed, one soldier ripping a cross from the wall, holding it long enough for the videographer to take a close-up, then crushing it with his boot.

In Miami, a camera equipped with a light amplifying lens revealed a man in a small apartment over a closed restaurant. He was holding a small child, lowering him into the waiting arms of a woman standing in the shadows of the alley below. The woman caught the child, easing him to the ground. Then, as she looked up for her second child, she was roughly grabbed, forced to the ground, and handcuffed. In the apartment above, the remaining child was ripped from the arms of his father, who was struck with the butt of a pistol when he tried to resist.

A moment later, the family was reunited in the front of the building. The man's jaw was broken, his face covered with blood. He had to be held erect by two officers who showed no compassion for his intense pain. The children were crying, reaching for their parents but restrained by the other soldiers. And the woman, her hands cuffed behind her back, was being held by her hair, her face forced upward, as her neighbors jeered, ridiculed, and spat at her.

The soldiers ignored the woman's pleas for a doctor to help her husband or the chance to take her children to the home of a friend. "They're not haters. They believe in the Messiah. Please, check them out. Just let my children go."

Ignoring the pleas, the soldiers forced the couple in one patrol car, the children in another. "They'll be with you while the Messiah decides whether you all should live or die."

As the cars moved down the streets, the neighbors cheered, praising Macalusso.

There were other scenes, other arrests. In Minneapolis, a mob attacked a secret religious book store. One of the New Christians had quietly gathered as many of the possessions of the disappeared as he could, adding materials stolen from closed book stores whose stock of Bibles, tapes, and Christian books had not yet been burned. Then he built shelves in his basement, organizing what he had and brought other new Christians he met into the room. One of his customers had talked too freely with a believer in the Messiah, who had then gone to the police. But the man's neighbors, learning what was taking place, meted out their own justice by fire before the man's home could be secured.

In Los Angeles, Bibles were removed from churches, transported to MacArthur Park, covered with gasoline, and ignited.

Soon other burnings of New Testaments were taking place in Tokyo, Pretoria, Hong Kong, Rome, Sao Paolo, Paris, and elsewhere. As one reporter happily observing such a scene exclaimed on camera, "What is truly ironic is the fact that the very book that had once divided the world is now bringing it together. Every copy of the New Testament is being zealously hunted down and burned in fires like this one, across the country and around the world."

On late night television, one comedian began reading a list of the ten most outrageous quotes of the Deceiver. "And here's this one from the book of Matthew which all you book burners out there know we won't have to read much longer, praise Macalusso. Anyway, it says, 'Do not think that I have come to bring peace to the earth; I have not come to bring peace, but a sword.'"

"Read further, you jerk," shouted a man in the studio audience. He rose to his feet, oblivious to the security men moving towards him. "Read that whole passage."

"Hey, a hater among us!" shouted the comedian. "What, you got the book memorized? Trying to corrupt my audience?"

The guards grabbed the man, pulling him back towards the exit. "Why don't you shoot me?" the man shouted. "That passage ends with the words, 'those who lose their life for my sake will find it.' Read the book. Don't burn it!"

It was late morning when the violence of the night before was finally over, flames doused, the arrested moved to holding camps for processing in the courts. On an isolated hill overlooking the bay, Bronson Pearl stood alone, microphone in hand, speaking into the camera. "Don't worry about the timing," Bronson told the man running the satellite uplink truck. "Just use my code when you send this and they'll cut in to the broadcast to carry me live. It's a system we use when we've got a breaking story in the Middle East and a live report must take precedence. They'll understand in New York. No reason to call and coordinate." No reason to alert them to my actions, he thought, though he dared not tell them that little detail.

"If you say so, Mr. Pearl. It's not routine over here, though."

"It's not routine anywhere, Louie. I got permission to use it in this way when they sent me here to do a commentary on the aftermath of the day's events."

The camera operator adjusted the lens, took a sound level, then signalled the reporter to begin. "I'm Bronson Pearl, and for those of you who have watched my broadcasts over the years, you know that I've always told you the truth as I knew it. *Time* magazine called me the most trusted man in American broadcasting a few weeks ago, and while I'm not certain I deserve that title, I have never gone on the air without first looking at all the facts.

"I was in the valley of Armageddon when the war we all so desperately feared seemed to have begun. I was present when President Macalusso arrived, and I saw first hand the vanishing of the weapons of destruction. I heard him declare himself the Messiah, and I've seen the wonders he has performed. I have also investigated him quite thoroughly, which is the reason for my report to you tonight.

"Franco Macalusso is *not* the Messiah. He has not returned to save the planet from the forces of evil. The fact is that quite the opposite is true. Franco Macalusso is, in fact, the embodiment of evil itself. He is the one the Bible calls the Antichrist.

"I have always told you whatever is important, whatever you need to know to understand a world crisis on which I have reported. That is why I'm asking you today to please, listen to what I am saying. President Macalusso is the Antichrist. He is not who he says he is.

"Do you think the Messiah fears a book such as the Bible? Of course not. He has ordered the burning of every book that holds the truth about his lies. The Bibles do not promote hatred as he would have

254

you believe. Not even close. The Bibles tell the truth about God, about the real Messiah, and about the signs, actions, and ultimate evil of the Antichrist.

"President Macalusso is the Antichrist. He is..."

"Cut the sound!" shouted Len Parker. "And who in blazes allowed that hater to pre-empt our broadcast? I'll kill the..."

Suddenly Parker realized he was still on the set of WNN News. His words and actions were being seen by more than two dozen employees, all of whom had been shocked and fascinated by the broadcast.

"Sound is cut!" came a voice over the loudspeaker. "The patch code was used to signal a breaking story that had to take precedence over whatever was on the air. It's so routine, no one thought about it. We'll break the video feed in a moment."

"How dare he pull a stunt like this. I'll have him killed. I'll..."

The men and women in the room stared, shocked. Some were angry with Bronson for his words denouncing the Messiah. Some were angry with Parker. Some were confused. And a few, who had been nodding their heads as though in agreement with what they were hearing, quietly went back to work, saying nothing.

Bronson Pearl was fairly certain his broadcast would be stopped, but there was no way of knowing when. He continued talking even as he heard the sirens in the distance. He continued talking as the police cars arrived, a dozen guards rushing over to where he was standing. They grabbed him, slamming the microphone to the ground. They handcuffed the videographer who stepped away from the camera and raised his arms in surrender.

TWELVE

Day Seven

The "spontaneous" celebrations had been ordered by Franco Macalusso. They were to be part of a worldwide recognition of the Messiah. Government offices were closed. Schools were closed. And in those cities where parades had been arranged, businesses were ordered to let their employees have whatever time off was needed to let their families enjoy the show.

Billboards, banners, and signs flashing photos of Macalusso proclaimed, "He's back!" "The Messiah Is Here" and similar sentiments. Bands played joyous music.

Apart from the celebrations there was a less joyous sight. The number of arrests of followers of the Deceiver were growing beyond anyone's expectations. Local jails and prisons were soon filled to capacity. College buildings, stadiums, and areas through the country became make-shift prisons. By encircling them with razor wire, converting observation areas to guard ports, and using officers with attack dogs to constantly patrol the perimeter, instant prisons had been created.

The hand picked guards were totally loyal to the Messiah. They understood that their first concern was re-education. They also understood that though efforts had been made to assure the relative comfort of the detained during the re-education process, those who would not serve him were to die. It was a carrot and stick approach, the specially chosen men and women comfortable with either end.

Giant television monitors were wired throughout the makeshift prisons. WNN broadcasts would be shown throughout the day and night now that the network was firmly in the control of the Messiah. Taped programs, along with special speeches and successful group counselling sessions, would all be shown to help the people understand why they should embrace the Messiah. Then, in a few weeks or a few months, the people who finally understood Macalusso's version of the truth would be returned to society. The remainder would be killed as surely as a laser vaporizes a cancer when a surgeon aggressively attacks the deadly growth. Len knew that the Messiah believed that all but a handful of the very weakest believers among the haters would have to be put to death.

Transportation had originally utilized vans and police cruisers, but again such items were too limited. For a while Len Parker thought about commandeering city buses to transport the haters to these "re-education centers. However, the Messiah had vetoed such a suggestion, reminding Parker that if they used enough buses to be effective, public transportation would be crippled and people would want to know why. Men and women taking baby steps towards their full conversion to unquestioning belief in the Messiah might stumble in their walk. They would question why, after so many had disappeared because of impure hearts, there could be so many more being arrested. That was why they had chosen to use cattle transport trucks. The prisoners would ride standing up, their bodies pressed together, allowing the maximum number of people per vehicle. The slats in the trucks provided air yet also revealed the prisoners in a way that invited taunting and humiliation.

APOCALYPSE

The New York holding facility was approximately forty miles outside of Manhattan in the stadium of a large community college. Women had been separated from men, children from parents. Isolation, fear, and worry were to be used to assure cooperation.

Bronson spotted Helen as soon as he arrived. She was with the women being taken from one of the trucks to the processing area.

Bronson hurried to Helen's side, taking her hand as she stood in line. "I should never have doubted your courage, my darling," she told him. "I didn't see your broadcast, but the women who were just brought in talk of nothing else. They praise the Lord for your bravery."

"I have the awful feeling that all I did was assure my arrest."

"It doesn't matter. The Lord knows what was in your heart when you did it. Oh, Bronson, I..."

"Break it up, you two!" shouted one of the guards. "This isn't the nightly news. You, Hannah, stay with the women. As for you, Pearl..." He reached out and jabbed Bronson in the stomach with an electrified cattle prod, pressing a button and jolting him with the electricity. As Bronson doubled over in pain, the guard mocked him.

"Bronson Pearl, the most trusted journalist in America. I hereby dub you King of the haters!" And with that he jolted him again, this time on the head. The newsman fell to the ground in agony.

"Stop that! You're going to kill him!" shouted Helen from across the yard. She started to run, was grabbed, handcuffed, then chained to a post in the women's section. "You don't understand."

"Don't worry. We're not going to kill him," laughed one of the guards. "That would spoil the fun we have planned for them."

. "These new followers of The One Who Came Before Me are passive fools," Franco Macalusso had explained to Len Parker and his top security aides. "Remember how he went to his own death? Even carried his own cross? They are all like that. We will have no trouble with them."

Agents Probert and Parker had been ordered to stay at the prison where Helen and Bronson were being kept to assure they did not get away. The Messiah was using WNN extensively. He did not want any surprises from the haters. He also wanted the two most important voices on the network to face punishment in prime time. For the believers, it would be an occasion for joy. For the hidden followers of the Deceiver, it would be a warning to change their ways or suffer the same fate.

In the warden's office, actually a converted press box with an excellent view of the make-shift prison camp, the television was tuned constantly to WNN. As the two agents spoke, the announcer was saying, "Even though every word that comes out of the Messiah's mouth is both glorious and vital, tonight's message promises to be the most moving of them all. Not only will he tell us of his continued outpouring of love to every corner of the globe, he is also going to show us the way to godhood."

Agent Probert had been ignoring the talk, standing by the window, staring at the regular arrival of the cattle trucks, each unloading more and more of the followers of the Deceiver. The number of people who no longer questioned Jesus was enormous, especially considering the fact that the same scene was being played out in all fifty states and throughout the world.

"There are more of these haters than any of us dared to believe," said Probert. "If they keep pouring in like this, I don't know how we're going to manage to process them all."

Parker ignored his concerns. He knew that ultimately this was not about re-education. The new followers of the Deceiver came to see the disappeared as proof of the ideas they had discovered, ideas that were now certainties in their hearts. Instead of being impressed with Macalusso, they were convinced that he was the antichrist, not the true Messiah. They would happily go to their deaths before considering renouncing Jesus.

It was the ones who remained undecided, who had learned

enough from the papers about the disappeared to question the Messiah, but were not yet committed to the Deceiver, whom he was determined to change. "Maybe once they see their beloved Bronson Pearl executed on national television, they'll take a step back and realize that this is not a game. You're in or you're out. There are no other options. And if they'd rather die than worship the Messiah....well, that's their choice. But make no mistake, the Messiah will crush anyone who stands in his way."

In the holding area, a loudspeaker was broadcasting the latest speech by Macalusso while an elderly woman sat on the ground, her head down as though sleeping.

"This is a day of unity, of love, and of peace," said the amplified voice of Macalusso. "It is time for you to join me as I show you the way of total love and harmony."

"Hey, over there on the side. What is that old woman doing?" asked one of the guards watching with binoculars from the top of the stadium/holding facility.

"Sleeping, it looks like," said a second guard, straining to see.

"Her lips are moving, and the way she's holding her hands.... Radio Figby to check her out."

"It was written long ago that God is love," said Macalusso's voice. "Have I not shown you great love?"

"It's a Bible," radioed Figby, racing over to the old woman, grabbing the small book from her hands, and tearing the pages. Then he hauled her roughly to her feet. "That should have been burned before you got here. How'd you hide it?"

The woman was silent.

"Get Allison over here," Figby radioed. "I want this one taken to the infirmary and strip searched to see what else she's hiding."

The guard put the woman in a painful wrist hold, dragging her towards one of the side areas. As he pulled her, another prisoner tried to stop him. Before he could grab Figby, the female guard, Allison, rushed over, striking the male prisoner with the butt of her rifle, dislocating his jaw, breaking his nose, and sending him sprawling to the ground.

"Do you not feel a new love burning in your hearts? A new love for life and for others? That is the love of God. And I can give it to you, for I am the Lord."

It was nightfall when the guards began forcing the prisoners back into the cattle cars in which they had been brought to the New York stadium. There were hundreds of followers of the Deceivers being held there, and they greatly outnumbered the soldiers who kept them prisoner. If there was a riot, there was a chance the prisoners could gain control of the holding area, then move back into the city. That was why Parker insisted they be caged during the hanging of Bronson Pearl.

There was no time to build a proper gallows, and one really wasn't necessary. A gallows was designed to offer a quick death, the prisoner standing on the trap door with a noose around his neck. When the door was opened, the prisoner would drop, his neck would break, and he would die.

A less sophisticated hanging had the same results, but sometimes the victim would dangle a bit as he suffocated more slowly. The dance of death it was sometimes called, a punishment usually reserved for the most dastardly of criminals. Bronson Pearl may not have fit the profile of a prisoner deserving such a death at the time the form of execution originated, but a lingering dance on the gallows would shock the world. That was why the noose had been rigged between two of the cattle cars, a camera in place to record the event, the trapped prisoners able to see through the slats without being able to go to his assistance.

"Hey, Pearl, ready to show the world what kind of hero you

really are?" called one of the guards as he prepared a step ladder on which Bronson would have to stand for the execution. The noose would be placed around his neck, tightened securely, then the ladder kicked out from under him.

"Get ready to meet this God of yours, Pearl," laughed another guard. "Mine's already down here with me."

The men who were crowded together in the same holding container as Bronson Pearl were silent. Some were praying. Others were trying to find words that mattered. A few wept openly, unsure whether their tears were for God, Bronson, or themselves.

"Hey, it's okay, you guys. Our hope is not in this world. Never has been. We all know that.

"So I'm leaving this place a lot earlier than I planned. At least I know the truth I was too blind to see before the Rapture. Certainly we should thank God for giving us all a second chance."

"Amen," said one voice. "Praise the Lord," said another. "Amen to that." "Thank you, Jesus."

Len Parker and several guards walked to the truck. Four men positioned themselves, two on each side of the door, their automatic weapons pointed at the prisoners who were crowded together. Two other guards opened the door, the rest flanking Parker.

"In case any of you have any thoughts about rushing us, I have to tell you that the orders are to shoot you in the legs, then leave you in the cattle cars for the next 24 hours. The wounds will be very painful. They will bleed and fester. Many will become infected. Those of you who are lucky will die from shock, blood loss, and the trauma of the bullets. The rest of you will probably never walk again except in great agony. So if you think you want to either take control of the camp or die, think again. There is a third choice, it is mine, and the guards are prepared to act accordingly."

The door was opened, two guards roughly taking Bronson Pearl from the truck. As the door was slammed shut again, one of the guards kicked Pearl in the back of his knees, knocking him to the ground. His wrists were bound behind his back, then he was pulled to his feet and dragged towards the gallows.

Inside one of the women's trucks, Helen watched with horror. She knew she should not have waited so long to tell Bronson she would marry him. Her grandmother had been right. She should have grabbed for life while she could. Now her grandmother was gone, and soon...

One of the other women began singing the first verse of *Because He Lives*, her voice growing louder, bolder. By the time she reached the chorus, others throughout the holding yard had joined in. Len Parker was livid, yet there was nothing he could do short of killing them all to silence them, and such mass murder would have to wait. Too many of these haters still had families who might turn against the Messiah. It was better to wait until everyone was so committed to the new world order that the idea of killing a former loved one who persisted in following the Deceiver seemed a well reasoned idea.

Bronson looked over at Helen, their eyes meeting. Their love for each other was obvious, yet it was too late even to speak again. As Bronson was forced up the small step ladder, the noose placed around his neck, Helen suddenly screamed, "No! No! You can't do this!"

"But we can," said Parker. "Tonight is the ultimate ratings test. From what I hear, the death of Bronson Pearl will dominate the world. This is a bigger audience than the Olympics. In fact, we just might make this a two night event. Would WNN's leading anchor like to repeat tomorrow night what her boyfriend gets to do tonight?"

"My hope...Our hope is not in *this* world, Len."

Parker turned to the guard preparing to kick the ladder from under Bronson. "Just a few seconds more. The Messiah said to wait exactly for midnight."

On one wall of the holding area, a giant screen television was showing a close-up of Bronson, his neck in the noose. It was the same image that was being broadcast throughout the world.

"Twenty seconds to go," said Parker. "Nineteen. Eighteen. Seventeen."

APOCALYPSE

"I'm Bronson Pearl, and for those of you who have watched my broadcasts over the years, you know that I've always told you the truth as I knew it." The voice was coming from the speaker for the giant monitor. Parker looked up in horror, watching a repeat of the tape that had forced Bronson's arrest. "*Time* magazine called me the most trusted man in American broadcasting a few weeks ago, and while I'm not certain I deserve that title, I have never gone on the air without first looking at all the facts."

"Who in Hell put that into the broadcast feed?" shouted Parker. "I'll kill him. I swear, I'll kill him."

"I was in the valley of Armageddon when the war we all so desperately feared seemed to have begun. I was present when President Macalusso arrived, and I saw first hand the vanishing of the weapons of destruction. I heard him declare himself the Messiah, and I've seen the wonders he has performed. I have also investigated him quite thoroughly, which is the reason for my report to you tonight."

"Somebody get through to New York. Find out what's going on. Tell the guards to kill anyone they see. Tell the guards...." Parker suddenly realized he was powerless. He was too far away to handle whatever was happening, yet he was also responsible for the execution scheduled to take place.

Suddenly Bronson started to lose his balance. "Grab him!" shouted Parker. "Don't let him die until the whole world is watching. The Messiah will kill us all if he dies without an audience."

"Franco Macalusso is *not* the Messiah. He has not returned to save the planet from the forces of evil. The fact is that quite the opposite is true. Franco Macalusso is, in fact, the embodiment of evil itself. He is the one the Bible calls the antichrist."

One of the guards grabbed Bronson, helping him regain his balance. Then, as a precaution, he took the noose from the reporter's neck, leaving him on the stepladder, his wrists still bound.

"I have always told you whatever is important, whatever you need to know to understand a world crisis on which I have reported.

That is why I'm asking you today to please, listen to what I am saying. President Macalusso is the antichrist. He is not who he says he is."

"The 12 second delay," shouted Parker. "There was supposed to be a 12 second delay in my office." And then he realized he was not in his office, not anywhere near to where he could do anything about whatever was taking place.

"Do you think the Messiah fears a book such as the Bible? Of course not. Yet Macalusso has ordered the burning of every book that holds the truth about his lies. The Bibles do not promote hatred as he would have you believe. Not even close. The Bibles tell the truth about God, about the real Messiah, and about the signs, actions, and ultimate evil of the antichrist.

"President Macalusso is the antichrist."

In the WNN control room, Agent Domi sat smiling, looking at the two Parker loyalist guards he had handcuffed and gagged on the floor in front of him. "You men didn't go through the academy, did you?" he asked. They stared at him, silent, unable to reply.

"One of the things they taught us was to understand a man's weakness. Learn what he fears, then see why." He paused, listening to Bronson's comments. They were being broadcast to every part of the world, and the only way to stop them was to break into the control room at WNN where he was sitting with his two hostages. Several angry people had gathered outside his door, but they were unable to enter.

"Some fears are justified, of course. A man roaming the wilderness may fear large predators like bears or mountain lions. He may have been attacked or had friends attacked. He may carry a .44 magnum or a rifle for protection. That's a justified fear and you can't really use that when he becomes your enemy.

"But some fears reveal a weakness you can use. A man might be afraid of the dark, so you know that if he is your enemy, you should plan your attack by night. Then he not only has to combat you but also what is inside himself.

"And so we come to Franco Macalusso, this self-proclaimed Messiah."

The guards looked startled. Agent Domi had been one of the inner circle, a man of importance. For him to mock the Messiah was startling.

"I have known Franco Macalusso since I was with the United Nations. I was one of his special unit people and he brought me along with him when he became President of the European Union. I witnessed the miracles he did, and yes, I do believe they were miracles. One day I'll ask the real Messiah how it happened, but as I understand things, we have a few years before that takes place.

"Oh, I can see by your eyes that you have some questions. Well, if I live through this, you may be able to ask me. If not, I'll be in our Father's house and hopefully you will come to an understanding so that you can join me when it is your time.

"Anyway, when Macalusso began getting obsessed with destroying the New Testament, when he wouldn't bring himself to say the name of Jesus, I got to wondering. That's why I kept a few souvenirs from our search of that Edna Williams home after we arrested her granddaughter. That's why I read the books and watched the video. That's when I came to understand how a man who can make missiles vanish from the sky can also be terrified of a few words printed on paper or a scroll or whatever it was they were using a couple thousand years ago.

"Do you know what Franco Macalusso's real weakness is, gentlemen? It's truth. He is the antichrist, and as my late mother used to say when I was too stupid to get it, Jesus is Lord! Hallelujah!"

Len Parker was terrified. He had lost all control, not only of himself but also of the events of the moment in which the Messiah had placed him in charge. On the giant screen, he was watching a carefully made broadcast of audio and video material secretly recorded over the past few days. Only an insider with access to the tapes could have done it, and the only insider whose background included specialized electronic training was Agent Domi. But Domi was totally loyal, a true son of the Messiah. There was no way...

This time the voice being heard was Parker's. It was recorded during the conversation with Helen Hannah. "Don't mistake our talk of peace and unity for weakness.

"People want peace at any price, and so we will give it to them. They want to believe that they are more than just flesh and blood, and we'll tell them they are."

Helen's voice came on, saying, "I think the serpent did the same thing in the Garden of Eden."

"Child's play, Miss Hannah. What we have done is beyond anything written until now. And all anyone has to do is worship the Messiah."

"You mean Franco Macalusso, don't you? And if they don't worship this man?"

"Then they die. The choices were gone the day of his coming.

"You have never seen the wrathful side of Franco Macalusso. Do you really understand who he is and what he's capable of? You worship him or you die what might be a death more horrible than you can ever begin to imagine. The choice is a no-brainer, Miss Hannah. It's too bad you don't see that.

"Take her away."

Alerted by Parker and others, security officers and technical personnel were trying to break into the control room where Agent Domi was broadcasting. Because of the importance of WNN and networks like it, a decision had been reached many years earlier to make control rooms high security areas. The windows overlooking the studios were made from a special plastic that was stronger than Lexan, the material used in airplane windows. The doors were reinforced steel with special locks that could seal out keys from the outside. There was an independent oxygen filtration system and back-up power supply. While entry was possible, even the best prepared assailants would need at least an hour of constant effort to break through.

As the voices coming over the studio monitors reached the angry workers, they began stopping their efforts to break through. Instead, they began listening, then drifting over to the monitors. Instinctively they knew that the broadcast was not a fake. They knew that whatever was taking place was the result of Agent Domi or someone else having gotten a hold of tapes that were never meant for broadcast use.

At the prison camp, the guards had gathered below the screen meant to aid in re-education. What no one had expected was that Macalusso would lose control of what was shown. This time it was from the Jack Van Impe tape Domi had carefully copied for re-broadcast.

"True salvation and everlasting life are God's gift to everyone. And all you have to do is ask Him, with an open mind and an open heart. If you want Jesus to come into your life right now, then bow your heads and join me in praying the sinner's prayer."

In Mexico City, in a crowded cantina, several men had been watching a television screen, seeing the images being broadcast. A few of the men laughed derisively. One man grabbed a handful of Jalapeno Peppers and hurled them at the screen. But off to the far end of the bar, a worker in worn coveralls, his boots muddy, his face caked with dried sweat, set aside his beer, slid to his knees, and oblivious to the rest of the men, bowed his head in prayer.

Others from around the world joined the Mexican worker, and together they recited along with Jack Van Impe, "Dear Lord, I know that I am a sinner. But please come into my life...."

Len Parker was running around, screaming hysterically at the guards, telling them to turn off the monitor. Not everyone of course, was moved by the message they were hearing, but many could be seen reciting the last of the prayer, "Come into my heart and live there inside of me."

Parker grabbed a rifle from one of the guards, aimed at the monitor, and began firing. The monitor exploded, shards of glass littering the yard. But the sound continued from the speakers, the words of praise and truth still not silenced.

Then a light appeared. It was not lightning, though lightning was Parker's first thought when he saw the flash. It was more like a searchlight from a helicopter. It struck one of the cattle truck with laser like intensity. There was a crashing sound, and when Parker could see clearly, he realized that the giant door of the truck had fallen open.

"Shoot any hater who tries to escape," he ordered, looking frantically to see who was the traitor among his security force who had opened the door.

The spell of the broadcast broken for them, even the guards who had been praying began doing as they were trained. Some took strategic positions, aiming their weapons at the truck. Others raced to see if the door could be replaced.

There was a second flash and a second door dropped to the ground. In the background, some of the prisoners began singing Amazing Grace.

"Shut up!" screamed a guard holding a machine gun. "Shut up or I'll blow a hole in every last one of you."

Another flash, this one striking the weapon. The guard screamed, dropping the machine gun, his hands suddenly blistered as though they had been thrust into fire. The weapon lay on the grass, sizzling in the night dew, steam rising all around it.

The prisoners began filing from the trucks, moving quickly yet not running, no longer afraid. They would not die tonight. They knew that. The time of trial was just beginning, of that they were sure. But they would endure because the Lord was with them. This was His battle, and He had triumphed.

Helen ran to Bronson and untied his wrists. As the two of them clung to one another, Len Parker rushed towards them, brandishing his weapon, ready to kill them.

One of the released prisoners tackled Parker, knocking the rifle from his hands. Parker was dragged into one of his own cattle cars, his hands cuffed around the slats.

"You can't stop the inevitable!" Parker screamed. "You know that, don't you? There's nothing you can do to change that."

Bronson and Helen walked over to the cattle car. "Aw come on, Len. I'm sure you read the book. Didn't you get to the end? Your buddy's got a little time for bluster and parlor tricks. But he's the antichrist, Len. Don't you get it? He's in the book. Jesus is in the book. In a sense, we're all in the book. And you know what? No matter what you do. No matter what your false Messiah says. In the end, God wins!"

Before Parker could respond, a patrol car came racing onto the prison grounds, sirens blaring, lights flashing. It pulled to a stop in front of Helen and Bronson, the driver leaning across the seat to open the door. "Get in, you two," he said. "It took a miracle to get out here. I don't think I'm going to have another one tonight."

"Agent Domi?" said Helen, surprised.

"Yes, now will you get in? I'm all alone here, and you remember what it says, wherever two or three are gathered in my name..."

"Hallelujah," said Bronson, helping Hannah, then getting inside and closing the door as the car picked up speed. "I can't wait for Macalusso to hear about the ratings for tonight's broadcast."